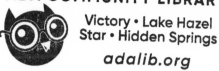

SEVEN PERCENT of Ro Devereux

ELLEN O'CLOVER

An Imprint of HarperCollinsPublishers

HarperTeen is an imprint of HarperCollins Publishers.

Seven Percent of Ro Devereux
Copyright © 2023 by Ellen O'Clover
All rights reserved. Printed in the United States of America.
No part of this book may be used or reproduced in any manner whatsoever without written permission except in the case of brief quotations embodied in critical articles and reviews. For information address HarperCollins Children's Books, a division of HarperCollins Publishers,
195 Broadway, New York, NY 10007.
www.epicreads.com

Library of Congress Control Number: 2022938552
ISBN 978-0-06-325503-6

Typography by Chris Kwon
22 23 24 25 26 LBC 5 4 3 2 1
❖
First Edition

To Tucker, who believed in this version of the future
when I couldn't see it myself.

0 1

The only time I see Miller that summer, he's walking straight at me in a tuxedo.

"Code red," Maren says, and tugs me sideways into the math hallway. School is quiet—a little over a week before the start of classes, only open this afternoon for senior presentations. I risk a peek around the corner just as Miller's looking up, a clothbound book tucked under one of his arms. When he sees us, his eyes narrow.

"Maren," he says, nodding tightly as he approaches. His gaze skates right over me, and I get busy studying the locker Maren plastered me against. A rudimentary etching of the word *dickhead* is carved like a rainbow around the combination lock.

"Miller." Maren's voice is icy, and after Miller passes us she sticks her tongue out and makes a vulgar hip thrust in his direction. He's cut his hair since May, his usual mop replaced by a short-on-the-sides, tsunami-wave-up-top situation that makes him look like a boy-band front man wannabe.

"Sick tux," I mutter, and Maren snorts.

"Of course he wore a penguin suit to his presentation." Her arm's still hooked through mine, and she guides us back into the main hall. It's empty now, late-August light slanting in through tall windows that overlook the parking lot. "Has that boy *not* taken something too far even once?"

I can hear his dress shoes retreating—*click, click, click, click.* Steady and measured, unshaken by me.

"Come on, Ro." Maren elbows me in the ribs. "Don't let him throw you off your game."

"He didn't," I say, even though my chest has gone all tight, that suffocating feeling only Miller ever gives me. A natural side effect of being so thoroughly hated, maybe. "I'm ready."

"Good," she says, and nudges me forward. We've reached the end of the hall, where a printer-paper sign is taped to the auditorium door: **Group A Senior Presentations 12 p.m.–5 p.m.**

"Hey," I say, turning toward her. "Thanks again for coming." She didn't have to be here: It's summer, still—the last few precious days. But here she is nonetheless, just like always.

"You know I wouldn't miss it." Maren reaches for the door, swinging it wide so I have to step through. "Now let's go, you're stalling. The future awaits."

I could've waited until May to present my senior project. Maren hasn't even decided what to do for hers yet. But here I am, instead: ten days before the start of senior year, in a room full of teachers I'm not legally required to listen to for over a week, with my unruly hair tamed into a bun and my toes cramped into flats Maren made me borrow.

I could've waited until May, like everyone else. But not everyone else has a dad breathing down their neck to apply to college when it's the last place they want to go. And not everyone else needed all summer—literally every waking moment—to finish their project. I couldn't have pulled this off during the school year, with eight hours of all my days spoken for, plus homework. Between all-nighters spent coding and mornings studying behavioral science with Vera, I needed all the time I could get.

I definitely needed more time than Miller, but of course when I step onto the stage his presentation's still up on the big screen, leaching overachiever pheromones into the whole auditorium. His title slide's plain white, Times New Roman font:

THE ILIAD'S SECOND HERO:
THE GREAT WAR THROUGH HECTOR'S EYES
ALISTAIR MILLER
SWITCHBACK RIDGE HIGH SCHOOL
SENIOR PROJECT GROUP A

What a fucking nerd.

"Can you pull my thing up?" I hiss toward the sophomore manning the screen. He's sitting in the front row with his shoes off and a Styrofoam smoothie cup the size of my head. He takes a long sip before looking at me.

"Name?"

"Rose Devereux," I say, and after a couple of lazy clicks my presentation blinks up onto the wall. There's a panel of six teachers sitting behind Smoothie Boy, and behind that Maren's made herself comfy in the very center of the auditorium, legs folded up in her seat. Otherwise, shit's empty as Antarctica. A classroom would've been kinder, but instead I'm presenting to ninety-two empty seats. *Cue the applause*, I think, and then my dad walks in.

He holds the door for Vera, and as she teeters in behind him I can see she's gone the whole nine yards to be here: cloud of gray hair teased into a neat bob, lilac sweater set, her favorite columbine brooch. Maren waves them over to sit with her, and Dad offers Vera his arm to help her down the narrow aisle. He's still wearing his apron and I'm pretty sure there's whipped cream on his face.

"Rose?" Mr. Gupta, the AP English Lit teacher, prompts. I'm so busy thinking about how he must have gone googly-eyed for Miller's faux-intellectual literary escapade that I miss what he says next, and he has to repeat himself. "I said, we're ready when you are."

"Right." I grip the sides of the podium. My notes are fanned out in front of me, but by now I could do this in my sleep. Dad flashes me a thumbs-up from the audience, and I think, *This is all for you. Pay attention.*

"I love computers," I say, leaning into the mic so my voice fills the room like a god. "I always have. And the weird truth is, we're more like them than we think." Smoothie Boy coughs on air from his straw, doubling over to hack into his hand, and I wait. When all six of the teachers are looking back at me, I tell them what Vera's been telling me for years. "Human behavior is ninety-three percent predictable."

Pause for effect. "And in theory, if we knew all of someone's nature and nurture information—who they come from and how they were raised—we'd be able to accurately predict their behavior. So I built an app that asks the right questions, then tells you your future. It's called MASH."

Maren lets out a whoop, and the logo she helped me design animates on-screen: a hand-drawn spiral, spinning over the letters *M A S H* arranged in a square.

"My app takes the idea of the kids' game Mansion Apartment Shack House and pairs it with a science-backed survey to accurately predict your future. I worked with Vera Kincaid, renowned human behavior expert, to develop the survey. Once you take it, MASH chews up your data and spits out four key aspects of your future: the city you'll live in, your profession, how many kids you'll have, and who your partner will be."

Not gonna lie, I get chills just listening to myself. And I can tell I've got these teachers on the hook—some of them aren't even blinking.

"But instead of telling you about MASH, I want to show it to you." I walk around the podium, pulling my phone out of my pocket. "So if you don't mind, go ahead and download MASH from the App Store. And see for yourself."

"Rose," Ms. Thompson says, peering at me over her readers. Her phone's lit up in her palm, download in progress. "This seeing-your-future thing. Is it really possible? Accurate, I mean?"

"Oh, yeah," I say, and I can't help it—I smile. "It's really possible."

5

"Crushed it," Maren says. She kicks off her Birkenstocks and plants her feet on my dash. "Gupta's voice when MASH told him he's fated to be a novelist? I thought he was going to cry."

"I thought *I* was going to cry," I say, shifting the truck into drive. "I can't believe it's over."

"You pulled it off." Maren's head lolls back against the top of the passenger seat; the headrest busted years ago but she's short, fits just right if she scoots down. "Miracle of miracles."

Miracle of miracle of miracles. I barely slept this summer between afternoons at Vera's to talk science, nights in my bedroom writing code, anxious hours waiting for the App Store to finally approve my beta. Clicking that MASH icon and having it open an actual app on my actual phone in my actual hand was pure magic.

"Now we just have to hope my dad's convinced," I say.

"How could he not be?" Maren looks at me, late-afternoon sun hitting her hair like alpenglow. "You found a way to see the future, Ro. Coded it all on your own in three months." Her eyebrows hike up into her bangs. "You've got the goods—you don't need a bachelor's degree to prove it."

"God, *agreed*." I stop at the four-way intersection at the bottom of the hill. There isn't a single traffic light in Switchback Ridge. "Can you say that again, but record it this time and text it to my dad?"

She laughs, rolling down her window to stick an elbow out. "No. But I bet if he takes the survey it'll tell him he's going to run his own restaurant one day, and he'll be so happy he'll let anything go."

I sigh and don't tell her what I'm thinking—that maybe he'll take the survey and it *won't* tell him that, and it'll be more than either of us can bear. My dad inherited Beans on the Lake from his dad, who inherited it from his dad before that. The Devereuxs have been slinging coffee in Switchback Ridge for three generations, but Dad went to culinary school. All he wants is a restaurant, but all he's got are double-shot mochas, the occasional grilled cheese, and a full pastry case of muffins. What he also doesn't have is money. So.

"When are *you* going to take the survey?" I ask. There's a beep, and when we look up Dad's passing us in his SUV, hand lifted in a wave and Vera riding shotgun.

"Still never," Maren says, rolling her eyes. "My future's a mystery and that's how I like it."

"Fair," I tell her. "Only, your best friend in the whole world made an app all on her own, and it would be super best-friendly of you to experience it for yourself. That's all I'm saying."

"I *love* you," Maren says, drawing out the *o*. "So much. But there are some things we just shouldn't know."

I wave her off. "Some of us prefer a little insight, but okay."

"Get the partner match up and running, and then we can talk." Maren looks at me. "I'm *definitely* game to circumvent the whole dating thing for the entire rest of my life if I can nail down my partner now, then go find them when I'm ready."

Partner match—my biggest hang-up. I could only get MASH to hit three of its four categories: city, job, and number of kids. (My results: San Jose, software developer, zero. Check, check, and check.) Those three things follow from a user's own survey responses. The partner match, though—you need more users, a critical mass of people to pair up. Get their consent, mine their data, and unleash the algorithm to match them based on their surveys. I could do a lot on my own, but not that. Which was a bummer, because figuring out who you'd marry was always the best part of playing MASH.

When we were in middle school, I'd sleep over at Maren's and her mom would teach us all the stuff my mom wasn't around to—how to French braid our hair and how to stop the microwave before the popcorn burned and, best of all, how to play MASH: a paper-and-pen future-prediction game she'd played growing up in the eighties.

We'd make lists for each category: four cities we'd want to live in, four jobs we dreamed of having, four boys who made our heads spin. A throwaway list of four numbers to represent how many kids we'd have. And, of course, the final category: mansion, apartment, shack, or house?

From there, one of us drew a spiral at the bottom of the page. And when the other told us to stop, we tallied the lines to the center and used that number to count down, checking off options on each list until we were left with the picture of our far-off adult lives.

Every category was fun—finding out you'd live on a beach in Florida, in a mansion with six kids, whatever—but knowing the name of your future husband? That's where the real power was. We'd pick the cutest kids in our class, leaving ourselves with no bad options (save for the few times Maren snuck Miller's name into my list as a joke).

We knew—distantly, somewhere—that the game was outrageous. We probably weren't going to marry Eli Kim, the absolute dreamiest boy at Switchback Ridge Middle, and live with him in an apartment in New York City. It was unlikely either of us would make it out to San Diego to be lead ornithologist at the zoo. And that was before Maren told me she was bi; we didn't even put girls on her list.

It was all completely fantastical, but seeing those new-penny-shiny futures written out on paper made them feel possible. It was like bottling up a daydream and drinking it straight. I wanted to re-create that feeling with the app, and I got there—seventy-five percent of the way.

"Unless a million people download my buggy beta," I say, "you're out of luck."

Maren shrugs. "A girl can dream."

When I pull into her driveway, red-sand gravel and pine-tree roots, Maren slides her shoes back on and hops out of the cab.

"Hey." She leans through the open passenger window, her face constellationed with freckles. "Good luck with your dad. You got this."

"Right," I say, shifting into reverse. "I totally got this."

02

Turns out I do not, in fact, got this. This becomes immediately obvious when Dad plunks a plate of celebratory pasta carbonara in front of me and says, "I'm so proud of you, Ro. This is going to really make you stand out on your college applications."

I look at Vera, but she just smiles. She's Team College, too, that traitor.

"Hold up," I say. Vera slides the container of parmesan toward me, but I don't reach for it. "You saw what I made. I don't need college; I'm *already* doing what I want to do. Why would I waste all that money when I can go get a job?"

"Ro." Dad rubs his forehead. "What you did is so impressive. Let's just celebrate it tonight, okay? We don't need to fight about you leaving Colorado right now, let's—"

"I'm not trying to fight." I lift my hands in peace, and my forearm scar catches in the light. "I'm just saying. This project was the proof I don't need college. That's the whole reason I did it."

"That's the *whole* reason," Dad repeats, raising his eyebrows at me.

"No," Vera says firmly. She's silhouetted by the window behind her, sun lowering through the pines. "You did this for *you*, Rosie. Because you had a good idea and you wanted to see it through."

I groan, because she's right, as usual. Vera's been our neighbor forever, since before my parents got married or had me or my mom left. I spent most of my childhood in her book-buried living room, huddled in front of the wood-burning stove while Dad worked and Vera told me about brains. About what it actually means—factually, biologically—to be human.

She ran a behavioral research lab at the university in Boulder until I was fifteen, when her cancer slowed her down too much to keep at it. Then she just taught me, instead: every little tidbit I begged her to share with me about how predictable behavior is, the lanes we're born into, the patterns we follow. With my mom gone, Vera raised me and educated me. I was her shadow and her student—she'd make me a peanut butter sandwich, and then she'd teach me that there's logic to all the rash, emotional, human choices we make. I gripped on with white knuckles, never speaking of my mother but always hoping there'd be a pattern in what I learned that could explain why she'd left me.

"Okay," I concede. "It was *a* reason. A big one."

"Eat your pasta," Dad says, but he's smiling. Five-o'clock shadow coming in, laugh lines around his eyes. "We'll argue about this tomorrow."

An hour later Dad walks Vera home, down our gravel road to her house at the end of the street. I watch them through the vaulted windows, his arm bent so she can hold on to it, her steps measured and slow. College is something Dad's always wanted for me that I've never wanted for myself; if I move out to Silicon Valley and start working, we're set. Money for me, money for his restaurant one day, maybe. If I go to college, I push all that off for four years and Dad goes into debt. Seems pretty clear to me, but Dad's stubborn. We have that in common.

My phone buzzes with a text from Maren. **Any luck?**

None, I think, but it's too depressing to share with her yet. Instead I cross the living room to our lumpy old couch and collapse backward into the pillows, startling Esther out of the way. She's eight now, a tabby we found behind the café. She's got bristly whiskers and a serious attitude problem, but she's ours.

Esther snarls and then curls up to give me the cold shoulder.

"Same to you," I say, unlocking my phone and opening Instagram. It's almost eight o'clock, the second-to-last Friday of summer. My feed is full of people in front of bonfires at the lake, camping in the Rockies, sitting on the hoods of their cars with their arms around each other. Normal, normal, all the way down. But then, suddenly, I see her.

Sawyer is my cousin, twenty-three and fully blessed in the genes department, beautiful as all hell. After she graduated from the University of Minnesota she couldn't deign to take an entry-level job so she started selling her lifestyle on Instagram instead. Usually she's out here shilling #ad eye cream to her nearly-a-million followers, but as I scroll across a video of her face something stops me, and then I realize what it is. The MASH logo, superimposed in the upper corner of her screen. I hit full volume.

"Hey, babes!" Sawyer says. She's wearing fake eyelashes and her lips are as glossy as twin candy wrappers. "I wanted to share something a little different with y'all tonight—ready to go on a ride with me?" Her green eyes bug, lashes flaring. Distantly, I wonder when she started using *y'all*.

"So there's this new app called MASH, and it's legitimately the coolest thing I've ever seen." She pauses, leaning toward the camera and lifting a hand to whisper conspiratorially. "I'll admit I'm a little biased, because my genius baby cousin made it. But y'all remember that game we played as kids? Where we'd draw a spiral on a piece of paper and—"

She's still talking, but I can't hear her over the blood flushing in my ears. What the fuck is this? I scroll through the comments, heart climbing into my throat.

Just downloaded!

OoOOOoooOOOoo this sounds so cool. I wanna see my future.

OMG getting this now. MASH + science??

Thanks for sharing @sosawyer this sounds dope af

No. No, no, no. I text her immediately, the last message in our thread from just this morning when she wished me good luck with approximately fifteen thousand emojis.

Sawyer, you have to delete that post, I say. The app's just a school project, it's not meant for anyone to actually use. I sent it to you for your eyes only!!

The seconds tick past. My skin's gone all hot. Next to me, Esther starts snoring.

But it's fucking amazing, Ro-Ro! And then, It says I'm going to be an actress in LA, can you believe??

Yes, actually. Sawyer lived in Switchback Ridge until I was nine, when Uncle Harding moved the whole family to Minneapolis for his new job. Since then we've mostly kept up over text and DM, but even when she's pared down to pixels, Sawyer's the most theatrical person I know.

Before I can respond, she sends another: **Josie's all over it, too. She just shared it to her Insta story!**

I scramble back into the app and click through to Josie Sweet's profile, Sawyer's most A-list friend. She dropped her third album last year and, lo and behold, has just posted a story about MASH. I watch it with my jaw on the floor.

Dude you hav to delete and ask her to delte to. I fire off the text so fast half the words are misspelled. **It's not ready Sawyer seriously.**

Looks ready to me, she replies, embellishing with three heart-eyed emojis. **Check your downloads, lady!!!**

Frantically, I open my app analytics. And there's MASH, the logo Maren made, my stupid senior project, with twenty-six thousand downloads. As I sit there, the numbers tick up. Forty-four thousand. Fifty-two thousand.

By the time my dad walks through the front door, shuffling gravel into our hallway, there are one hundred ninety-two thousand downloads.

We look at each other, and his eyebrows draw together. "Ro?" he says. "What's wrong?"

I look back at my phone: two hundred thirty thousand.

Shit. *Shit.*

03

My mother was half-computer. Or at least, that's how Dad always describes her.

She grew up in Slate Lake, a vacation town even tinier than ours, three hours from Denver and buried in the mountains like flint in a riverbed. She was twenty-two when she came into Beans on the Lake with a backpack and a book about the Epson HX-20, the very first laptop.

She read that thing like it was poetry, Dad told me. Like it was beautiful.

They were married by twenty-three and parents by twenty-four and then she was gone by twenty-six, across the country to California without either of us to weigh her down. She reverted to her maiden name and disappeared into the ever-growing fold of Silicon Valley—every so often I'd come across an article that mentioned her, always unintentionally, always with the kind of jolt that felt like putting my finger in an outlet.

Technology's beautiful to me, too. That's one thing between us. The other is I look just like her.

There's a picture from their wedding in the drawer of Dad's desk, sepia-faded and folded in half right across their abdomens. They're standing on the dock across the street from the café, past the pebbly beach. Dad's smiling at something out of frame but my mother's looking right at the camera, sharp-eyed in her white dress. Our hair curls the exact same, sun-lightened and wild, and even then—on a day like that—she looks ready to leave. Or that's how she's always looked to me, at least, biased by the knowledge of her going.

The way Dad tells the story, she did ask him to go with her. But he had the café, and back then his dream of turning it into a restaurant was right around the corner, something he could taste. And I was just two, and I had family here, and what was in California that we couldn't get at home in our mountains? But my mom knew, same as I do now: the future. We weren't the version of it she was looking for, so she went.

It was a clean break, muddied only by the birthday presents that showed up every year like clockwork. Colorful, noisy robots that taught me block coding before I could read. Board games with names like Hackerz and CodeMode. STEM books when I was old enough, and then software for the desktop Dad and I shared in the upstairs office.

When I was small I didn't see the gifts for what they were: a bid to turn me into her, a once-yearly sowing meant to grow me into someone worthy of her attention. I only knew how their arrival changed my dad—the way his relaxed, six-five frame stiffened like a drought-season pine needle when he saw her return address. How all of him went brittle and unfamiliar.

So I pretended to hate the gifts, of course. Hid them under my bed, closed out of the coding computer game she'd sent me when I heard his footsteps on the stairs. Dad was my entire life: he'd built our A-frame cabin with his dad and brother; he drove me everywhere I needed to go; he cooked all my favorite foods. We talked about everything, the flow of his love like a conversation that never stopped. But my mother was the one thing that cast a pallor over him, that made him sad in a way that felt like a gut-punch.

I hated it. But right alongside that hatred, I loved the world she'd shown me. The clean logic of building code, the intangible magic of technology. So I hid it from Dad, and when I was eleven and sent her a letter for the very first time, I hid that, too.

Miller proofread it for me, tongue poked between his lips in concentration as he added in all the commas I'd missed. It was a long note, full of questions about her life. It ended pathetically, a shaky-handed scrawl of *Will you come visit me?*

She didn't come visit. She didn't even respond. And then I turned twelve, and instead of a gift, she sent an unsigned birthday card with a hundred-dollar bill inside. I had failed her, somehow, by breaking the pattern—ending the unspoken truce that we'd never be in contact. I burst into tears in front of my bewildered father and it was Miller who found me, snot on my lips, in the woods behind my house.

I tried to give him the cash but he shook his head, helped me burn it in a pile of winter-crisp pine needles. The cards came every year after that, and every year we burned them together, right up until we didn't.

Life kept moving: Dad didn't convert the café, at first because Grandpa was still alive and loved that place just the way it was. Then he died, and Dad didn't convert it because he wanted to honor his memory. We did every family moment there: birthday dinners, anniversaries, holidays with Sawyer and me snug between her parents and my dad. He and Uncle Harding are nearly identical in the photos, bearded and solid as tree trunks. But then Sawyer moved away, and it was only Dad and me, and there just wasn't money. I watched Dad's dream fade to gray, knowing my mother was out there somewhere living hers in full color.

And even though I don't want anything to do with her, loving what she loves is right here in my genes. My predictable, human behavior. I love tech. I can't help it. And I've got to get to California to make a name for myself in that world, make it mine the way she made it hers. I want it so bad it burns—to prove I don't need that money we reduced to ash in the woods. That I could've done it without her all along. That I can give my dad the dream she stole from him.

He's over forty now and if I let him, he'll put it off forever. Take out a loan he can't afford to send me to school, spend the rest of his life paying it off, never get out from behind that espresso machine. Dad knows how to make anything taste delicious—it was a game we played growing up, me and Miller and then me and Maren, gathering the weirdest ingredients we could find between our kitchens and presenting them to Dad for consideration. He transformed them like magic every single time.

And that's what he's doing now, when my phone rings. In the twenty-four hours since Sawyer posted about MASH, the app's been downloaded 972,000 times. My server crashed. I didn't sleep last night.

It's a California number I don't recognize, and Dad glances up from the bell pepper he's dicing. I've been hiding from my phone all day, but something makes me shrug at him and pick up the call anyway. Not just something, really—it's that familiar itch at the back of my throat, the one that feels halfway like tears. The one that says: *It could be Mom.*

Of course, it isn't.

"Rose?" The voice on the other end of the line is serious and clear. I stand up taller, and Dad quirks an eyebrow at me. "This is Evelyn Cross from XLR8 in Mountain View. Do you have a moment? We'd love to talk to you about MASH."

The woods behind my house are age-old and whispery. The wind moves differently here, fingering through the shivering aspen leaves. It's not a forest, exactly—you can't get lost in it. If you walk for too long you'll get to John Able's house, and his big black dog will howl up a warning from the back porch. But if you stand in the very middle—seventy-two paces in—it goes quiet. And then, like a radio switching stations, the noise picks up again. Only different, now. *You can hear the heartbeat of the earth out here,* Dad told me once when I was small. Miller was with us; I watched him press his palm to the pine-needle floor of the world, feeling for it.

I hate that these woods belong to both of us—that even here, three summers after he last spoke to me, I'm thinking of Miller. The firelight playing across his pale cheeks, and the echo of his laugh on the wind, and the rooted way he was always nearby. It's Miller's face blinking back at me when I close my eyes, grab right onto the earth until my fingernails hurt. That last way he looked at me, before he never looked at me again.

Out here wind moves like the ocean across the aspen trunks, shushing me. When I can't breathe, when my brain feels like the gash of a trapped scream, the woods root me down. Trip my lungs like a breaker so they remember their rhythm and keep me alive.

I'm sitting on the mossy patch between two gnarled trees when Dad finds me on Monday morning—right in the middle of the woods with my eyes shut, my makeup done and my blazer on and Maren's too-tight flats again. School starts in one week. I'm meeting with XLR8 in one hour. Miller's the last thing I should be thinking about, and I try to remember: the trees are all just out here breathing, and I am, too.

"There'll be traffic," Dad says. He's not the nervous type, but still—he tugs a little at his collar. I can count on one hand the number of times I've seen him in a dress shirt. "We should hit the road."

"Yeah," I say, standing up. I brush the dirt from my palms, wishing I could bring it with me.

"You got everything you need?"

We look at each other, and the sun is pale yellow the way it only ever gets in the woods, in the morning, in summer. "I don't need anything," I tell him. I already answered every question XLR8 had about MASH; I was on the phone with Evelyn Cross for an hour.

Thanks to Sawyer, my app has gone from a school project to a serious prospect. And once Josie Sweet latched on, it was a forest fire, photos of the MASH interface flaring up across Instagram like so many sparks. I spent all weekend on XLR8's website, reading and rereading their mission statement until it was seared into my eyeballs: *XLR8 provides seed funding and unparalleled resources to help entrepreneurs build the next generation of innovative applications.*

Am I an entrepreneur? I built MASH in my pajamas, in my bedroom, with Esther in my lap. And at the exact same time, XLR8 was setting their sights on an expansion into Colorado. *Serendipitous* was the word Evelyn used. *We just opened a Denver office. Come in on Monday and we'll talk about the possibilities.*

I think it's all those possibilities that are making it hard to breathe. What if this thing takes off even more? What if—I trip over a tree root and Dad's arm shoots out to catch me—it doesn't?

"You okay?" he asks.

"Totally." A through-the-teeth lie, but I'm hoping we'll both believe it. "Just these stupid shoes."

"You can take them off in the car," he says, glancing down. And then we leave the woods, and we don't say anything else the whole entire drive to Denver.

0 4

The XLR8 office is in a high-rise right off the river, wall-to-wall windows glittering like sun on water. We park in the underground garage and Dad hands me the ticket so we can get it validated, pointing right at me as he does it.

"Don't lose that," he says, and this small warning is what finally—after a forty-minute drive in silent panic—calms me down. No matter what happens here today, we'll still need to get the parking validated. Life isn't so unfamiliar.

In the lobby, everything is smooth and white. No hard edges, nothing out of place. There's a monstera plant on the coffee table in the seating area and I think, *You're far from home.* I want to touch it, see if it's fake.

"Rose?" We aren't even through the door when my name fills the room. It's the receptionist, who walks around the desk to greet us in low-top sneakers and a stop-sign-red hoodie. "We're so excited you're here. I'm Mia."

She shakes my hand and then reaches for Dad's. "You must be Rose's dad."

"The one and only," he says, and I clench my jaw to keep from wincing.

"Can I get you anything while you wait for Evelyn? Water? Tea?" She gestures to a glass door, her ponytail swinging. "There's kombucha on tap in the back. Blueberry lavender, pineapple turmeric, or apple ginger."

"Water's great," I say, and Dad nods.

"On it." Mia sweeps a hand toward the white leather couch, and we drift over to it. "I'll be right back. Evelyn's just wrapping up her nine o'clock."

I settle next to Dad, smoothing my blazer. He reaches for the monstera and rubs one leaf between his thumb and forefinger. "Fake." He tips his head, smiling. "But convincing."

"Surprised you didn't go for the pineapple turmeric kombucha," I say, and he starts to laugh before covering his mouth with one hand. My phone buzzes, and when I pull it out of my pocket it's Maren: **Sending every good vibe in the whole universe! But I think my amazing logo will seal the deal so nothing to worry about!!**

Before I can respond, Mia's back with our waters, placing them on the table in front of us with little napkins.

"Thank you," Dad tells her, and she chirps a "You're welcome!" before slipping behind the desk.

"It feels like a spaceship in here," Dad whispers, but as I tuck my phone away all I can think is that this could be my life next year. That I could come to a place like this every single day. Beyond the glass door there are long rows of desks arranged to face the windows, mountains rising jagged and commanding in the distance. Every chair is occupied, people in headphones leaning close to their monitors. I can hear the buzz of their chatter from all the way out here, low and thrumming. It's like a hive, all the pieces moving in unison. And then, the queen.

Evelyn Cross is wearing a rust-colored jumpsuit and has blond hair cut to her jawline in a pin-straight bob. She's holding a tablet in one hand and pushes open the glass door with the other, her face slicing into a smile.

"Rose Devereux," she says. Her voice is more imposing in person, like she's used to having people's full attention. "Evelyn. We couldn't be more thrilled to have you here."

"Excited to be here," I tell her, which isn't exactly right. The emotion I'm feeling is part excitement, part disbelief, part serious impending stage fright, and part nausea. I swallow. *Don't you fucking dare puke in this place.*

"Pete," Dad says when Evelyn shakes his hand. "Thanks for having Ro."

"We should be thanking her," Evelyn says, and turns to hold open the glass door for us. "Please, come on back. Everyone's gathered."

Everyone? I think, and then she leads us to a conference room with twenty people inside.

When Dad and I sit in the two empty seats at the middle of the table, every single chair swivels toward us.

24

"Everyone, meet Rose and Pete," Evelyn says. She takes the chair at the head of the table. There's a tall, skinny glass of water in front of her and glass carafes of water and fruit down the center of the table—lemons, limes, oranges. I kind of want to pour myself some but extremely don't trust myself to move.

"Rose, this would be your team." Evelyn sweeps her hand in front of her, and as I look from one person to the next, everyone smiles at me. My desire to be one of them hits pure and strong, all at once. They're wearing T-shirts and cool watches and chunky glasses and half of them have tattoos. "Well, part of it."

Evelyn turns to wave along the wall of glass that separates us from the floor of employee desks. "We have three floors here in Denver, and MASH would be one of them." She looks at me pointedly, and her eyes are like a bird's: sharp and keen. "Entirely."

I swallow. "How many people is that?"

"Fifty or so. We'll be hiring, of course. The board would like three teams on this: here in Denver, London, and Shanghai. We'll be working on MASH twenty-four seven."

"Wow," Dad says, taking the word straight out of my mouth. And then, another word that makes me deflate a little: "Why?"

Evelyn smiles, and when she speaks, her words are directed at me. "We want in on this idea, Rose. It's a smart one. And the amount of public interest you've received without any marketing or funding is astounding. Imagine what you could do with our resources." She pauses, glancing at Dad. "You'll need a team if you want to make this work. And you should. Want to make this work, I mean."

"She built it on her own," Dad says, before I can respond. "Why does she need all this fancy stuff?"

Okay, I love this man. But oh my god. I almost lift my hands so I can hide behind them.

Evelyn's eyes flick to a guy at the opposite end of the table, who smiles. He's wearing a black T-shirt and has a baseball cap propped backward over his hair.

"Rose's code is good," he tells Dad, then looks at me. "But we can make it better. Also, the UI looks like shit." A couple of people laugh, and I feel heat pool in my cheeks. I think of Sawyer, her cheery text from Friday: *Looks ready to me!* "We'll bring in a design team, make this as beautiful as it should be."

"And there's monetization," another woman says, sitting right across from me. "We'll put together a sales team to get moving on sponsored results. MASH tells you you're going to be a doctor, we serve you an ad for Harvard Med. You know the drill."

"Marketing." When I turn toward the third voice, a woman with perfect braids hanging to her elbows offers me a friendly smile. "We'll set you up with press—interviews, guest blogs, all of it. And, if they're interested, bring Sawyer Devereux and Josie Sweet on board as brand ambassadors."

"And of course," Evelyn says, drawing everyone's attention like a bow string pulled taut, "there's the issue of funding." She nods to the guy next to her, who hits a button on his computer that activates the projector behind Evelyn. Suddenly, we're all looking at the next six months. "We've built out a workback plan."

There's a Friday in February, circled in red with the words *Goal*

Celeritas meeting date above it. Even I know Celeritas—one of the most powerful venture capital firms in Silicon Valley.

"You think Celeritas is going to want this?" I blurt, before I've even looked at anything else on the calendar.

"We do," Evelyn says, smiling. "They would be the goal for your Series A funding. We'll take a few months to make MASH its best before pitching to them. Prove just how powerful this app is going to be, how it's going to change the way human beings exist in society."

Change the way human beings exist in society? I blink up at Evelyn, my mouth open like a trout. I didn't set out to change the world; I was just trying to graduate. But if I *could*, if this thing I made really has so much potential—

"And this is how we're going to do it." Evelyn swivels toward the projector, pulling a laser pointer out of nowhere and drawing my attention to a date less than a week away. *Launch partner match*, it says.

I think of Maren in my truck, just three days ago. *Get the partner match up and running, and then we can talk.*

"If we have a shot of getting Celeritas to buy in, we need to dial up the partner match." Evelyn looks at me, serious and certain. "This is a dating app that sees the future."

"We'd gate the partner function at eighteen," someone else says, and I turn to look at her. "Allow people to set their own age ranges. Then pair them with their best match within their designated parameters."

"It's already set up," I say. My heart is ping-ponging against my ribs, but I realize I'm not nervous anymore. I'm freaking *excited*. "I wrote the algorithm to match people based on their survey results; it's all there, I just didn't have—"

"Critical mass," Evelyn finishes for me. "With over a million downloads, we're there, Rose. We just need to prove that it works, that you're hardwired to fall in love with your MASH match."

"I developed the questions with a behavioral scientist," I tell her, glancing around the table. "But it was just for a school project. I don't know if it'll be right one hundred percent of the time, for every single user. I don't know if it'll work perfectly."

"It doesn't need to work perfectly," Evelyn says. "People just need to believe that it does. And you'll make them believe."

Breath swells inside of me, full to bursting. I *want* this.

"How?" Dad says. When I look at him, there's something worried in the set of his jaw, like he's hearing something here that I'm not. "How will she make them believe?"

"With the ultimate proof point," Evelyn tells him. "She'll take the survey, and she'll fall in love with her match."

05

"Absolutely not," Dad says as soon as the elevator doors close. He kept it together in the conference room, deflecting us out of there with a neutral *We'll think it over*. But now that we're alone, he's almost apoplectic.

"This is too much to take on with school, Ro." He jabs the garage button once, twice, three times before we finally start to move. "You can't be expected to manage both. You saw that workback plan, there are milestones every week from here to February. You have other priorities that are more im—"

"They're not more important," I say, and a muscle jumps in his temple.

"There's nothing more important than your schoolwork."

"The whole point of my schoolwork is to get me here," I say, gesturing toward the elevator doors. "Do well in school so I can graduate so I can get a job. Right?" He doesn't say anything, because he knows where I'm leading him and he doesn't like it.

Still, I say it again. "*Right?*"

He's quiet, so I keep going. "I can come in after school. I'll work here in the afternoons."

He shakes his head. "You didn't even want to do your project during the year because you knew it would be too much with school."

"Dad, this is different—"

"Yeah, it's *more*. It's unreasonable, Ro."

"I can handle it! And by the time I graduate we'll be funded and I'll be able to come on full-time and—"

"You really want to give them half of what you made?" His brown eyes are dark in the shadowy elevator. "You did this, Ro. It's yours. You give them fifty percent, that's not true anymore."

I swallow, and the doors slide open. I *don't* want to give XLR8 fifty percent, is the truth. When I saw the number on the contract it tickled at the back of my brain, suffusing my pure-white excitement with a bloodred drop of doubt. Fifty percent is orders of magnitude higher than any other accelerator I've researched—but then again, I'm only one person. I don't have a team behind me yet, or any resources to bring to the table at all. XLR8 is ready to give me everything I need.

And besides, the contract held so much more than that jarring fifty percent figure. It promised dedicated, full-time teams. All the funding it takes to get us to Celeritas. And, impossible to ignore: a job waiting for me when I graduate.

I won't make any money up front, but with XLR8's help, we can win over Celeritas. And if we win them over, MASH will take off—I'll own fifty percent of a successful app and make more money than I can hardly stand to dream of.

This contract is my ticket to everything I want: bypass college, enter the tech industry with a bang. Evelyn was right, what she said in that conference room overlooking the mountains: I can't scale this without a team. And nothing is perfect. This is close enough for me.

"Dad, with their resources—"

"Their *resources*." He practically spits the word. "Their big, genius strategy to pair you off for profit like some contestant on that ridiculous show you and Maren watch." He unlocks the car, waving one hand around.

"*The Bachelor*?"

"Yeah, *The Bachelor*." We slide into the front seat and he looks at me. "You're not a proof point, Ro. You're my kid."

"I know," I say, and his eyebrows shoot up. "I know, I know. But it's temporary, Dad, the dating thing will be fake, I just have to pretend for a few months and then—"

"Pretend to love some stranger for a few months? Do you hear yourself?"

I do hear myself, and—okay. It doesn't sound great. But it's just a detail, the sort-of-awkward means to an end that I really, really, really want. And besides, I wrote a smart algorithm. It'll pair me with someone I'll like—that's its whole job. So maybe this could even be fun, maybe we'll even—

"It's a no," Dad says, and the finality in his voice makes my hands start shaking. Panic. "And bringing on Sawyer? She has her own work. She's—"

"No, no, no," I say, but he's already starting the car. "Dad,

Sawyer will *eat this up*. This *is* her work. And look—if I do this, I don't have to leave Colorado, okay? If we get this funding in February we can really make this thing work, and I'll be here after I graduate. I'll live in Denver and I'll see you all the time and I don't have to go to California at all." That muscle jumps in his temple again. He's not looking at me, but he's not driving away, either. I think of my mother, cutting out on him to chase the same dream I'm chasing now. Of all these months I've spent trying to convince him that I should get to leave, too. My voice goes quiet and pitiful. "I won't have to leave home. Dad, *please*."

Silence falls between us, and for a minute there's nothing but the rumbly engine humming under our feet. Dad hesitates for so long that I think maybe I've actually convinced him. But when he finally cuts the gas and looks over at me, what he says is, "We didn't get the parking validated."

I ride the elevator back up to the eleventh floor alone. When the doors slide open into the XLR8 lobby, Mia smiles at me.

"Forget something?"

I hold up the parking ticket, wave it around like an idiot. My hands are still shaking. "Need our parking validated."

"*Oooh*, good catch." Mia circles her big white desk to take it from me. "They charge eighty bucks for lost tickets. Can you believe that? I've got the stickers in the back, just one sec."

When she bounces through the glass door and disappears, I look around the sleek, sun-filled lobby. I want so badly to think of it as mine—a place I go to and belong in. I stare unblinking at the fake monstera, and by the time Mia comes back I've made up my mind.

"I also need to sign the contract," I tell her. My fingers close around the validated parking ticket. "Is Evelyn free right now?"

Mia's eyes widen a little. "Oh my gosh, totally. Let's seal this deal! Let me grab her." She pushes a button on the intercom behind her desk. "Evelyn? Rose is back to sign her contract." The words are distorted, half washed out by my own heartbeat roaring in my ears. Evelyn gets to the lobby in what feels like point two seconds, a slim stack of papers in her hands.

"Rose." She smiles as she comes through the door. "I didn't expect you back so soon. Where's your dad?"

"He's in the garage," I tell her. "He just, um. He just—"

"Preferred to wait in the car?"

"Yes," I say, and she motions me over to the couch.

"We may need his signature." She spreads the papers across the white table. "Do you think he'd be willing to come back up for a moment?"

"We don't need it," I say, but I can't quite look at her. This feels like simultaneously the most shameful and most exhilarating moment of my entire life. "I'm eighteen."

Evelyn studies me for just a beat before handing over a pen. "All right, then. Perfect."

"There's one more thing," I say, and she stops shuffling the papers to look at me. I tug my blazer sleeve over the fish-scale-silver edge of my scar. "My partner, Vera Kincaid. I couldn't have designed the survey without her—she taught me all the science. She needs a percentage of this, too—from both of our halves."

Evelyn's eyes don't leave mine. "What number did she have in mind?"

"I don't know," I say, trying to wipe my sweaty palms on my pants without being too conspicuous. "I have to talk to her."

"Well, we'll need to negotiate a percentage," Evelyn says evenly. "Let's sign these today, and we can draw up a new version if—"

"No." I sound a whole lot more confident than I feel. "It needs to be here before I sign."

Evelyn blinks, but if she's surprised, she hides it well.

"How about this," she says, pulling another pen from her jumpsuit pocket. "I'll add a note indicating negotiations to come, and we'll draw up a new version of the contract if she decides she'd like equity."

Her handwriting is clean and precise, scrawled across the bottom of the contract: *Negotiated equity percentage for Vera Kincaid TK*. She initials next to it, *EZC*, then slides the paper toward me.

"Initial here, then on the flagged lines throughout."

I nod, duck my head, and sign everywhere I'm supposed to. When I stand up and shake Evelyn's hand, her skin is smooth and cold.

"This is the right choice, Rose." She smiles, and I take what feels like my first full breath in minutes. "We're going to do great things together."

06

Vera doesn't have kids of her own, but she's always treated Dad like a son. Which makes me her honorary grandchild, which means she lets me get away with more than I should. So when I tell her how everything went down with XLR8, I'm expecting her to give me a signature Vera Kincaid wink and tell me I've got spunk. Instead, she frowns. Like, deeply. This is a *withering* frown.

"What?" I say. We're on her back deck, a pine platform Dad built for her a few summers ago. The sun's low in the sky and there's barely a breeze, the air still and summer-lazy. It's Wednesday and Dad isn't speaking to me.

"There were other ways, I think, to go about that."

"Maybe," I say. "But maybe he'd never have come around, and all that work I did would've been for nothing."

"For nothing?" Vera's voice is more papery than it used to be, which is something I don't like to think about. "A week ago you didn't even know you'd get interest from an accelerator. That's not why you made MASH, Rosie."

She's right—I never imagined this would happen. All I expected from MASH was a passing grade on my senior project and a stamp of approval from Dad. It was only ever supposed to be a demonstration, something I could hold up to show him what I'm capable of without a college degree. The last week has been like drawing a stick figure and having the curator of the Louvre offer to buy it—it's so unlikely you don't even think to want it, but once you know it's possible, you feel like a failure with anything less.

"Okay, true," I say. "But how could I pass it up? And how could he expect me to? Working for a company like XLR8 is my dream, and he knows it. And he *still* said no."

"This is one iteration of your dream," Vera says. "Maybe he wants a better version for you."

Better than a high-rise office in my own hometown? Better than a road map that takes us to Celeritas? Sawyer summed it up when I texted her after the XLR8 meeting: It's all happening!!!

"I'm not sure it gets better than this."

"You're eighteen," Vera says. "How could you be sure of anything?"

I roll my eyes, and she finally cracks a smile. "You betrayed him, Rosie. It was unlike you, and he's hurt."

And there, suddenly, is Miller's face again: right behind my eyelids, stricken and silent as I turn away from him. Saying, *Maybe betrayal isn't so unlike you*, though in reality he never says anything to me at all.

I blink, clearing him away. Vera watches me expectantly.

"*Hurt* isn't how I'd describe it," I say. My dad's stony silence has felt like a fortress—it's hard to believe he's the same man who listened to me buzz about MASH all summer long. Who met me at the dinner table after full days at Vera's house so I could tell him about everything we were building together.

MASH has been my world for months; creating it felt like cracking some kind of sacred code. With every hour spent in Vera's sun-drenched living room, life came into closer and closer focus. *You ask this type of question*, Vera taught me, *to learn this type of variable about a person, to predict how they'll behave in this type of scenario.*

It was so clean. I'd found a way to make a math problem of human beings, to forecast every predictable behavior and translate it into code. A simple survey on a seamless, digital interface. An app that could give you the answers to life's biggest questions.

We can explain it all, I told my dad in late July, when the algorithm was almost finished. *There's a way to make everything make sense, right here in our minds. You were meant to build this house, and be a chef, and everything else. It's coded right into you.*

He'd laughed, as bowled over by it as I was. The mood was light every time we talked about MASH. I didn't tell him the other thing this algorithm was helping me explain away—the fact that my mother was always going to leave us. That her absence was just as logical and predictable and black-and-white as the rest.

MASH gave me a reason for everything, explained the unexplainable so tangibly. It was magic that demanded to be shared. And now, for whatever reason, my dad couldn't see that anymore.

"Give him time," Vera says, reaching over the table to pat my hand. For my whole life it's been the three of us, and everything feels off-kilter with him mad at me. "And be careful. Not everyone you meet has your best interest at heart. But your dad always will."

I groan, slumping in the patio chair. "Okay, I get it, I'm the worst daughter who has ever daughtered."

Vera laughs, and it turns into a cough that she hides behind her hand. "No, but he is afraid to lose you. And you seem to have stopped caring about his approval earlier than he was expecting."

"I *do* care."

"You just care for other things more."

I'm not sure if that's true, if I care more about XLR8 or if I just did something crazy in the moment because it felt right. It still feels right, if I'm being honest. It felt right to spend my whole day at the XLR8 office yesterday, pinging from conversation to conversation about code, product design, match parameters. It felt right to post the graphic XLR8 made to my Instagram this morning, the MASH logo and Big news coming Friday nestled right there under my own handle, @rodev. It feels right and it feels like flying and *god*, if my dad could just get on board, it would feel pretty close to perfect.

"Speaking of *more*," I say, "you deserve equity in MASH. Whatever you want, I'll talk to Evelyn."

I expect her to roll her eyes at my clunky segue, but instead her face darkens, some unfamiliar storm passing over it. She straightens, pressing her small frame to the back of her chair. "Rosie, I don't want to be part of this."

I blink at her. "Why? I could never have figured out the science without you. It's yours as much as it's mine."

"I helped you design a survey for a school project." The breeze picks up, rustling through the fine gray hair that hangs to her shoulders. "Not something I expected to be tested on the world at large. It's an imperfect science. Human behavior, it's—"

"Ninety-three percent predictable," I say. "Almost a hundred percent."

"Almost," Vera says. "*Almost* leaves a gray area, room for error. It won't be foolproof."

"I already told them that." I wave my hand, smiling to encourage her. She doesn't smile back. "They know it's not going to be totally accurate for every single person."

"But they'll pitch it that way," Vera says.

"It'll be implied." We're meeting with the legal team tomorrow, getting our claims in order before the partner match launch. "And it'll mostly be true! Ninety-three percent."

Vera's eyes search mine, pale blue and watery. There's something there I don't recognize, sharp-edged and insistent as a doubt.

"No," she tells me finally. "I don't want equity."

"Match day!" Maren shouts, swinging herself up into the cab of the truck. She has her hair in a neat bun, bangs perfectly arched over her forehead. "Today my virgin Rose falls in love for the very first time."

"Okay, let's manage our expectations." I shift gears and reverse down her driveway. "He could be anyone."

"Not just anyone," Maren says, leaning toward me. "Your *one*."

It's four o'clock on Friday and we're headed to Denver for the MASH match party, XLR8's idea to launch the partner match. We'll push the function live and I'll find out who my match is, the mysterious person I'll be navigating the next six months with. It's totally casual and very normal and I feel fine. Sawyer and Josie are on tap to amplify the announcement on social once it breaks.

"Man, you're blowing up." Maren picks my phone out of the cupholder, scrolling through my notifications. Since I posted the news this morning—GET READY TO MEET YOUR MASH MATCH—my DMs and comments and texts have been out of control. Sawyer's called me no fewer than three times, mostly just to squeal.

"It's because XLR8 put money behind my post," I tell her. "I'm pretty sure everyone with even a fleeting interest in MASH has seen it at this point."

"Wild." Maren's pointer finger hovers over my phone screen. "Rose Devereux from Switchback Ridge, Colorado—America's tech sweetheart." She flutters a hand over her heart, looking up at me. "How blessed am I to bear witness."

"Shut up," I say, and Maren laughs. She drops my phone back into the cupholder.

"Seriously, though. You're doing the damn thing, Ro."

I feel a rush of pride swell up my throat. I *am* doing the damn thing. And now I just have to fall in love.

Which, to Maren's point, isn't something I've done before. There have been boys, sort of—a senior from Elk Grove that I made out with at a party last summer on the lake, a tourist that took me for ice cream before his family went back to Texas, Declan Frey in the spring of my freshman year. Maybe I'll have better luck with my match, someone algorithmically perfect for me. Maybe, at least, I'll be better at faking a relationship than I've ever been at nailing one down for real. How hard can it be? Hold hands a little, laugh at their bad jokes. I've seen *The Bachelor*. I know how shit works.

Maren whistles when we step into the XLR8 lobby, but it's drowned out by music thumping from the back. Through the glass door, all the desk chairs are unoccupied—streamers hang from the ceiling and everyone is milling around, dancing, laughing, holding beer. She looks at me. "Is this a frat party?"

"Nope," a voice says, and Mia emerges from behind the desk. She's grinning. "Just launch day. Come on back."

Maren widens her eyes at me, hooking her arm through mine as Mia ushers us into the fray. A whoop goes through the crowd when people realize I'm here, and before I know it I'm introducing Maren around with a glass of kombucha in one hand and a party horn in the other. (The kombucha's grown on me this week, okay? It's not bad. Just kind of sour.)

"All right, let's get you set up." Jazz from marketing grabs my wrist, and I reach for Maren to tug her along.

"Get me set up?"

"We're going to livestream you revealing your match," Jazz says. Her hair looks as incredible today as the first time we met, back in the mountain-view conference room when she suggested bringing

Sawyer and Josie on board. Half her braids are shot through with gold thread, and she has the widest, easiest smile of anyone at XLR8. She's maybe the most beautiful person I've ever met.

Now, she guides us toward a corner of the room that's staged with a blue couch, a fig tree (fake), and *MASH Match Day* in looping calligraphy across a whiteboard. "Don't forget to smile."

My lips pull wide automatically, and Jazz laughs. "Great, just like that."

"Is it already time?" Maren asks. Her cheeks are flushed, and she's holding a MASH-branded water bottle. The swag came out of nowhere, showing up at the XLR8 office so quickly I'm half-convinced they had it made before I even signed my contract.

Jazz glances up at a huge screen on the wall, where a count-down's running in emphatic red numerals: 3:22, it says. 3:21. 3:20. "Yep, it's already time."

She turns to me, then reaches to smooth a wrinkle in my shirt. "We gated your match parameters, just like we talked about, so it'll be someone nearby."

The matching functionality is self-gated, so users can select their own age ranges and location radiuses. Because we'll be the poster children for this whole affair, my match and I need to be close—so we can work with Jazz and Evelyn and everyone else all the way up to Celeritas. He'll be a Colorado kid, just like me.

Jazz raises her eyebrows. "You ready?"

When I nod, she turns to Maren. "You good to be on camera?"

"Oh yeah," Maren says, scooting closer to me. "I'm ready for my fifteen minutes of fame."

Jazz flashes her a smile, then gathers her skirt to climb onto the coffee table. She cups her hands around her mouth. "MASHers! Listen up! Ro's about to match."

The room erupts into cheers, and Maren reaches for my hand. When she squeezes, I squeeze back. This is *happening.* Silence falls, and Evelyn parts the crowd to come stand with us.

"All good?" she asks, and I nod.

Jazz has her phone out, already recording. Maren peers down at my screen over my shoulder. I open the app and it's right there, a push notification with the words **Ready to meet your MASH match?**

I click through, taking a deep breath. **Reveal match.** I look at Evelyn, who nods. Then at Maren, who squeals and says, "Come on, come on!"

The countdown clock hits ten seconds, and everyone starts chanting. It's like New Year's Eve on steroids, a hundred people in a high-rise screaming *"Ten, nine, eight!"* When they get to zero I grin like a maniac and hit the button.

At first, I think it's a glitch.

My face freezes in its smile; I couldn't move my lips if I wanted to. My entire body suddenly feels like plastic—like I'm fake, like this is a dream or a joke someone's playing on me. It isn't until Maren whispers "Oh my god" that I remember everyone's watching me.

I look at Evelyn, the expectant set of her mouth, then back down at my phone.

Alistair Miller.

"She's matched!" Jazz cries, deflecting. She turns her phone camera around and cheers, sending up applause and shouting from everyone on the floor. Jazz is still talking, telling people on the livestream to reveal their own matches, to share them on social with #MASHmatch. But I can barely hear her, and when Evelyn cuts the distance between us a high whine splits my eardrums.

"What is it?" Evelyn asks. "What's wrong?"

I swallow, forcing the words. "This guy and I—"

There's no good way to explain what Miller is to me. I look at Maren, her wide eyes, her hand lifted to her mouth. *No*, I think. It repeats across my brain like a marquee. *No, no, no.*

"We have a history," I manage, finally.

"A history," Evelyn repeats. Her eyes move from my phone screen, to Maren's face, to mine. Her gaze is puncturing in its intensity. "A history of what?"

When we were kids, Miller was sweet as a toothache. Almost painful in his purity, so sincere he was like an exposed nerve. He'd cry at a dead bird in the forest, or a tree gored black by lightning-strike. He cried when my mom left, though we were both too little to understand the permanency of her going. Or maybe he did understand, more than I did, and that's why he was so upset.

I grew up temperature-testing the world by his reactions to it. If something set him off, it deserved my attention. If I couldn't fix it, I moved on. We could do nothing about the dead bird, the black tree. But they were sad, he was right—and Miller always concerned himself with what hurt him, even if he could not solve it. That's how we were different.

My mother was his mother's best friend. They moved from Slate Lake together, got a little apartment behind the post office and found jobs—still half an hour from Denver but practically the big city compared to where they grew up. Her name was Willow, after an underappreciated tree in a state known for its aspens and pines. She married Alistair Miller, the new high school math teacher, and when their son was born they named him Alistair, too—like every other boy down the family line. She called him "the littlest Miller." So I called him Miller, too.

I was born a month later. You can imagine it: two girls from the mountains sitting at the lake in their sun hats, their fat babies grabbing at sand in front of them. Miller and I did every milestone together, almost in sync, always him first. *Miller took his first steps*, Willow would tell my mom. And a couple of days later, I'd take mine. We shared all of it. When my mother left, we shared Willow, too.

She's in the photos from my first and second birthdays, standing next to my mom. And from then on it's just her, huddled behind my shoulder with Miller and Vera and my dad, sometimes Miller's dad, too. Smiling into the pop of the flash—her kind, familiar face.

When I was thirteen it was Willow who taught me how to use a tampon, what a tampon even was. I sat in Miller's house with hot tears in my eyes and his mother on the other side of the bathroom door, her voice patient and close. *You okay in there, honey?* I wasn't okay, but I wasn't Miller with the dead bird, either. My own mother was gone but I could swallow that pain, keep it inside me where no one could look at it.

I didn't talk to Willow, or anyone, about my mom. It was too embarrassing to admit that Miller had a mother who loved him and I didn't. I couldn't imagine a single thing more shameful than revealing how much it hurt me. And underneath it all was what I knew so well: that Miller was the better of us.

The adults in our lives gravitated to him; his quiet thoughtfulness drew them in all the same ways it drew me. Miller was entirely without pretense, absolutely knowable because he showed all of himself to everyone. He was unlike anyone else and impossible not to love, my very favorite person on the entire face of the earth. Next to him, what was I? It made sense, I thought, that if only one of us could have that kind of love, he deserved it and I did not.

And so Willow was ours, but she was always Miller's first. She loved books and read us all kinds of stories, but my most vivid memories are of bone-cold Colorado winters huddled in Miller's living room as Willow told us about mythology.

They had a round, spinning lounge chair across from the fireplace, soft from years of use and big enough for both our growing-up bodies. Miller and I would burrow there under quilted blankets and Willow would sit on the couch, reading to us from Edith Hamilton's *Mythology*. We loved those stories—Achilles with his spear, Circe with her spells. Miller would nudge me under the blanket at the good parts, gasp at every twist and look over to check that I was dazzled, too. I was.

We'd play at gods in his yard—me always Athena, the most powerful woman of all. If I'd been Miller I'd have picked Zeus, no question, the king of the gods. But Miller liked Hermes best—quick-witted and wily, light on his feet, the only god to straddle both worlds. We made weapons from fallen branches and smacked them against each other, laughing at the *crack*. We had our own kind of power, just for the two of us.

We got older and things changed around us, but we stayed the same: I read the world through Miller's reception to it, and he showed me what to do by always doing it first. We heard each other in that language between two people who've never known a life without the other in it. He didn't have to speak to tell me he was upset. I didn't have to show him my hurt for him to believe it was there. When we fought, there were no teeth to it—Miller was like air, a given. He'd be there the next day, and the next.

He grew up bony and blue-eyed and pale as river mist, all dark hair and delicate lashes. I was the mess of us—dirt under my fingernails and scabbed elbows and curly hair that never cooperated. We lived just blocks apart and spent sun-soaked summers rollicking from my woods to his attic bedroom to Vera's kitchen for snacks. We were like wedges of the same fruit, the skin between us nearly translucent. Our lives blurred together.

There were others, of course. Maren, who I met in fifth grade, and Sawyer, and Miller's friends from all the activities he buzzed between: piano lessons, classes at the library, Boy Scouts (shortlived). But Miller was different, not so much my friend as a part of my own self. I knew it was the same for him.

Which only made what happened all the worse.

Freshman year was the first time I'd felt invisible in my life. Miller, Maren, and I had gone to a tiny middle school where everyone knew one another. But Switchback Ridge High was the river every other tributary flowed into, and there were three hundred kids in our class. We sat in the lunchroom like sailors in a life raft. Then Maren started spending her lunch period in the art teacher's darkroom, and Miller's whip-smart, bespectacled friends used lunch to tutor the football team. Like so many times in our lives, it was just Miller and me.

Which had always seemed okay, when our world was so small. When we loomed large within it. But here, at Switchback Ridge High, it suddenly felt like there was a whole gem-bright side of life I was missing out on. I wanted to join it and I didn't know how. And, of course, there was Declan Frey.

The first time I saw him was at a pep rally. The Switchback Ridge athletic department wasn't much to look at, but our basketball team had made it to state the year before. Declan was the captain, and that fall he had really come into himself: six foot three, finally a senior, already signed with a scholarship to an East Coast school. He reminded me of a jungle cat, that first time I saw him—his long, powerful limbs and the graceful way he moved. The threatening elegance of him. My heart cracked open like an egg, pooling in my stomach.

I got pretty into basketball after that. Miller came with me to the games, glancing up every now and then from whatever book he was reading to watch me watch the court.

"This is new," he said in his mild way. We were at our second game of the season, halfway up the bleachers.

"What is?"

"Sports." His pointer finger held his place on his page. As a kid, he'd trace every line with his fingertip when he read. He'd grown out of the habit, but sometimes it still twitched out of him. "You've never really cared about sports."

"The team's just so good," I said, feeling like they were the stupidest words I'd ever uttered out loud. "It makes it fun to watch."

Miller glanced at the court, where Declan made a basket from an impossible distance, then back at me. He nodded and looked down at his book. I didn't give a single, solitary shit about basketball, and he knew it.

That first semester, I only ever saw Declan on game days or at a distance. He was a senior, and our classes weren't even in the same part of the building. But every sighting confirmed my suspicion: he was perfectly made, faultlessly coordinated. This was true, I would come to learn, every time and every place except for one. Pottery class.

It was an elective Declan needed to graduate, an easy A he'd set like the cherry on top of his basketball scholarship. It was my only class that wasn't all freshmen, spring semester, January to May. When he walked in that first day my stomach dropped out of my body, and when Mrs. McMahon assigned him the seat across from mine, I had to scoop it back up off the floor.

He was different in that room, or so I let myself think. Dressed in slacks and a button-down for game day, the sleeves rolled up past his elbows. The crude way he tried to shape his very first pinch pot made me fall in love with him even more, his athlete's hands covered in wet clay. He was so defenseless there that it endeared him to me, fooled me into thinking he was like me. He was exposed in that art room, plainly bad at something. I mistook his clumsiness for vulnerability, kindness. It wasn't, but I wouldn't know that until later.

He called me "Flower," which was a brainless nickname. I blushed under it anyway, and by the time April came and he mentioned the party, I was a goner. He didn't invite me, exactly. He mentioned it to a friend, sitting at an adjacent pottery wheel. But he said it *in front of* me. He knew I was listening, I was sure. He smiled at me after, and it was like he'd sunk his teeth into my arm—the idea of this party latched on and did not let me go.

"I don't know," Miller said. We were walking home, same as we always did. "How would we even get there?"

Declan lived on the opposite side of town from us, a ten-minute drive. But we were only freshmen and didn't even have learners' permits. "We'll bike," I said.

"In the dark?" Miller looked at me, and as it usually was with him, I felt like he was asking me something else entirely.

"*Please*, Miller." I grabbed his elbow, shook it. "Don't you want to make more friends? Not sit alone at lunch every day?"

"I don't sit alone," he said, but he didn't look at me then. "I sit with you."

Time had made Miller different: he was still that little boy in tears over the dead bird, but hidden now. I'd watched the change over all three years of middle school, Miller folding himself into smaller and smaller versions that became harder and harder to see.

In fifth grade we'd had a class hamster, Dumpling, that traveled to different rooms to be "adopted" by a new class every quarter. Miller cried when it was our turn to give Dumpling up, and our teacher, stricken, asked what was wrong. *I'll miss him,*

Miller had said. And of course he would. It was that simple—Miller was grieving. But Aiden Sharp had the whole class laughing in two minutes flat. What kind of loser cared so much about a rat?

I stole Aiden's brownie at lunch and smashed it under my shoe, but the damage was done. Miller zipped into himself, saving his big feelings for the times we were alone.

I knew all this, and still, I pressed on.

"We could sit with *more* people," I said.

It wasn't why I wanted to go to the party; Declan and his clay-speckled forearms and his lithe, towering body had consumed my brain like a virus. I didn't say it out loud, but I felt it sharp as a splinter: *This is my chance.* For what, I wasn't exactly sure. But Declan was leaving soon. And what other option did I have?

"I won't know anyone there," Miller said. We were the exact same height at fifteen, the shadows of our strides falling together.

You'll know me, I should have said.

"We'll know Declan," I said.

08

We biked to the party in the dark. Dad thought I was at Maren's and Willow trusted Miller too much to worry where he'd be. He was wearing dark jeans and a black hoodie, like we were going to commit a burglary.

"Are we going to drink?" Miller asked when we dropped our bikes on the front lawn. All the lights were on in Declan's house, a pristine cabin on towering stilts with a wraparound porch. The question was another symptom of the change in Miller—it wasn't always him, now, doing things first.

"I don't know," I said, rubbing my hands together. It was early spring and ten o'clock, cold as winter. Miller's cheeks were pink and windburned from the ride over. "We'll just see what happens, I guess?"

I was trying to sound confident, but from the way Miller looked at me, it clearly wasn't working.

"Right." He looked up at the house. When he swallowed, his Adam's apple bobbed in his throat. "We'll see what happens."

Inside it was humid and loud. Everyone breathing the same air, music thumping through the soles of my sneakers. We wriggled through to the living room and I had the sinking feeling that Miller had been right—we didn't know anyone here. I recognized faces, could've named ten people, maybe. Declan was nowhere in sight. Miller's expression was neutral when he looked at me, which was a gift I didn't deserve.

"Let's get drinks," I said, just to say something. He followed me wordlessly to the sticky-floored kitchen and took the room-temperature can of beer when I held it out. I opened my own, taking a long drink. It was disgusting and tasted vaguely like bread and burned a little on the way down. I took another sip anyway. Miller didn't open his, just let his arm fall to his side and kept it there against his palm. Like it was a rock or a textbook, something he'd keep in case he needed it later.

We moved back to the living room, if only because its vaulted ceiling made the air a little cooler. Miller started scanning the bookshelves above the fireplace. My beer was almost gone and I was starting to feel cored-out by my own humiliation when I heard Declan's voice.

"Flower," he said, and when I turned he was there.

His face was flushed, a crooked smile on his perfect mouth. He moved in a pack, just like he always did, even in his own house. I recognized the four guys surrounding him from the basketball team.

"You made it," he said, and I accepted the words like a trophy. *He did want me here.* "Let me get you a beer." His words were loose and languid. Relaxed, I thought.

When he cracked the tab and handed it to me, beer dribbled in a thin line across my palm.

"Ro," Miller said. I turned and he was grinning, a rare show of feeling for the careful, muted person Miller had become. He'd put his beer down somewhere and was holding a book—tattered, the jacket torn at one edge. On the cover: a man on a flying horse, his arrow nocked against an ink-black sky. Heracles, maybe. Miller would've known.

"It's *Mythology*," he said. "A first edition." He opened the cover and pointed to the thin, black scribble inside. "Signed, too."

His face was lit up and totally open, defenseless. I remember that the most, the way he looked at me—like he knew I'd understand him, like he was safe. It was the last time he ever looked at me like that.

"Cool," Declan said, drawing out the *o*'s in an exaggerated display of sarcasm. His friends laughed, and Declan reached one of his long arms toward Miller. Just like he'd tip the other team's ball away from the basket, he tipped the book out of Miller's hands so it toppled to the floor. Miller jerked inelegantly to catch it, and missed.

When he picked it up and straightened to look at me, his cheeks were red. There's so much I could have said, but I only told him, "Not now." He blinked rapidly, and I had to look away.

"There's a whole library in the office upstairs," Declan said, and as he did his hands landed on my waist. "Knock yourself out."

I looked down at his fingers, curled at the bottom of my rib cage where my T-shirt met my skirt. I thought of them smudged with dried clay in Mrs. McMahon's class, and how much bigger they looked on my body. My brain felt fuzzy and slow. When I looked up, Miller's eyes were moving from Declan's hands to my face.

"Are you okay?"

He asked it right there in front of all of them, no coding to it at all. A cleverer friend would have hidden the question in a different one—did I want water? Did I need some air? But Miller wasn't clever, he was only Miller: honest and unguarded and, in that moment, unsure. I didn't know if I was okay, but I knew I could never say so plainly if I wasn't. Declan's fingertips had dipped below the waistband of my skirt.

"Chill, Miller." I said it on a laugh that wasn't my own. My voice was high and sharp-toothed, something that belonged more to this moment and this place than it did to me. "I don't need you to protect me."

Declan made a noise like air hissing through a cracked window. When he pulled me closer to him, I had the hideous thought that I'd said the right thing. His friends were laughing.

"We're not kids anymore, okay?" It was a cutting, unnecessary thing to say. But everyone was still laughing, and Miller was holding my gaze, and I didn't stop. "Just leave us alone."

Declan's thumb brushed a line across my hip bone. "Take your fairy tales and go, man."

Miller didn't even flinch—he just stared at me. I knew him well enough to know he was waiting for me to say something else, and I should have. Of course I should have. But instead I took a sip of my beer and turned in Declan's hands so we were facing each other.

Later, when I glanced over my shoulder, Miller was gone.

It only took half another beer for Declan's friends to wander off, leaving the two of us pressed into the alcove in the hallway off the living room. Kissing him wasn't what I'd thought it would be—I'd dreamed it as this crystalline thing, but in practice it was wet and warm and sloppy. It made it hard for me to breathe. Declan's body was much bigger than mine, and when he led me toward the bedroom at the back of the house it felt like I had no choice but to follow.

His fingers dipped into the front of my skirt before the door closed behind us, skimming the elastic of my underwear. I felt it like an eel sting, and when I jolted in Declan's arms he laughed breathily in my ear.

"Easy," he said, and something about that word landed on me like cold water.

"Stop," I said, and he didn't. His fingers tugged at the zipper on my skirt, the noise of its undoing like a beacon in the dark. I said it louder, "*STOP*," but it was like he couldn't hear me, or didn't want to, or wasn't listening. I let out a noise like a wounded animal and felt myself go small, shrinking against the inside of the door. He pressed against me and the doorknob ground into my spine. I scrambled for it, jerking against the suffocating weight of him.

When the door swung into the hallway I stumbled backward and Declan blinked, bewildered, into the shock of the light. There were three people leaned against the wall by the bathroom and they looked up, stopped talking. I zipped my skirt, righting it on my hips. I couldn't breathe. My face was sun-surface hot.

As I put distance between us, Declan held his hands up, palms out. Those hands I'd found so beautiful for so long. It was clear, what he was saying to the people watching us: *Look, I'm not touching her. Look, I didn't do anything at all.*

When I finally gasped out onto the lawn, gulping in the sharp night air, Miller's bike was gone. Even after what I'd done, I couldn't believe he'd left me there alone. My bike was by itself at the end of the driveway, its back tire spinning lifelessly in the wind. I made it home only because I'd lived in Switchback Ridge my whole life and knew it well enough to navigate blind.

The next day, when the beer haze was gone and all I had was cotton-mouth and a headache, I tried to call Miller but he didn't answer. I was made of shame. I wanted to tell him sorry a hundred times and I wanted to yell at him for leaving me behind. I'd never done anything without him and I didn't know how to do this— how to wake up into my life after the night I'd had—on my own.

I kept calling, and Miller kept not answering. And he never answered again.

I didn't hear from Declan after that night; he switched seats in pottery class and soon he graduated, disappeared from Switchback Ridge and my life. Still, he lingered longer than I wanted him to. I donated the skirt I'd worn to his house, the best one I owned, because I couldn't look at it without imagining his fingers on the zipper. I didn't tell anyone what happened; not my dad, not

Maren. I could barely admit it to myself.

That fall Miller came back to school six feet tall, fuller through the shoulders, sturdier than I'd ever seen him. In every single way, not my Miller anymore.

Then Maren was all I had. We'd been friends before, but with Miller gone we spent all our time together. *I could never get closer to you*, Maren said, when we were sophomores and I finally told her his half of what had happened. *You were always saving that spot for Miller.* I'd still have given it to him then, was the truth.

The space he left in my life was like a negative in the woods— the blank that remains on the forest floor where something heavy's sat for centuries and finally disappears. Nothing grew there anymore, trained to the absence. I left room for him—never moving the log he always propped his bike against, never touching the deck of cards he'd forgotten in our living room. I dug through my desk drawer every six months to put new batteries in the walkie-talkies we'd used since we were seven, just in case his voice ever crackled over the line.

But it didn't, and the more time passed, the more hardened I became. We were second-semester sophomores and then juniors and then two years had passed, two and a half, nearly three. Miller cut me out of his life so cleanly I could only assume it had been easy for him. And I was too proud, too angry, too—something, not to hate him right back.

We grew apart, I told my dad. *It happens. It was bound to happen eventually.*

09

Maren and I drive home from the match party in near silence. It's that awful time of day, the worst time to be driving, when the sun is low in the sky and glares everything flaming orange. I'm thinking about what Evelyn said on Monday, that I'll get us Celeritas's buy-in by falling in love. About everything that's happened in the last week, how the marketing team has been grooming me to become the face of all this—boosting my social posts, adding MASH branding to every single one of my profiles. And about how my match needs to be my partner for the next six months, to spin this story with me.

I'd hoped it could at least be half-real. That even if we didn't fall in love, we'd *like* each other. Now it'll be a lie, and Miller would never lie. He would never, ever lie for me.

"We have two options," Evelyn said, after pulling Maren and me into a conference room to press us for the truth. I didn't tell her all of it, just the shadowy outline of a story: we grew up together,

I hurt him, he abandoned me, and now we're worse than nothing to each other. "We can fabricate a different match for you, or we can get Alistair Miller on board."

Lying about the algorithm felt off-limits to me, a line we'd never be able to uncross if we breached it now. *And besides*, said the small voice inside me, *the algorithm works. That's the whole point of this.* Which was, of course, the spikiest truth to swallow: Based on everything I knew, everything Vera knew, everything I'd spent all summer studying about human behavior, Miller was my match. We were meant for each other; the algorithm had decided. And if I believed the algorithm worked, well. It had to be true, no matter how much I hated it.

I told Evelyn I didn't want to fabricate anything, and she looked at me with her x-ray eyes and said, "Then we'll need to make this work as it stands. Are you prepared to do that?"

I was keenly aware of Maren next to me, the worry that rolled from her in waves. She was the one who stood by me when Miller disappeared, who watched the wall come up between us and hardened to it right along with me. Evelyn knew what this story sounded like, but Maren knew what it felt like.

"Ro." She touched my wrist, just her fingertips. "You don't have to put yourself through this."

"We could do it with someone else," Evelyn said. "Make someone else the face of MASH. Maybe Jazz, she's media-trained already and single as far as I know." She didn't mince her words. "But if you want to give this app its best chance, you are its strongest narrative: a teenager, a *woman*, who built something on her own that works so well it handed her true love on a silver platter. You make MASH irresistible. It may work with someone else, but it won't work as well."

I'd already sacrificed for this: committed to a hectic-as-hell senior year, made my private life public, pissed my dad all the way off. And I believed in it. I was proud of what Vera and I had done. Evelyn played right into that pride: *If you want to give this app its best chance, you need to do this.* If I didn't, and it all fell apart, it would be my fault and my fault alone. I didn't know if I could handle Miller, but I knew I couldn't handle that.

I looked at Evelyn. "How do we get him on board?"

She nodded, her shoulders relaxing. I'd pleased her. "Given the circumstances, our team will reach out to him first. Ideally, we'll come to a resolution this weekend, before you're seen together at school."

By the time we pull into Maren's driveway, the sun has dipped below the horizon. I can see her parents in the kitchen making dinner, one of her younger brothers at the table on his phone.

"Ro," she says, and I look over at her. "This is batshit."

"It'll be okay." I don't know if it will, but I say it anyway. "They'll tell us what to say, how to act. It'll be like reading a script."

She studies my face, and it makes me want to hide. "You think Miller will stick to a script?"

I bite my lip, then set the scary truth in the air between us. "I have no idea what Miller will do."

My phone buzzes between us. Sawyer Devereux: **Who is it???**

Maren glances at the screen, then up at her house through the windshield. "I don't know if this is good or bad," she says, "but I was just thinking, on the drive home. MASH has only been live for a week, and half that time it was glitched out and wouldn't even load. It's not like it's Facebook or Instagram. I mean—not yet." She offers me a little smile like I might be offended, but I'm not. "So, it's not this universal thing yet. Not everyone has it."

I'm not sure where she's going with this, so I just say, "Right."

"But Miller had it," she says. "He took the whole survey, or he wouldn't have been there for you to match with."

I blink at her, trying to parse what I'm actually feeling from the roil of emotions in my gut.

"He cares," Maren says. "He's paying attention."

Esther is in one of her rare cuddly moods. When I come in from the driveway she's curled in my dad's lap like a ginger croissant, snoring softly. Vera's in the armchair across from them, and she mutes the TV when I close the front door.

Dad hasn't spoken a full sentence to me all week, but now he says, "We watched the livestream." I'm still in the entryway, sandals kicked off and my feet bare on the cold tile. "What happened? Who is he?"

We stare at each other. I can imagine what he's imagining: some faceless guy with his arm around my shoulders, an unpredictable stranger, capable of anything. Someone like Declan Frey, maybe.

"It's Miller," I say. I have no commentary to add, so I don't.

All the tense air rushes out of my father, his shoulders slumping. For a moment, he actually closes his eyes. "Oh, thank god," he says. Because to him, Miller is safe and familiar. Someone he can trust with his one remaining nuclear family member. To me, Miller's something else.

"Dad," I say, not moving any closer. I glance at Vera and she nods, like she knows where I'm headed with this. Dad looks up at me, one hand on Esther's rounded back. "I don't want to go through all this with you mad at me."

"Honey," he says, "I'm not sure I want you to go through all this at all."

I bite my lip, and he pats the couch next to him. When I sit down, Esther cracks an eye open to register my presence, then shuts it again.

"I'm doing this," I tell him. He hasn't turned any lights on yet and the living room is getting dark, crickets just starting to sing through the cracked windows in the kitchen. "I have to try. Vera understands," I say, gesturing at her. She gives me a little look, like, *Do I?* But I barrel on. "Why can't you?"

Dad looks at Vera, but if she disagrees with what I've said she doesn't show it. A gift she's always given me: she'll correct me in private, but never in front of someone else.

"I understand how important this is to you," Dad says slowly. He's still in his work T-shirt, *Beans on the Lake* stitched on the pocket and a smudge of jam at the hem. "But I'm also your dad, and it's my number one job to keep you safe. Can you understand that?"

I nod. "I am safe." It feels true in the bodily sense, all my limbs intact.

"This is going to be overwhelming," Dad says. "You know that, right?"

"It's going to be worth it."

"I hope so." He rubs Esther between the ears, and she lets out a gravelly purr. He looks at Vera again, sighing before he turns back to me. "I know I can't keep you small forever, Ro. Or keep you in this cabin with me forever, or keep you the same forever. But I thought I'd get one more year before you left for the real world. Before all that stress found you."

"I can handle stress."

He smiles, but there's something sad about it. "I know you can. Of course you can."

"Then what?"

He drops a hand onto my shoulder, big and warm and familiar. "I'd just rather you didn't have to."

I swallow, think of Maren. *You don't have to put yourself through this.*

"Pete," Vera says gently, and we both look at her. "Mind if I have a moment alone with our girl?"

Dad hesitates, but then nods and stands from the couch. He places Esther in my lap and brushes a hand over my hair, leans down to kiss the crown of my head before he leaves the room. I close my eyes as he does it: smell his aftershave, feel the scratch of his stubble. We're okay, I know.

"So." Vera eyes me once he's out of earshot. "Alistair Miller."

I look at Esther, rubbing a hand down her back and earning an irritated snarl in return. I tuck my hand under my thigh instead. "Yes," I say.

"Tell me."

"Tell you what?"

Our eyes meet and for a moment she just holds my gaze, a standoff. Vera's a little trickster, five foot two and frailer by the day. Still strong enough to steer me.

"What you're feeling," she says, finally. She coughs, then reaches for her water glass and takes a sip. "It looks big."

What I'm feeling: devastated. That my dream is right at my fingertips, and Miller could ruin it. That I achieved something so purely good and now it's tarnished. That I'm scared, under all of it, of every way I've convinced myself not to miss Miller, and that I don't know how I'll keep it up when he's close to me again.

What I tell her: "How can this be right?"

"Which *this*?"

"How can it be Miller?" My voice cracks, a hairline fracture on the last syllable of his name. Vera loved Miller once, too: he was my shadow, the two of us always at her house, tumbling through her yard. She'd asked, of course, what happened between us back then. But after so much shrugging her off, she finally stopped asking. "It doesn't make sense for it to be Miller. Did we get the algorithm wrong?"

Vera looks at me for a long time. Finally she says, "Does it not make sense?"

Suddenly, stupidly, I feel like I might cry. "Of course not."

She reaches out a hand, and I scoot to the edge of the couch to take it. Her fingers are cool in mine, surprisingly strong when she squeezes my palm.

"Was your fight so insurmountable?" she asks. The same question I've had since freshman year, the one I've held against my heart like shrapnel.

"I think so," I whisper.

Vera's thumb brushes over my knuckles, and her eyes meet mine. "Maybe it's not the algorithm," she says, "that got this wrong."

We're having trouble making contact with Alistair.

The text comes less than twenty-four hours later, early Saturday afternoon. I've spent the morning in bed, reading through old texts with Miller like an idiot with a sunburn lying out at the lake. Just worsening the problem, adding to my pain.

I'd forgotten the shorthand I always fell into with him, no full sentences anywhere, sending Miller a smattering of disconnected words that he always, somehow, understood. He'd respond in complete paragraphs with proper punctuation. Our last texts are the hardest to look at—I should say, *my* last texts. From the morning after the party, and the days after that.

Pick up

Please i want to talk to you

I am an ass, just please call me back

Miller

Miller

Really?

The glaring absence of the words *I'm sorry* makes me want to fling myself from a cliff. Surely I said it in a voice mail, in the rambly, pleading messages I left him for days after we left Declan's house.

Now, my phone pings again. This is Evelyn Cross. We've left him several voice mails. Ideally, we need to meet tomorrow to capitalize on your first appearance together at school. Could you initiate contact?

To be honest, I'm riding the fence about Evelyn. She's smart, clearly, the kind of woman I'm hardwired to admire. Midthirties but leading a whole office on her own. Commanding, sure of herself, great haircut. But she also loves to call herself *Evelyn Cross* even though we know each other now, which is weird. And I do not want to initiate contact.

I'm halfway mad at her for even asking before I realize that assertive Evelyn can't be my intermediary forever. If all goes well, she won't even be my intermediary for another forty-eight hours. At some point, very soon, it'll be just Miller and me. I smash my pillow across my face, empty my lungs into it, and send Miller a text message.

Did you get a voice mail from XLR8?

After years of resolute silence I assume he'll make me wait for an answer, so I force myself out of bed and head to the kitchen for a bagel. But it's only minutes later, as I'm popping the tab on the toaster, that his reply comes through. It's quick and brutal: I did. I'm not interested.

I look at the window over the sink, stare out at the trees in our backyard. They shiver in the wind, moving to music I can't hear. *I'm not interested either*, I want to scream. My body's gone hot and angry. *I'm interested in you staying the hell away from me, you selfish, silent asshat.*

He didn't even take a full five minutes to reject me. He didn't even have to think about it. I want to break something, but instead I smash out the words: I know you don't owe me anything, but this is really important to me. Would you consider taking the meeting? No obligations, just hear them out.

It's painful, but I send the next text anyway: Please.

Hours go by. I eat my bagel, label my binders for the new school year, give Esther a brushing she does not want.

The sun is low in the sky when his text finally comes through. Six characters total.

Ok. 3pm

10

I tell Dad about the meeting, but he has no one to cover for him at Beans, so I go alone.

Call me immediately after, Maren says. *Better yet, livestream it for me.*

I have a feeling it will be a thing like that: the kind of train wreck you want to watch in real time, something you can't rip your gaze from. I haven't been able to bring myself to explain the situation to Sawyer, and her texts are growing more frantic by the hour. It would make absolute sense for Miller and me to carpool the forty-minute drive from our blocks-apart houses into Denver, but of course we do not.

I get there half an hour early, anxiety-chug an entire glass of kombucha, and spend fifteen minutes breathing in the bathroom with my eyes closed. The office is quiet on a Sunday, dust motes catching the light between empty desks and a few people puttering from the kitchen to the conference room where This Will Go

Down. Evelyn's here, plus Jazz from marketing. There's a third person I haven't met, a skinny guy in a short-sleeved, palm-tree-printed button-down who introduces himself as Felix. They have all that infused water set out, just like before.

I take a seat in the conference room and try to still my trembling hands. Once he's here, I know, it'll be okay. Once I can see the shape of this, all I have to do is run with it. But now, not knowing—the anticipation feels like a triple-shot espresso right to the veins. I'm jittery as hell.

"You good, Ro?" Jazz's braids are piled in a knot on top of her head. "Need some water?"

"I'm good," I say, and then Evelyn walks in with Miller and Willow.

Of course she would be here. I don't know why it didn't occur to me before. Miller doesn't look at me, but her eyes find mine immediately.

"Hi, honey," she says. She smiles, and I manage something smile-adjacent in return. Seeing her face is half a relief and half harrowing, a nauseating blend of muscle memory from all the time I spent growing up in her house and all the shame that floods me knowing that she must know, that Miller must have told her all of it.

It was Willow who'd finally called me after Declan's party, when two weeks had passed and Miller still wouldn't answer the phone. The voice mail she left wrapped right around my heart and wrung me out completely. *I don't know what happened*, she'd said. *But I want you to know I'm always going to be here if you need me.*

I knew, though, that Willow was Miller's before she was mine—and that in losing him I'd lost my right to both of them. I didn't reply, and she didn't call again.

"Please have a seat," Evelyn says, gesturing them into chairs across from mine. I'm next to Jazz, with Miller, Willow, and Felix facing me. Evelyn takes the head of the table, same as always. "We're so grateful for your time."

Everyone's murmuring introductions, but I can't rip my eyes off Miller. I half expected him to show up in that stupid tux again, but he's in jeans and canvas sneakers and a threadbare black T-shirt. His new haircut makes his cheekbones look sharper, more raised in his face. I haven't looked at him for this long in years, but if he can feel me staring, he doesn't give in. He looks at me not even once.

"Before I launch into the full spiel," Evelyn says, "how familiar are you with MASH? I don't want to waste any of our time if you're already up to speed."

"I'm familiar," Miller says. His voice is even and steady, the Miller special. Classic freaking Miller, calmer and more in control than anyone else around him. I have a sudden, desperate urge to know the rest of his MASH results.

"Great," Evelyn says, swiveling in her chair to face the presentation on the wall. She skips past her intro slides, wireframes of the MASH interface, and lands on a slide titled *The Road to Celeritas: How We Get There.* "Then we'll cut to the chase. This is where you come in, Alistair."

"Just 'Miller' is fine," he says, and Evelyn nods.

"Miller, we're targeting a February pitch with Celeritas, a venture capital firm in California." She glances at him to make sure he's following, but his eyes are on the presentation, not on her. He's already reading. "For all its exciting facets," Evelyn continues, "we know the most marketable component of MASH is its partner-matching functionality. That's where the money is. And while anyone can make a dating app, Ro is the only person who's made one that's foolproof."

I feel a swell of pride, and hop the fence firmly into Evelyn Cross fan club territory. A not-so-small part of me is thrilled to have her talk me up in front of him.

"Almost foolproof," I say, and Evelyn's eyes dart to mine. "Ninety-three percent."

"A detail," she says, looking away from me. "Ninety-three percent may as well be a hundred, and we'll market the app as entirely foolproof."

I think of Vera—*It's an imperfect science*—but Evelyn's still talking, leaving no room for me to object.

"The partner match is how we'll get consumer buy-in, build buzz, and scale MASH into something shiny enough to catch Celeritas's eye." Evelyn clicks to the next slide, where someone's pasted Miller's yearbook photo in next to mine. And seeing us there, grafted together like two halves of a whole, makes my brain go entirely blank. I stop thinking about MASH's marketing, the promises we'll make, anything at all. Miller's face stares back at me from the wall: his guarded blue eyes, the freckled bridge of his nose, the indecipherable slant of his smile.

"You two will be our proof point," Evelyn says, and I finally blink. "Ro is quickly becoming the face of MASH on social, and soon we'll start scheduling media interviews. Our hope is that you'll be by her side for all of it, and that together you'll show the world just how well MASH works."

Both of us look at Miller, but he's still staring up at the screen. At our two pictures there together, side by side.

"Felix Gutierrez will be your guide," Evelyn says, gesturing to the guy in the palm-tree shirt. He offers a sharp little wave. "He's going to handle your media training, plus considerations like wardrobe that may come up as we go along. We'll have the two of you start with some public appearances, nothing formal, and post a few things to social media. Then we'll book you for an interview here in Denver at the end of September."

Evelyn looks between us. "If that's all tracking so far, we can get into specifics."

Wordlessly, Miller nods.

The next slide is a list of bulleted sentences, each one pressing my ribs tighter and tighter against my lungs.

- Unscripted public appearance (e.g., ice cream, hiking, museum visit)—1x/week
- Social media posts to @rodev—2x/week
- Social media posts to @MASHapp—1x/week
- TV, radio, print interviews—as opportunities arise

I stop reading when it gets truly painful to breathe. *Ice cream?* Miller's eyes are still on the screen. Willow's face is pinched with worry, but when she leans close to whisper something in Miller's ear, he just shakes his head.

"This is an initial list Felix put together," Evelyn says. "He'll walk you through all of it, and we can make adjustments as necessary."

Silence falls at the table. I resist the urge to stare down at my hands, remind myself that this is *my* app. My meeting.

"Miller," Evelyn prompts. "Tell us what you're thinking. What can we do to get you on board?"

Miller looks at Evelyn. In that same, even voice, he tells her, "I want forty-seven thousand dollars."

I'd been running a thumbnail over my knuckle, and I press so hard the skin splits.

Evelyn blinks. "That's a very specific number."

I look at Willow, who's watching her son. On top of the table, her hands are squeezed together so tightly her fingertips have gone white.

"Enough to cover half my college degree after financial aid," Miller says. I wonder how much they talked about this, if they spent all weekend strategizing what they could get out of me. *Fair is fair*, I think. I'm trying to get something out of him, too.

"Understood," Evelyn says. She rises from the table. "Give me just a moment to make a phone call."

The room is underwater-silent while she's gone. Nothing moving, the five of us like amber-trapped bugs waiting for the verdict.

"All right." Evelyn returns less than five minutes later, reclaiming her seat.

Miller speaks first. "Who were you talking to?"

"The head of the board in Mountain View," Evelyn says. "She has an idea."

She, I think. You love to hear it.

"How about this." Evelyn looks at Miller, and he looks right back. His posture is relaxed, like this is the last thing that matters to him in the whole entire world. "We'll pay for your degree," Evelyn says. "All of it. *If* we get the funding from Celeritas. Otherwise, nothing." She points between Miller and me. "You'll have to sell this."

Miller doesn't look at me, doesn't even flinch. "Deal," he says. Confident, I realize, not in me, but in his own ability to pull this off.

The word lands like a mosquito, featherlight and piercing. *Deal.* We're doing this.

"Sweetheart," Willow says softly. Miller looks at her, something inscrutable passing between them. "Are you sure?"

Miller swallows, then jerks his head in a sharp, definitive nod. I watch him sign three different pieces of paper, his mother reading each one before he wraps his name over the dotted line. After that he stands, shakes Evelyn's hand, and walks out of the office. He says nothing to me, does not look at me, makes it clear I am not a going concern at all.

"Well," Felix says. There's a smirk warping the lines of his mouth. "This'll be fun."

11

When I walk to my truck the next morning, Miller is idling at the end of the driveway. Dad's been gone for hours—Mondays start at five o'clock at Beans on the Lake. The air is crisp and clear, that good end-of-summer weather, and I've got twenty minutes until the first bell of my first day of my last year of high school.

Miller's car is his dad's old one, a white station wagon with fake wood grain on all the doors. Miller stares up at me through the windshield. Not so shy about eye contact today, apparently.

I look from Miller's face to my truck and back again. I've got my backpack on, a thermos of tea, and my car keys around my pointer finger. This is not how I imagined this morning going.

Miller rolls down his window. "If you're supposed to be my girlfriend, you should probably get in."

The word burns like acid in my ears.

"Match," I tell him, circling my flatbed and opening his passenger door. "I'm your match, not your girlfriend."

Miller cranes his neck to reverse down our driveway. He's wearing a thin hoodie and the same jeans from yesterday and his hair's still wet. His shampoo smells good, which I hate.

"Functionally," he says, "what's the difference?"

There isn't one, probably, but he's such a smart-ass it makes my skin sting. I can't believe *this* is the first conversation we're having.

"If you're going to do this with me, you need to use the right vernacular."

"Vernacular," Miller repeats, glancing at me as I try to get comfortable. The passenger seat has no padding left and feels like sitting in one of those plastic chairs at a baseball stadium. "Okay, Ro."

My name in his mouth is familiar in a bad way.

"Why are you doing this?" I look at him, then decide it's easier not to and stare straight ahead. "We could've just met at school."

"Is that what we'd do if we were in love?"

I almost spit out my tea. He's just going to throw that word out there, when we're only two minutes in?

"I have absolutely no idea what it would be like if we were in love." I look at him, and he's so unrattled it makes me seethe. "I cannot even *begin* to imagine that scenario."

"Well, you should probably start trying." He comes to a stand-still at a stop sign, waiting a few seconds even though there are no other cars around. "You have a lot riding on this, and I do, too."

I grip my thermos, look out the passenger window. A hawk lands on a fence post and stares at me, blinking his yellow eyes as we roll away. Already, somehow, we're back where we've always been: Miller with the clear vision, keeping us to plan. Me, too wild, veering off course. Even though all of this is mine. Even though MASH and our fabricated relationship and his tuition money wouldn't even exist without me.

"I know that," I say. Last night, Jazz posted a graphic to the @MASHapp handle—pictures of Miller and me spliced right next to each other with a little pink heart connecting them. Like we were fourth-grade valentines, passing cardboard notes with candy glued on. One match to start them all, the caption said. Sawyer and Josie boosted it, just like we'd planned. And like lights blinking on at sundown, like dominoes clicking down the line, my feed filled up all night long: one match after another. People I didn't know, using what I made to find each other.

Sawyer had texted me at nine thirty, the pout radiating from her words: You reunite with your adorable childhood boyfriend right off the bat and I get no match? :(Keep pressing the button but just get a "Love is on the way! Check back soon" message

Just means there isn't a good match in your param-eters yet, I told her, willfully ignoring her incorrect uses of the words *adorable* and *boyfriend*. Sawyer knew Miller when we were young but assumed, like most people, that the only thing to come between us was time. I didn't have the words to explain to her what had happened back then, and I never found them. Can't pair you up until your match joins MASH

What if he never does??

I don't know, I thought. *Date like a normal person?* I wasn't a matchmaker; I was a programmer. And half of me wished MASH had served me up the same message—*Love not found. None for you, Ro!* Maybe it would've been easier than this.

"But we don't need to be in *love* yet," I say, finally, every word sticking to my teeth like taffy. Like some trapped, sickly thing. "We just matched a day ago, and everyone knows it."

"Don't you want to start on the right foot?" Miller says, glancing at me. There's no good answer to a question like that, but he doesn't even give me a chance to respond. "At any rate, we should align on our strategy."

I want to mock him, his stupid boardroom-speak even though it's just me and him alone here in this shitty old car. But this will be easier, I know, if we play nice.

"Agreed," I mutter.

Miller nods. "I think walking you to classes makes sense, and sitting together at lunch on Fridays when I'm not helping in the writing center. I can drive you to school every day but Thursdays; I have to be in early for National Honor Society. Holding hands feels reasonable to me. And we should pick different days to do our public appearances each week so they don't seem scheduled."

He says this like he's delivering the weather report. *Holding hands feels reasonable to me?* I stare down at my fingers, wrapped around my chipped gas-station thermos. I think of Vera, clear-eyed in my dark living room. *Does it not make sense?* And I think of Miller and me, seven years old, rapt in his round chair listening to Willow read about the gods.

"Sure," I tell him. "Sounds logical to me."

Later, as Miller waits for me at my locker, he takes my hand. My fingertips curl over his knuckles and I'm pretty sure I'm sweating, but his skin is cool and dry. Even with a hallway full of people watching us, he is so calm—so impossibly, impossibly calm. I study his face, searching for the boy I knew once who wore the full contents of his heart outside his body for everyone to see. He smiles at someone over my shoulder, and I can't find him here.

But then I remember: This means nothing to Miller. He's doing it for money. He can hold my hand and fake a smile and all the rest because he doesn't care, because there is nothing of his heart to show here at all.

"You're different than you used to be," I tell him.

"Yeah." Miller doesn't look at me. "So are you."

First period, I have Environmental Science. Maren is waiting for me at one of the long black tables, and kicks a stool out when I come through the door. She watches Miller walk down the hallway with round, unblinking eyes.

"Oh my *god*," she hisses, leaning close as I sit down next to her. I feel like I've just run a marathon, though it's not even seven thirty and I left my house less than fifteen minutes ago. "What did he say?"

"He's like a robot," I whisper. Everyone's still coming in, getting settled, comparing new sneakers and campfire burns from the summer. "He showed up at my house unannounced and drove me here and we held hands in the hallway like assholes."

"*What?*" Maren's voice rises and I shush her, looking around. No one cares. Quieter, she says, "You held hands?"

"Like, in the literal sense, yes." I flex my fingers, trying to shake him off me. "Not in a meaningful way."

"Jesus, Ro." Maren's in a white T-shirt and jeans, red scarf tied around her topknot like Rosie the Riveter. I wish, furiously, that I could've just driven to school with her. We were on the phone for an hour last night, dissecting every moment of the tense meeting with Miller and Willow at XLR8. *It sounds like he was scared to look at you or something*, she'd said. *Like you're Medusa.* But Medusa was a force, awe-inspiring and powerful. With Miller, trapped in the car this morning, I'd felt the opposite. "How do you feel?"

"Fine," I say, and Maren rolls her eyes. I try again. "I don't know. Kind of sick, maybe."

"Ro," someone says, and I look up. It's Macy Sakamoto, holding up her phone and grinning. She has MASH open, spiral swirling in the center of her screen. "Are you kidding me with how cool this is?"

And that's how it begins.

12

By lunch, I've texted thirteen people the MASH download link and taken two selfies with other seniors who matched over the weekend—Abbi Gold and Marley Bosnick, Zara Chapman and Noah Young. Abbi and Marley are shy together, careful how they touch each other, Abbi laughing nervously when Marley's arm loops her waist for the photo. Zara and Noah just look relieved, like maybe they were always headed here, and I gave them an excuse to cut to the chase.

"Ro," Noah says, his hand light around my elbow as I'm about to turn away. "Don't tell her, but I've been crushing on Z for years." He smiles self-consciously, the joy of it sparking in his eyes. "I feel like I'm cheating or something. Getting this lucky."

"It's not luck," I tell him. I can imagine it feels that way, though—Noah hitting the button to meet his MASH match, hoping beyond hope it would be Zara and then seeing her name there. It's not luck, exactly, but he's lucky. Luckier than me. "It's just science."

There are others, unmatched—Zack Price nudging me in Spanish to tell me he's going to play pro hockey, Ameena Lazaar stopping me in the hall with a smile like a lightbulb gone off to say she's finally, actually going to get out of Switchback Ridge. "Chicago," she whispers, putting it in the air between us like a gift, or a promise. It feels like everyone who didn't know about MASH before today certainly does now—in every class period I watch at least one person download the app with their phone hidden under their desk.

I feel like I'm in a simulation. It's maybe the best day of my entire life.

I'm sitting down for lunch with Maren when Sawyer texts me again. This time, for once, it's not about her.

Dilemma: she sends, and I wait as the three dots ripple on-screen. Maren peels plastic wrap off her sandwich and leans toward me, reading along.

Let's say you're already in a committed relationship. You want to know your MASH results, but won't the matching fuck things up with your boo?

You have to opt in to be matched, I tell her. You can get the rest of your results without it.

She should know; XLR8's paying her to post about her other predictions until she matches.

Sure, Sawyer sends, but who would be able to resist? Then, the purple devil emoji.

I roll my eyes. Sounds like a personal problem. Who's asking?

Josie, she sends, and Maren cries, "Sweet?"

Josie toured with Hayes Hawkins, twenty and Texan with a voice like honeyed gravel, for her second album. They've been together ever since, and there's probably not a single other couple that America loves more.

Is she gonna break up with Hayes?? I send, but Sawyer quickly dashes any hopes we might've had of being first to the news.

Obv not, she says. **She doesn't want to match, and put it in her XLR8 contract. But MASH is gonna break some hearts. Just something we were texting about so thought I'd take the question to the source.**

That's me, I realize. I am the source of this thing that's crawling across the country phone-by-phone, that's buzzing on people's lips right here in the cafeteria of my own high school.

"She's right," Maren says, chewing. "Have you thought about that? Like, people could break up because of this."

I shrug, popping open a bag of chips. "If you're dissatisfied enough with what you've got going on to pursue your match, that's on you."

"Harsh," Maren says. "But I respect it."

I hold the chips out to her, and she dips her hand into the bag.

"So," I say. "Partner match is live. When are you taking the survey?"

"I will," Maren says, chip poised in one hand. When my eyes narrow, she repeats it. "I *will*. It's a long survey, Ro. 'What one thing would I bring with me to a deserted island?' 'Is it more important that my partner be fun, or reliable?'" She pops the chip into her mouth, crunching. "Why can I only bring one thing to the island? Why can't my partner be both?"

"It's hypothetical," I say, rolling my eyes. "You have to pick for the algorithm to do its job."

"I know, I know." She waves her hand at me. "But I don't know the answers off the top of my head. I opened it and got instantly overwhelmed; I just need a minute."

"Fine, but—"

My phone vibrates on the table between us: *Jazz Richards*. When I swipe it open, her texts are still coming through.

The Denver Post wants to do a profile on you.

Does next Wednesday after school work for the interview?

Maren knocks me in the arm, nearly toppling me out of my seat.

We'll do it at the office.

There's a brief pause, and then: **How's day one with your man? Nice post, btw.**

My man, I think. Miller is neither a man, nor mine. I posted the first of my two requisite weekly social posts about him this morning, a video of him opening my car door in the school parking lot with the overlay **Chivalry?? Dead? Nah, meet Miller. #MASHmatch.** He's smiling in it, sweeps his hand out like a butler. Charming as all hell.

Afterward we walked into the building with two feet of dead air between us, not saying a word to each other.

Miller waits for me at my locker after last period. Maren's with me, calculus textbook tucked under her arm, and she smacks

Miller with it as soon as he's within range.

"What's up, Alistair?" she asks, and he grips his elbow where the book made contact. "Have a good summer?"

"Great," he says, his eyes moving to me. "Are you ready?"

"Loved your preso on *The Iliad*," Maren says. She leans into the locker next to mine. "Did you rewrite the whole book, or was it more of a fan fiction situation?"

I bite back my smile, reaching into my locker for the books I need while Miller's ears go pink. He's so pale that the change registers like blood in snow.

"What're *you* doing for your project?" he asks, and Maren shrugs.

"First proposal's not due for a month, so who knows. Maybe I'll mess around and make an app that predicts the future or something."

"Funny," Miller says, and Maren pokes me in the side.

"I'll see you tomorrow, Ro."

"Take the survey!" I call after her, and she lifts a hand in the air without turning back to look at me.

I close my locker as Miller says, "She hasn't taken it?"

"Uh, not yet." I glance at him, pulling on my backpack. I think of Maren in my car, just this weekend. *He cares*, she'd said, though everything about today has proven otherwise. Before I can help it, the question's out of my mouth. "Why did you?"

He doesn't say anything, just takes my hand, same as this morning. His fingers are bony, the hard knots of his knuckles threaded against mine. We haven't held hands since we were, what, five? I look up at him but he's staring straight ahead, like his hand's disconnected from his body and it's just this dead thing he's given me to hold on to. Like it's not even part of him.

I keep looking at the side of his face, and he keeps not looking back, and by the time we hit the parking lot my whole body's gone hot. When I checked my Instagram follower count during last period, it was close to nine thousand. The *Denver Post* wants to run an entire piece about just me. Josie freaking Sweet is out there in the world having casual conversations about MASH. But still, somehow, Miller makes me feel small. When we get to his car I slam the door.

"Okay," he finally says, after we drive all the way to my house in silence. I have not looked at him even once. He doesn't get to show up after years of shutting me out just to ignore my questions and make me feel like an idiot in the heat of my own success. He doesn't get to ruin this for me but somehow, already, I'm letting him. "You're upset."

"I'm not upset," I snap. I have the car door open, one foot on the gravel of my driveway.

Miller's eyebrows lift just the tiniest distance and it's there, finally, that I see him: the Miller I knew. Reading me whether I want to own up to what he sees or not.

"Don't do that," I say. The September breeze blows through the open door and rustles a parking ticket in his cupholder.

"Do what?"

"Look at me like that."

"I'm not looking at you like anything."

"Then just don't look at me at all."

He says my name again, but only once, and I'm already gone.

I get to XLR8 at three fifteen, headphones looped around my neck and car keys spinning around my finger. This is our arrangement: I get out of school and come straight here, Monday through Friday, until Celeritas.

In the conference room facing the mountains, Jane from the product team is leading a meeting. Up on the screen: a live view of MASH with the buttons off-center, everything a hair out of place.

". . . fix this as soon as possible," she's saying when I step in. "Just makes us look unprofessional."

Everyone turns to look at me, and Jane smiles. "Ro, hey. Come on in."

"What's up with the buttons?" I ask, nodding my chin toward the wall.

"Something's off with the code," she says. "They aren't lining up right, but we'll get it fixed today."

"I'll do it," I tell her, and when she starts to protest I say, "Just give me an hour with a computer. I'll fix it."

I drop my headphones over my ears and turn out of the room, headed for the nearest empty desk. I boot up the computer and turn up my music until I can't hear my heartbeat, or the people moving around me, or my own thoughts tumbling like current over river rock.

I don't know how to handle Miller, how to get through six months of his distant silence, how to thread out the coiling weave of my own stupid feelings.

But this, I know how to do. The computer blinks on.

13

When I get home it's almost seven, and there's music on in the house. It smells like shallots coming from the kitchen, sharp and heady with something smoother mixed in—sage, maybe. Vera's at our dining table with her usual glass of white wine. Dad cranes his neck around the upper cabinets and waves a spatula at me.

"First day!" he calls, and I dump my backpack to the floor. "Come regale us."

We do this every year, a big meal after my first day of school. Used to be Vera would come straight from work, her black brief-case stuffed with papers in need of grading. She'd shake her hair loose from its clip, let out a gusting breath, accept a glass of wine from my dad. Now, she just smiles and pats the table next to her.

"Good day, Rosie?"

"Pretty incredible," I tell her. Dad turns chicken in a pan, and we both look over as it sizzles. "The *Denver Post* wants to interview me next week."

"No kidding," Dad says, as Vera reaches to squeeze my wrist.

"What will you tell them?" she says.

Her expression is neutral and pleasant. When she lifts the wineglass, her hand shakes.

"Depends what they ask," I tell her. "But XLR8 has a whole press kit—key messaging and a bunch of stuff." The messaging leaves no gray area: *MASH accurately predicts users' futures.* I asked if we needed to be so firm, if we could leave a little room for unpredictability, but Evelyn was adamant. MASH needed to be a sure thing, or it wouldn't work at all. And I'm not willing to face a reality where it doesn't work at all—not when we've already come so far. "I should memorize it, probably."

Vera hums her agreement. "I saw the changes they made to the app, that new tagline."

The future's written inside your mind, MASH says now.

"And?" I prompt.

"Feels very Zoltar, don't you think?"

I roll my eyes. "It's not fortune-telling, Vera, it's science. You know that better than anyone."

She holds up her hands, and I watch them tremble. "Just an observation."

"Eat," Dad says, sliding plates in front of us. Vera smiles up at him, hand dropping to his forearm.

"Looks wonderful, Pete."

I lift my fork but I'm still watching her, that face I know as well as my own. She's different now—softer-spoken, slower to laugh, weary in a bone-deep way. But she's still Vera. Who taught me to swim, who made me stovetop mac 'n' cheese for lunch every growing-up summer, whose scared eyes raked over mine when I biked so far from our street I got lost and she found me, crying, outside the 7-Eleven.

"I saw Miller drop you off after school." She says it lightly, like a feather skimming the lake. But she knows me, and when I tense her chin lifts, eyes unwavering on mine.

"How was that?" she asks.

I reach for my fork and knife. "It was fine."

When she and Dad both just stare at me, I repeat it. "It was *fine*."

"You two haven't spent much time together since high school started," Dad says. He takes a bite of chicken, watching my face while he chews. "I'm sure you had a lot to catch up on."

I stare at my plate, slicing my food with surgical precision. "There will be no catching up," I say. "What we're doing is a business transaction."

Over my head, I know they're looking at each other. I don't indulge them by acknowledging it.

"In a way," Dad says, slowly. "But he's also your friend."

"Miller is not my friend." I look up at Dad, his surprised eyes. When Miller stopped coming around he believed the simplicity of it: Miller was just busy, I was just better friends with Maren. "Not even close."

"No," Vera says. She's always known it wasn't so simple. "He's your lover."

"Oh my god," I say, nearly gagging. "Please do not ever use the word *lover*."

Dad's gone red, but Vera only shrugs. "That's what XLR8 is saying, isn't it?"

"I can guarantee they aren't calling him my lover."

"Your beau, then."

I cut my eyes at her, and she sighs. "Whatever word they use, it's not how you feel. Is it?"

I draw a slow breath. I could tell her that sitting in Miller's car this morning felt like dipping into the frozen lake, like going numb and being on fire at the same time. I could show her the half-moon cuts in my palms from my own fingernails, my hands fisted together on our silent drive home just to give me something, anything, to hold on to. I could.

But in the end, I just say, "Miller's my match."

Vera looks at me for a long, silent minute. She doesn't even glance at Dad; it's just the two of us in this, staring each other down. Her thin voice is threaded with steel when she finally speaks. "Don't let them force you into what you aren't ready for, Rosie. Don't lose control of the narrative." She doesn't move, doesn't blink. "This is your story to tell."

The next week, I get to tell it. The *Denver Post* sends a reporter and a photographer to XLR8, and Jazz sets us up in a cushy back office I didn't even realize existed. I sit on a brown leather couch in front of a mountain-facing window, and because we're doing pictures first, Felix flits into the room with a rolling rack of clothing. I look down at what I'm wearing—white T-shirt, corduroy miniskirt, black boots—and then back up at him, eyebrows raised.

"There's nothing wrong with it," he says quickly. He slips a leather jacket off a hanger and hands it to me. "Just add this."

It matches my boots, soft and worn-in with fringe at the shoulders. As I slip it on he moves closer, fluffing my curls out of my face. They're different day by day but this afternoon's not bad, all things considered—low on the frizz and still sun-blond from summer. Felix has blue nail polish on and his eyebrows are immaculate, every hair perfectly in place when he leans close to unstick a curl from my cheekbone. He smells expensive.

"Okay." He leans back to take me in, then nods. "You're a vision."

I roll my eyes and he holds up a finger to stop me. "Always take the compliment." Then he turns to the reporter, a midthirties woman in a navy pantsuit. "She's all yours."

The photographer moves in, directing me to look this way, then that way, cross my legs and then uncross them. Felix and Jazz stand at the corner of my vision, leaned against the wall with their heads together, whispering. I'm starting to feel like a tiger in a cage when Jazz flashes me a smile, both thumbs up.

"Fantastic," the reporter says. She introduced herself earlier as Vanity Jones, which sounds maybe fake but also pretty cool. Her blond hair is so shiny that I can practically see my reflection in it. "I'm going to ask you some questions, Rose, and Jeremy's going to keep taking photographs. You can ignore him."

I glance at Jeremy, who's wearing a huge green hoodie and kind of looks like he just rolled out of bed. He gives me a sleepy smile, then takes another photo as I'm staring right at him.

"Um, okay," I say to Vanity. "And it's just Ro. My name."

"Okay, Ro." Vanity smiles, her teeth white as milk glass. "Can you tell me how you came up with the idea for MASH?"

"Based on the game," I say. "Mansion Apartment Shack House. I used to play it growing up with my best friend, Maren, and I thought: 'Wouldn't it be cool if it was real?'"

"And is it?" Vanity asks. Her eyes on mine are like the sun through a magnifying glass. "Real?"

Across the room, Felix whistles. No softball questions here, apparently. But Jazz put together a five-page key messaging document, and I've spent the last week poring over it. I know this shit back to front.

"Sure it is," I tell her. "Human behavior's ninety-three percent predictable. MASH peers into your brain, takes a look around, and uses those predictable patterns to show you what the future looks like."

"So you're saying it's based on science."

"Yep."

"Whose science?"

There's a brief, held-breath pause. I've been clear with everyone since Vera asked me for that promise: her name can't come up. She wants her privacy, and even if I don't agree with it, I can understand it.

"I worked with a behavioral scientist to build every part of the survey," I tell Vanity. She's recording me and taking notes, and Jeremy's orbiting us like an incredibly slow-moving satellite. "I can promise you MASH uses the latest research to predict users' futures."

"Great," Vanity says. But her voice is like a honeypot: sweet with a knife underneath. "Can you give me a name?"

"No," I say, and Vanity's eyes come up from her notepad to find mine. She says nothing, like she's waiting for me to elaborate. I don't.

"So we're just supposed to take your word for it?"

I glance at Jazz, who mouths, *You got this.* When I look back at Vanity, she's watching me expectantly. "Have you taken the survey?" I ask.

Something in the set of her smile goes rigid. "I have."

"And?" I fold my hands together in my lap. "Any surprises?"

She clears her throat and glances at Jeremy, who's leaned between us to snap a photo at a deeply unflattering angle. "A few, yes."

I raise my eyebrows, and for a moment no one speaks. Finally, Vanity says, "I got 'kindergarten teacher.' For my profession." She crosses her legs. "So you can imagine why I'm dubious about the accuracy of all this."

I shrug, unshaken. "You're not exactly ancient, Vanity. There's time."

"So you're saying I'll be making a career change?"

I offer her a smile, don't break eye contact. "I'm saying time will tell."

14

They run the article the following week, a photo of me on that couch beneath the headline: "Time Will Tell: How Switchback Ridge Senior Ro Devereux Built an App That Sees the Future." In the picture I'm gesturing with one hand, looking directly at Vanity out of frame. Felix was right about the jacket. I look cool as hell.

The article is grudgingly complimentary, and when I read it I can imagine how every word must've nagged at Vanity Jones's skeptical sensibilities.

With nearly six million active users and over two hundred thousand matches, MASH has taken the country by storm. What started as a high school senior's school project has turned into America's favorite app—and Ro Devereux is only getting started.

Even Dad is proud Thursday night when I slap the paper onto the kitchen counter as he's making dinner. He reads the headline leaning away from the stove, stirring onions as his eyes skim the page. His smile spreads slowly, and when he looks up at me I start laughing.

"Can you believe this?" I ask him, and he just says, "Yeah, I can."

The story gets picked up by all our local news channels, syndicated to every corner of the internet. And every time, it's my face there with it, so no one can forget. *Ro Devereux built an app that sees the future.* It's mine. I did it.

I spend every afternoon at the XLR8 office, where momentum from the article hisses among us like woodsmoke. We're all breathing the same eager air, taking lungfuls of it. Every day, MASH downloads go up. Every day, people meet their matches.

And every day, still, there's the One Issue. Alistair freaking Miller.

We follow all the rules: He drives me to school every day but Thursdays, right on time at the end of my driveway like predictable summer rain. I post about him on Instagram twice a week—how he looks with afternoon sun coming through the driver's-side window, or a forced-smile selfie on the one day a week he eats lunch with Maren and me. We go on our dates: Dad eyeing us over the espresso machine at Beans on the Lake, the two of us sitting on the pebbly lakeshore long enough to take a photo and go. When we hold hands now, my palms don't sweat. Unless someone is looking directly our way, we don't speak.

Since that first day in the car, I've kept the heat out of my voice when I talk to him. He's doing his job, and I'm doing mine. The pinprick memory of our past stays where it is: unspoken, buried with the versions of ourselves we were back then. It lives between us like a translucent membrane. I can see Miller through it, but I can't feel him there. In some ways, it's impossible. In some ways, it's easier.

But in the most important way, it's working. Jazz books us, together, for an interview on *Rocky Mountain Live*, the Saturday morning show on Denver's NBC affiliate. Miller doesn't have Instagram, but my account hits fifty thousand followers. I get verified, that little blue check blinking up next to my name. *Officially a big fat liar*, I think, when it happens. When I can't sleep I scroll through the #MASHmatch tag and look at people's beaming faces, one after another after another, and remind myself that I've done something good.

The day after the *Denver Post* article drops, Miller and I get ice cream after school. This date's on a Friday, clearly differentiated from our previous Saturday and Sunday dates in Miller's carefully kept Very Genuine and Totally Normal, Nothing-to-See-Here Date Calendar.

We cross the parking lot with Maren after last period, headed toward Miller's car with his cool palm flush against mine. I feel people watching us as we go: heads lifting from phone screens, cross-country runners glancing up as they lace their sneakers near the track entrance. The senior class president, Sophie Zhao, mentioned the *Denver Post* piece during morning announcements, and Principal Armistead taped a copy to his office door, which everyone has to walk past to get basically anywhere.

All of it's been equal parts mortifying and amazing, but things definitely start to tip toward *mortifying* when we reach Miller's wagon and Aiden Sharp eyes us from the hood of his Jeep. Aiden, who hasn't changed much since fifth grade's Dumpling the Hamster Incident. Aiden, who's looking at us like we're the butt of a joke he can't wait to tell.

"*Ro Devereux's only getting started,*" he quotes in a snide, nasally voice. He chuckles at nothing and props a sneaker on his front grille. "What's next, then, Ro?"

"Flattered you memorized the article, Aiden." I throw my backpack through Miller's open passenger window. "Means a lot to me."

Miller's already sliding behind the wheel, avoiding Aiden just like he has for years. Aiden looks at him pointedly, then back at me. "Weren't you guys friends in middle school or something?"

"Or something," Miller says at the exact same time I say, "Well, we're not just friends now." Miller glances up at me and then quickly away, turning the keys in the ignition.

"When's the wedding?" Aiden asks, and Maren reaches over to smack the brim of his baseball cap upward, sending it flying onto the roof of his car. "Spare us, Aiden."

He goes scrambling after it and Maren turns to me, rolling her eyes.

"Come with us for ice cream?" I ask. XLR8 made us promise to go on dates, but they didn't *explicitly* say she couldn't come, too. I beg her with my eyes over the roof of the wagon, where Miller can't see.

"Actually, I can't." She glances at her phone, and when she looks back at me her cheeks are pink. "There's, um. I've been meaning to—"

"You ready?" Miller calls from inside the car. "I've got tutoring at five, remember?"

I shoot Maren a look, mouthing, *Sorry*. "I'm *coming*."

"Trouble in paradise?" Aiden shouts, throwing open his car door and chucking himself inside.

"Oh my god," Maren says. She thrusts an arm out and shuts his door, nearly clipping his elbow. "You're literally like a very loud mosquito."

"Ro," Miller says again. "Come on."

"Okay, okay. Jesus." I duck into the car, sending a wave at Maren.

"Enjoy the ice cream!" she calls as Miller shifts into reverse. When I look over at him his face is calm and impassive, zipped into himself just like always. Aiden winks at me as we pull out of the spot, and I roll my eyes, and we drive away in silence.

Downtown Switchback Ridge is one block long and five stores strong, the Fast Freeze plopped at the end of the strip like a sprinkle-topped afterthought. It's got a drive-through and a cracked-asphalt parking lot and a towering sign shaped like a cake cone. There are six picnic tables out front, all of them occupied when we get there except the one right next to the trash cans. We sit, thrown into shade by the cone sign.

Miller's in a polo shirt with the National Honor Society logo stitched along the collar, his sunglasses pushed up into his hair. I got a waffle cone but he eats his ice cream from a cup with a spoon, like a big jerk.

"No cone is incredibly lame of you," I tell him.

He doesn't look at me. "That feels like something my match wouldn't say to me."

I indulge in a dramatic eye roll, safely hidden behind my sunglasses where no one can see. When there are people around, Miller and I usually talk about something inane—homework he has, the new recipe Dad's trying out at Beans, how bad we need rain this year. Small talk with him makes us feel like strangers, which is what we are now. I'm debating whether to bring up Aiden when Miller opens his mouth and says, "I read the article."

I lick at my cookies-and-cream. "Keeping tabs on me, huh?"

He looks at me through the dark fringe of his eyelashes. "I have a vested interest." A pause, and then: "I noticed you didn't mention me. Aren't you supposed to?"

I actually recoil a little, leaning away as I look at him. "Excuse me?"

"I thought that was the whole goal of this." He spoons a bite of ice cream, taking so long to finish his point that I want to hop the table and strangle him. "To talk about our relationship as often as possible, communicate how meant-to-be it all is."

I blink, and a small spluttering noise escapes me before I can help it. "The profile was on me," I say. "About the tech and the science and how I made MASH all by myself." He looks up, and I keep talking without even considering the words. "And anyway, Miller, seriously forgive me if you aren't exactly top-of-mind after you haven't spoken to me in three years."

Miller goes absolutely still. He stares at me and it feels like the volume's been turned down on the whole entire world, like the clock's stopped for all of us. I'm not sure I could move even if I wanted to.

Slowly, Miller says, "Which was your choice."

Ice cream drips onto my hand. "I called you *every* day after it happened. You didn't pick up."

He puts his ice cream down, like a parent about to dish some discipline. If I could breathe, I'd use the air to laugh at him.

"You called me every day for one week." When he looks at me, there's a controlled calm holding his features in place. "I was hurt, Ro. I wasn't ready to talk about it."

Every word settles on me like a shovelful of sand, like the lake bed rising up to bury me. I haven't blinked in so long my eyes burn.

"And then you just stopped calling," Miller says, "like you didn't even care anymore."

I thought this pain was dormant in me, impassive as wet wood. But I shock myself, shock both of us maybe, with how fast my fury sparks to flame.

"No," I say, louder than I should. At the table next to us, a woman looks up from her sundae. "You're the one who completely disappeared from my life." More ice cream drips onto my hand, and I wipe it furiously with a neon-pink Fast Freeze napkin. "*You* didn't care, Miller."

"How could you possibly have thought that?" His voice is blade-sharp, everything about him suddenly, crushingly familiar. His hand fisted on the table, every muscle in his forearm gone rigid. The simmer of his hurt, right there on the surface for me to see. "After everything we—you *literally* told me to leave you alone, Ro."

"I clearly didn't mean forever!"

"That wasn't clear!" Miller shouts. His eyes are angry and unblinking on mine. His chest rises and falls, the breath forced and shuddering. And then he shakes his head, just a little, and glances around. The woman watching us looks quickly away.

"We shouldn't be doing this," he says. He stands and throws his ice cream, unfinished, into the trash can. Mine's still dripping all over my hand, a sticky mess these napkins won't fix.

Miller doesn't look back at me, just pulls his car keys from his pocket and turns away.

His voice is flat, like nothing even happened here at all. "Let's go."

15

There's one month out of every year when Miller and I are different ages. Growing up, that four-week span from July to August felt like the twilight zone—a strange dislocation before we phased back into place. It was during that weird, off-kilter month, when Miller was eleven and I was ten, that he saved my life in the woods.

Dad's A-frame is five minutes from the lake if you take the shortcut. Which, of course, we always did: through the trees behind my cabin, around John Able's house and over the gravel drive, down the embankment to McGough Pass Road and around the edge of the dam before scrambling up the hill to the lakeshore. The shortcut was strictly forbidden from a parent perspective. It checked all the major boxes—cutting through private property, crossing busy streets, the dam.

The Gossamer Lake dam looks innocuous from any angle, just a concrete wall with a slow spill of lake water that siphons off to the stream trickling toward town. It's a chipped-rock, rusted-out barrier skeletoned with rebar. It does its job, keeps the lake where it's supposed to be. And pretty much every parent in Switchback Ridge warns their kids away from it.

It's slippery, Dad would always say. *There's algae and uneven surfaces and sharp metal and even the water can change on you, Ro. You can get pulled under before you know what's happening.*

Sounded fake to me. It was just the stupid dam, the same one Miller and I walked the edge of nearly every summer day all our lives. I wrote it off as an adult worry, one that didn't apply to me—I knew the dam differently than Dad, always cooped up in his coffee shop. I was out there all the time. The dam was part of my world, not his. That big hunk of sloping concrete and I had an understanding, I thought.

It was early August, and Miller and I had backpacks full of sunscreen and chip bags and plastic-wrapped sandwiches from Vera's house. I could feel my walkie at the bottom of the bag, hitting my spine when I stood up to pedal. We carried the walkie-talkies with us everywhere: a set Dad had gotten me years before with a range big enough to span from my bedroom to Miller's. *Miller*, I'd asked him that morning. *Do you copy? Let's bike to the lake, over.* I loved that crackle of static before he answered: *Ro, I copy. Meet at your driveway in five. Over and out.*

I was wearing my swimsuit under my shorts and Miller had a baseball cap on, brilliant red with the Captain America logo. I could feel a sunburn starting on my shoulders, on either side of the thin swimsuit straps.

Race you up the hill, I shouted, which is the last thing I remember saying. We'd biked the thin edge of the dam reservoir and now I was pedaling uphill, grinding into my lowest gear as my fat bike tires yanked over uneven tufts of grass. We should've just walked it, like we usually did. It was too steep to bike, too close to the edge of the dam.

Miller yelled my name before it happened, like he knew. The whole thing spiraled at the warp speed of a car wreck, too fast to process. I was on my bike and then I wasn't, and I was falling until I stopped, and the pain exploded from my arm like something superhuman, too big to contain in my body. I don't think I screamed; in my memory the entire thing is empty, shock-wave silent.

When I opened my eyes there was just blue sky above me. Endless and Colorado-cloudless. The pain was too big to breathe through, absolutely too big to speak through. Miller's face appeared above mine, his mouth moving to form words I couldn't hear. I remember thinking his eyes matched the sky perfectly, that I'd have to tell him when I remembered how to talk. I remember that he looked terrified, which registered somewhere as a very big problem. When Miller was scared, I was supposed to be scared, too.

Later, he told me that it was my backpack that stopped the fall: one strap caught on the jut of the dam's concrete lip, interrupting my trajectory. Without it, who knows. My skull might've cracked against the floor of the dam, my brains flowing with the rest of the lake down the stream into town. That didn't happen, but as I fell my left arm caught an exposed thorn of rebar, rusted and vicious as a claw breaching the dam wall. It twisted open a gash from my lower bicep to the outer edge of my wrist. Miller told me he was sure I'd die, that he didn't know a body could hold so much blood.

And somehow, still, he shimmied the for-emergencies-only cell phone from my shorts pocket and called 911. He was eleven. We were stupid kids. If our roles were reversed, I would have called his mother if I called anyone at all. I would have let the panic eat me alive.

In the hospital, they pumped me full of tetanus vaccine and sewed the unpeeled pieces of my arm back together. I remember almost none of it, just flitting in and out of sleep to find Vera next to me, or my dad. I was in the ICU for two days, and when I came home Miller and Willow were waiting there with cookies and cartons of ice cream and a thick stack of DVDs that Miller and I spent the last week of summer watching in my living room. I was groggy and drug-addled, my arm always elevated on a pillow between us. I was bad company, probably, but Miller never left.

"Now you're like Odysseus," he told me the third day I was home. "With his scar from the boar fight." He hovered a pale hand over the Frankenstein mess of my arm, the long gash angry with stitches.

"Even if you're old," he said. "Even if you're different. Now I'll always be able to find you."

That's what I'm thinking about the next morning as a producer from *Rocky Mountain Live* clips a mic to my shirt. About eleven-year-old Miller, and ten-year-old me, and the carnage of my arm that didn't keep us together after all.

The producer steps back and Felix moves in, adjusting the clasp of my necklace out of sight and straightening the hem of my button-down. I have the sleeves rolled up my forearms and his fingers linger there, where the skin is carved silver and sensitive.

"What happened here, sweetie?"

We lock eyes, his perfectly lined and mascaraed. "Gnarly fall," I tell him.

Miller is within easy hearing distance, but when I glance over he's fiddling with his mic and doesn't acknowledge us. Felix has him dressed better than he ever is otherwise: navy chinos and brown leather shoes and a patterned shirt. I start to unroll my sleeve.

"Don't," Felix says, laying his hand on my arm. "We don't need to hide that."

I don't tell him that I wish we could. That the memory of Miller is eclipse-hot and impossible to look at. That in every moment that's passed since the Fast Freeze, there's been no room for anything between us except hatred.

After breaking our unspoken pact of silence about what happened freshman year, the polite distance that Miller and I achieved since matching is gone. He drove me home from the Fast Freeze wordlessly, turning up the radio so loud that it echoed in my skull even after I was home. I lay in my bathtub with my ears underwater for an hour, replaying our fight until all the words bled together but I was surer than ever that he was wrong. That *he* didn't accept my apology, that *he* removed himself from my life, that *he* chose this hateful space we live in now.

How could you possibly have thought that? he'd asked. And I thought, *How could I possibly have thought anything else?*

After a lifetime of sharing everything, Miller had chosen not to share my shame. Not to make space for that cowardly person inside me who spent a week crying into his voice mail. Miller had watched me wheedle for his own mother's affection from the moment mine left. Miller had pulled me bleeding from the Gossamer Lake dam. Miller had been there for every ugly, awful thing. But when we were fifteen, I made a mistake and Miller decided the relief of being free of me was finally bigger than the pain of losing me.

Miller picked that. And, like so many times before, picking it for himself meant he was picking it for both of us.

"Ro. Miller."

We look up in unison, and a guy in a headset waves to us through the doorframe. "Showtime."

16

"Ro Devereux and Alistair Miller." Ruby Chakrabarti is wearing a powder-blue dress and a million-dollar smile. "I'm so excited to have you here this morning on *Rocky Mountain Live*."

Miller beats me to the punch, punctual little teacher's pet that he is. "We're excited to be here, Ruby."

I bite the insides of my cheeks and smile, blinking into the stage lights. It's about two hundred degrees up here, Miller and me on a small couch across a coffee table from Ruby. There's a solid foot of space between us, and his hands are folded in his lap.

"Ro and Miller are seniors at Switchback Ridge High School," Ruby tells the camera. From where I'm sitting, I can see the words scrolling on her teleprompter. "But they're also the faces of MASH: a new app that predicts users' futures through a behavioral science survey. By telling you where you'll live, what you'll do for work, how many kids you'll have, and who your partner will be, MASH takes the guesswork out of modern life. And with MASH

111

matching having just launched a few weeks ago, Ro and Miller here are—dare we say it?—a match made in . . . algorithm."

Ruby turns to us, deftly avoiding the empty coffee mug by her knee. "Ro, Miller. Thanks so much for joining us."

"Absolutely," I say, before Miller can cut me off again. "Thanks for having us."

"Tell us what this has been like so far," Ruby says. That smile is stuck on her like permafrost; it barely moves when she speaks. "You two create an app for your school project, it suddenly goes viral, and you're all over the news." She widens her eyes indulgently. "That's got to be wild."

"Well, *I* made the app," I say. "To be clear."

There's a tense little silence, but then Ruby gives a rehearsed laugh and says, "Credit where credit's due."

"And yes," I say, glancing at the audience. The lights are too bright to make them out; they're a sea of legs and sneakers. "It's been completely wild. I knew MASH was a fun idea, but I never expected so many people to agree."

"It's really not so surprising," Miller says. His voice is casual and even as he shrugs at Ruby. "Ro took a kitschy kids' game, something universally popular with a lot of nostalgic value and very little complexity, and brought it into the digital age. It was bound to appeal to the masses."

In my mind, I watch my head turn to face him like the dummy in *The Exorcist*. But even as I stare at him, Miller keeps looking at Ruby. *What* did he just fucking say? This time, when Ruby laughs, it's even more uncomfortable.

"Kitschy as it may be," I bite out, "MASH as I've reimagined it is incredibly complex." I throw a look at Miller that I can only hope is scalding enough to hurt him. "I'm sure you know, Ruby, that to get your MASH results you have to take a hundred-question survey based on the latest research in behavioral science."

"That's right," Ruby says, and I watch her jump onto this info like it's the last lifeboat on the *Titanic*. "Tell us more about the science, here, Ro. Our brains can predict the future?"

"They sure can," I say. I cue up the right messaging point from Jazz's document and serve it to Ruby on a silver platter. "Human behavior is incredibly predictable. MASH's survey collects all of a user's relevant nature and nurture information, then runs it through an algorithm to predict their future based on dependable, human patterns. It's all rooted in science."

"Fascinating," Ruby says. She turns to Miller, and I think, *Don't look at him.* My skin is very, very hot. "Miller, what would you say to those who write Ro's app off as a gimmick? Who don't believe the science?"

"Come on, Ruby," Miller says. He's so calm and collected and I can't even believe him, how good of a liar he's become. "Ro doesn't need me to protect her."

I blink at the side of Miller's face, watch him smile as his words meet me like a torch. The instant, bone-deep way they burn.

"Defend her, do you mean?" Ruby offers that show-host chortle again, desperately trying to keep us above water. But I know, of course, that he did not mean *defend her*. He meant

Chill, Miller. He meant the horrible way I laughed at him in that hot living room freshman year, with Declan Frey's hands on the bare skin of my stomach. He meant, *I don't need you to protect me.*

"Ro," Ruby says, turning to me, "what do you have to say, then?"

I'm looking at Ruby but it's like I can't even see her—my vision's going blotchy with rage. I'm sweaty, and my body feels like my phone's started ringing while I'm sitting on it, like something's buzzing through me from the inside. I turn my chin so I can't see Miller in my peripheral vision.

"I would say, maybe those people should let it go." My voice betrays me, frayed and forced. "Because all evidence points to the contrary."

Ruby blinks like she's expecting me to say more, but I don't. She clears her throat, plastering on a scathing grin. "Why don't you tell us about MASH matching." She turns to her audience. "Who here this morning's got a MASH match of their own?"

A few cheers go up, some scattered clapping. Ruby's got to save this alone, and by now she knows it.

"A dating app that sees the future," Ruby says, turning back to Miller and me. She waves her bare left hand at us, then the audience. "Now that's something I can get behind."

Miller manages a laugh, but I'm just trying to keep myself from exploding off the couch and blowing this up for real. Miller's words are ping-ponging between my ears, rattling into every corner of my skull. I hate him. I *hate* him for doing this here.

"What's it like to be the first MASH match?" Ruby asks, which seems like a pretty stupid door to open considering how hard we've tanked this so far.

"We feel really lucky," Miller says, verbatim from Jazz's messaging. *Lucky* is the opposite of how I feel. "Getting to know each other without the stress of wondering if we're actually compatible is pretty awesome."

"Isn't that a lot of pressure?" Ruby asks, gathering her immaculately tweezed eyebrows in faux concern. "Especially for such a young couple? I mean, you two aren't even in college yet."

Miller laughs again, and it almost sounds good-natured. "That's right, Ruby. College is next year."

"Do you already have plans? Will you be going together?"

There is no pause, no hesitation. "I'm hoping to pursue Classical Studies at Brown."

It's another drive of the knife, a bow-wrapped reminder: *I am only in this for the money I need. Screw you, Ro, and everything happening here. Your dream isn't mine and I'll happily tank it because I'm off to pursue Classical freaking Studies at Brown.*

"Wow," Ruby says, her eyebrows rising. "How wonderful. Will Ro go, too? Are you worried about being apart?"

This time, Miller finally hesitates long enough for me to land one feeble talking point in this flaming mess of an interview. *The thing I want most*, I think, *is to be apart.*

"Not worried," I tell Ruby. My face is hot as midsummer asphalt, but my voice is steady. "MASH matches will always find their way to each other."

"I certainly hope so," Ruby says, smiling like a threat. "I truly wish you two all the best. We here at *Rocky Mountain Live* are looking forward to following the rest of your incredible journey."

She turns to the audience, who I've kind of forgotten about and who definitely deserve an apology. "We'll be back right after this."

I'm on my feet the moment the cameras cut, crossing to the stage door. I don't know if Miller's following me and I don't care. Ruby Chakrabarti is talking to one of the producers, probably asking for a raise or a security detail or a shot of hard liquor.

When I part the curtains they stay open, and that's how I know Miller's behind me, his footsteps echoing mine. I want to push him backward, get him away from me. I want to swallow up my shame, force it back inside me where it's lived all this time in the dark. I want to scream at him for unearthing a memory on live television he won't talk about when we're alone.

But I do none of these things, because Jazz and Felix are right there waiting for us. Their faces can only be described as *stricken*.

"Y'all . . ." Jazz says. The phone in her hand is blinking with one notification after another.

"To the parking lot," Felix says. His beautiful features are pinched and hard, almost unrecognizable. "Right now. Evelyn's going to die."

17

Evelyn isn't dead, but when I see how angry she is at us, I almost wish she was. When we meet her at the XLR8 offices the next morning, she looks like she hasn't even slept. Her hair is tucked neatly behind her ears, but there are dark circles under her eyes and one of her blouse buttons is in the wrong hole. There's a huge iced coffee on the table in front of her, and when Miller and I step into the conference room she doesn't even say anything for a full minute. She just stares us down, like she's inciting a moment of silence for the shame we should feel.

After cutting us loose from *Rocky Mountain Live* with a warning to keep our phones close, Felix finally texted us to clear our Sunday schedules and get to XLR8 by nine a.m.

I can't do tomorrow, Miller responded, in his typical shithead fashion. Have homework.

Before I could get a word in, Felix sent us a Google Drive link to a document titled *Crisis Monitoring Report*, full of tweets and headlines about our segment on *Rocky Mountain Live*.

The first link read: *MASH's Poster Children Have a Meltdown*.

The second was a Twitter thread—*Young love is so sweet*—complete with screen grabs of Miller and me throwing scathing looks at each other from across the couch.

The third was a GIF, presented without comment, of Miller repeating the words *very little complexity* on a loop.

And that was only the beginning. The document was six pages long.

Take a spin through this, Felix replied. **And clear your schedule.**

We don't drive together, so I'm not sure Miller's going to show up until he parks right next to me in the XLR8 garage. I'm reading a text from Maren, advising me to **Maybe punch him in the face?** when he knocks on my car window and scares the shit out of me.

"Come on," he says, and I don't even have the door open before he turns toward the elevator.

"Why so eager?" I slam the door, hiking my bag onto my shoulder. "Thought you couldn't deign to be here today."

"Well, I'm here." He doesn't look at me when I come to stand beside him. He's got his hands shoved in his jeans pockets and he's wearing some ridiculous T-shirt with a wizard on it and *god*, I really do want to punch him in the face.

"Guess you realized that being a dick to me on public television isn't the way to get your payout?"

"I realized," Miller says, stepping into the elevator, "that I don't have a choice in the matter."

"You have a choice," I tell him, pressing the 11 button. "You can leave any time."

"Really." Miller looks at me, and his gaze is like sun on snow. It hurts to look at. "Is that what you want?"

"Yep." I don't hesitate, don't look away. "That's what I want."

"Okay, Ro." Miller takes a step closer to me. "Let's play this out. I hit the elevator button, send us back down, get in my car, and drive away." His gaze flicks between my eyes, back and forth. "While I'm on the road, I call Evelyn and tell her I'm done. Meanwhile, you ride up to the office and sit at the table across from her. You're alone. You get to watch her react in real time to the news that now you guys are up the creek without a paddle, because you're already invested in this"—he points one finger at his own chest, then mine—"as a value proposition. We're already the promise of true love from MASH. And with me gone, you'll need to walk it back. And then what? You fabricate another match?" He shakes his head. "No, you can't do that now. Too many problems. Is MASH saying you can have more than one match? That your first one might not work out? What happens to the promise of finding your *one and only*?"

He steps back, and the temperature of my cheeks drops ten degrees.

"It doesn't work," Miller says. "You look like liars. People stop believing, and you don't get the money from Celeritas. So if that's what you want, I'll go." The doors slide open, and he sticks out a hand to hold them in place. "Just say the word."

My fingers are curled into fists. He's right: If he goes, we're fucked. If he stays, I'll die a small death every day from here to February. He's so calm, like this doesn't matter to him at all, like nothing that's happened over the last few days meant anything.

"Why are you like this now?" It's a stupid question to ask, but it comes out on its own. "I used to always be able to tell how you were feeling, and now you're like this—this robot, or something. Do you even remember what an emotion is?"

Miller stares at me. When he blinks there's something offended about it, like I spit in his soup or forgot his birthday. "Maybe you don't remember," he says icily, "but there's this thing called *other kids*, and when you grow up having huge feelings all the time, they sort of eat you alive."

My cheeks flame. Of course I remember—Aiden Sharp turning our whole class against Miller when we lost Dumpling the hamster. Those middle school years Miller spent transforming into the quiet, hidden version of himself. But if there's one thing I'm not going to do right now, it's feel bad for him after that stunt he pulled on live TV.

"You were an asshole yesterday," I tell him, and his shoulders stiffen.

"Maybe." Miller drops his hand from the door. "But you need me."

The doors start to slide shut, and Felix appears out of nowhere to stop them with his arm.

"What are you doing?" he demands, looking back and forth

between us. He's wearing a silk kaftan and has never looked more exasperated. "Get in here."

Evelyn waits in the conference room in absolute silence. When we file in and sit across from her, she just stares at us. Felix takes the seat beside her and rubs his temples. Next to me, Miller rests his hands flat on the tabletop.

"Well," Evelyn says. Her voice is low and exhausted. "You've seen the reactions by now. You two have made an absolute mess, and we've been running ragged for the last twenty-four hours trying to fix it. Fielding phone calls, answering inquiries, sending gift baskets to everyone at *Rocky Mountain Live*." She looks at me, then Miller. "What were you thinking?"

When neither of us speaks, she says, "The only positive thing—and I mean the *only* positive thing—is that people seem to have interpreted Miller's *protection* comment as some sort of feminist stand." She hits a button on the table and the projector blinks on, already open to a slide with screenshots of tweets. Miller in his button-down with the words overlaid—*Ro doesn't need me to protect her*—posted with glorifying captions like We stan a feminist king and Say it louder for the fuckboys in the back.

"Thank god," Evelyn says, "because we needed a silver lining here."

I stare unblinking at the screen. *This is not a silver lining*, I want to tell her. *This is the very worst part. This is the knife Miller put between my ribs.*

"We're sorry," Miller says. I don't want him to speak for me, but I'm having trouble speaking at all. "How do we fix it?"

"Great question," Evelyn says. "We've been working on a beta version of the survey, a new model that pulls in additional questions each week to predict new aspects of users' futures: projected income, pets, illness, etcetera."

"*What?*" My voice is loud in the empty office.

Evelyn laser-beams me with her gaze and keeps talking. "We weren't going to release it quite yet, but you two have created the need for a distraction. A new hook to keep MASH not only relevant, but beloved."

"You can't just add questions because you feel like it," I say, leaning toward her over the table. "Vera and I spent months refining those to make sure the predictions are accurate; it's not—"

"And with Vera out of the equation," Evelyn says, "we've been consulting with a behavioral scientist in Los Angeles. Rest assured, we've covered every base."

My mouth opens and closes, working to form a word. "Who?" I finally ask. Vera is the scientist behind MASH; there can't be someone else. "Why haven't you told me any of this?"

"His name is Dr. Blaise Wisener," Evelyn says. "And we haven't wanted to distract you from the matching narrative. Though it's clear you need to increase your focus, even still." Her eyes flick from me to Miller and back again. Then she looks at Felix.

"Which is why we'll be doing media training," he says. My brain feels like it's shuddering between tracks, struggling to keep up. Who the hell is Blaise Wisener? Why didn't anyone ask me about this? "You and me, all day. Then after school if we need it.

Then next weekend if we need that."

Felix leans back in his chair. He leaves one hand hovering in front of him, emphasizes his words with a finger tapped to the table. "We're going to talk about what to say in public, when to touch each other, how to look at each other—every little human thing that I did not think you needed to be told as two fully functioning young adults but that you *obviously* do." Felix looks between us, and I swallow. I feel about five years old. I feel like everything in this room is spiraling out of my control. "That was a disaster. And we also need to address why it happened at all."

We are silent. Felix's eyebrows yank up into his hairline. "*Well?*"

"It was a mistake," Miller says. I look at him, and he pulls his hands into his lap. "We had an argument and we let it affect us. It won't happen again."

How simple, stated like that. What a perfect cause-and-effect. *We had an argument.* Is that what it was?

"No," Felix says. "It certainly will not."

18

After that, Evelyn goes home. I wonder, watching her move toward the elevators, what else she's keeping from me. But I don't have too long to consider it because then it's just Miller and me in the conference room, listening to Felix deliver the most ridiculous lecture of all time.

"Body language," he says, after we've watched ten clips of rom-com couples with, as Felix describes it, *undeniable chemistry*. "It speaks volumes. And yesterday, your body language said, 'I have a clinical allergy to this person.'"

Felix raises the lights in the room and turns to Miller. "When you walk through a door, or sit next to Ro on a couch, or do *anything* in her vicinity, you need to be aware of her body."

Miller doesn't move, but the pale shells of his ears go pink.

"When you move through a tight space together—a doorframe, or a crowded hallway, or an aisle at the freaking grocery store—you touch her back, or her elbow. You *attune* to her." Felix points at me. "Ro is stunning. You are capital-B blessed to be matched with her. Act like it."

I swallow, staring at Felix because I absolutely cannot look at Miller.

"And you," he says to me, "need to meet Miller in the same ways. Reach back for his hand when you get separated in a crowd. Scoot closer to him on the couch. Lean into him like he's your partner and you draw strength from him, because he is and you should." He looks to Miller, then back at me. "You two are ninety-three percent compatible, all right? That's as sure a bet as anyone ever gets, and you're squandering it by letting this pettiness suck up all your air. It's time to get the act together." Silence falls between us, and Felix turns to raise his perfect eyebrows at me. "*Capisce?*"

"Capisce," I say, but my voice is hoarse and unconvincing.

"Similarly," Felix says, replaying a muted clip of a couple at a dinner party. "You need to work on your eye contact. By which I *do not* mean glaring at each other, because you've managed to nail that one with no help from me. Look how these two find each other in the crowd." On-screen, our hero and heroine connect eyes over a platter of canapés. "They're talking to other people, but they're always aware of their partner. They check in, because no matter who else is in the room, there's one person they care about most. They're attuned."

He looks at us, and I take a sip of my water. When Miller agreed to do this with me, I understood, somewhere, that we would need to behave like two people in love. But the actual mechanics of it, the elbow-touching and the eye contact and the *attuning*, feel huge enough to knock me out. With anyone else. With any given stranger. But how can I, possibly, with Miller?

"When one of you speaks," Felix says, "the other looks to them. When Ruby Chakrabarti asks Miller a question on live TV, Ro looks at him like what he's saying is a freaking siren song. If you're in public together and thirty seconds have gone by without one of you looking at the other, correct it." I glance at Miller, but clearly this diatribe has not inspired him to look at me, because he's studying his fingernails. "People in love love to look at each other. That's facts. Apply it."

I nod at Felix, and he says, "Good. We're going to practice right now."

For the first time in an hour, Miller speaks. "What?"

"We need to take a photo to post on social ASAP," Felix says. "Get some damage control going." He stands, readjusting his kaftan. "So we're going to go to the park down the street and stage an adorable little park date moment, and you're going to apply everything we just talked about."

Miller swallows, glancing at me. His cheeks are pink. "Okay," he says, and I wonder what happened to that confident person from the elevator. "Great."

"Great," I echo, though this is decidedly not great.

Felix claps his hands. "*Great.*"

When we step out onto the sidewalk, Miller holds the door for me.

"Nice," Felix says. "Good start, Miller."

He startles, and I know it's because it wasn't intentional. Miller has good manners like a reflex; they have nothing to do with me.

"Ro," Felix says, "take Miller's hand."

I do, and after everything that's happened in the last few days, it feels like I'm betraying myself. I hold Miller's fingers as loosely as possible, and he surprises me by tightening his grip. He looks down at me, and I look back at him, and in the second before I remember he's doing it because he's supposed to, I think, *What?*

"Look at that," Felix says, holding his fingers up and faking a camera. "The picture of young love." A chilly breeze blows his kaftan around his knees. "Very nice."

We walk to the park in silence, listening to Felix prattle on. *Hugs should linger*, he says. And, *Deepen your eye contact whenever possible.* Also, *Make each other laugh, even if you're faking it.* I feel like I should be taking notes, but part of me doesn't want to remember any of this.

The park at the end of the block is small and shaded, a hilly affair with scattered benches and a colorful playground mulched in at the far corner.

"Perfect," Felix says, directing us toward an unoccupied bench. It's green-painted metal dotted with bird shit, and the slats are cold through my jeans when I sit down. "Let's grab some photos here."

Miller sits next to me, goose bumps blooming over his forearms. The wind rustles his hair, and he pushes it back.

"Should've brought a jacket," I tell him, and he just says, "Yeah."

"People," Felix says. He's holding his phone and staring at

us, unimpressed. "Am I going to have to direct this moment by moment, or can you two at least *try* to apply what we talked about inside?"

I scoot closer to Miller, until the seam between our bodies collapses. *He's warm*, my brain tells me. It feels nice before I can remind myself to dislike it. Miller puts one long arm around me. *Also warm.* My shoulder notches into his armpit. I look at Felix, but he just waves his hand, like, *Keep going.*

This already feels like way more than enough, but I steel myself and then cross my legs, angle my body into Miller's, and look up at him. He's already looking down at me. His chin has disappeared into my curls.

"Great!" Felix shouts.

Miller smiles, soft and sincere and incredibly convincing, and then says, "Your hair is eating me."

I'd tell him to go to hell, but it honestly feels like we're already there.

After we post the photo, we stop for lunch. With Felix's careful art direction, it turned out better than I'd dared to imagine: my leg hooked over Miller's on the park bench, his arm looped around me, his fingers in my hair. We're looking at each other and he's smiling and it honest-to-god looks like I'm going to kiss him. Obviously, I did not.

Once we're back in the office, Felix goes to his desk to eat, and Miller and I sit at opposite ends of the giant conference room table. He pulls a textbook out of his backpack the minute Felix leaves the room, and I watch him take careful notes onto a grid-lined pad while he eats. *Interpreting Antiquity*, the book says along the spine. This boy loves a theme.

"Miller."

He doesn't look up, just keeps writing. "Yes?"

"Why Classics?"

His pen stops moving, but he hesitates a moment before responding. "If you're going to make fun of me, just come out with it."

"I'm not," I say, fighting an eye roll. *Jesus Christ.* "I'm making conversation."

He looks up, our eyes connecting over the empty length of the table. His hand is still poised over his notebook, pen just lifted from the paper. "Honestly?"

I nod. "Honestly."

He lets out a slow breath and looks away from me, speaking at the wall of windows. "Sometimes I have trouble making sense of things, how they are now. Why people act certain ways, or why they change. But in these stories, it's simple: there was war or there was peace. It's all about honor, vengeance, love." He looks back at me, and I find his gaze hard to hold. Like he's telling me something I'm not sure, after all, that I want to hear. "It's like humans stripped down to their base instincts. No phones, no social media, no apps telling you anything at all. I don't know." Miller taps his pen on the page, blinks once. "It feels safe to me."

I swallow. Miller's right in front of me, eighteen and unfamiliar and upset with me, probably. But I'm thinking of him as Hermes, laughing as he runs through the woods behind my house, the bright joy in his eyes at nine years old. I can almost hear it: the twigs under his sneakers, the way my name sounded on his voice before we grew up. Suddenly that faraway person feels close to me again, feels present in this room with an immediacy so sharp it makes it hard to breathe.

"Okay," I tell him, finally. He nods, like I said something more than I did. His eyes stay on mine.

"Okay," he agrees.

I look away, take a bite of my sandwich just to do anything at all. I'm pretending to read the stupid marketing copy on the to-go bag when Miller says, "Ro."

He hasn't moved—his pen's still there, hovering over his notebook. The wizard on his T-shirt's half-hidden beneath the table, so it looks like he's just a decapitated, pointy-hat-wearing head.

"What I said about MASH on *Rocky Mountain Live* wasn't fair or true," Miller says. "It's really impressive, what you did. I shouldn't have belittled it."

I could let it go. Accept the apology and look at him when I'm supposed to and reach back in the crowd for his hand and all the rest. It would be easier, maybe, to stay here on the surface. But I've always been the idiot of us, so instead I say, "Then why did you?"

Miller blinks. "Because I was angry with you."

I lift my chin. "I was angry with you, too."

The door pushes open, and we both look up. Felix tosses a stack of key messaging binders onto the table between us.

"Now that we've sorted that out," he says, "let's get down to business."

The training lasts a week. Every day after school, Miller drives me to XLR8 in the wood-paneled wagon and we play at loving each other until five o'clock. There are photo shoots, mock interviews, required viewing (romantic comedies that I watch alone in my bed, trying not to think of Miller watching them alone in his). Our public disaster on *Rocky Mountain Live* ended up driving a spike of MASH downloads, which Felix dismissed with a curt "You got lucky, but it *cannot* happen again." Every day, he gives us a letter grade. By Friday we're at a B minus.

"So we pass," Miller says, and Felix eyes him over the top of his chunky glasses.

"Well, it wouldn't get you into Brown."

"No." Miller stands from the break room couch and pulls his backpack on, white T-shirt collar blinking from beneath his sweater. "My actual grades will do that."

I roll my eyes and Felix gathers our empty cups from the coffee table, ferrying them to the trash. "What will my B-minus students get up to tonight?" he asks. "What are the youths doing with their Fridays these days?"

My plans are glamorous: dinner with Vera and my dad. Miller's are worse.

"Homework," he says. "I have a lot to catch up on after a week of this."

"On a Friday?" I scoff, but he doesn't even look back. Just opens the break room door, car keys in hand.

"On a Friday," he says. "Let's go."

We drive home the same way we always do: staring straight ahead, one of Miller's world news podcasts droning between us. We don't look at each other, touch each other, *attune* to each other. We've learned to be better, maybe, at faking it in public. But beneath the surface we're just the same.

"Well, this is quite sweet."

When I come through the front door, Vera's perched at the kitchen table with Dad's laptop open in front of her. She's peering at the screen and he's leaning over her, one arm braced on the table to read over her shoulder. They both look up.

"What is?" I ask.

"This profile the school did on you," she says. "Have you seen it?"

I forgot that was dropping today. Principal Armistead thought we'd make for a good home-page banner—senior project success stories. I step behind Vera to look at the screen, and there we are. XLR8 sent the photo to Switchback Ridge High directly from our new press kit: Miller and me in front of a pink MASH-branded banner with *The Future's Written Inside Your Mind* on it in white script.

Miller's arm is around my shoulders, his wrist loose, his fingertips brushing my bicep. He's looking down at me, mouth half-open like he's talking, and I'm laughing directly into the camera. We're standing in the photo and it strikes me that Miller looks twice my size: he's got at least eight inches on me, his shoulders wingspan-broad. We never used to be that way, so imbalanced. Like I'm something Miller could tuck away, instead of an equal version of his same self.

"It does look sweet," I tell Vera.

She looks up at me, pulling off her glasses with one slow, shaky hand. "Did you resolve your tiff from the morning show?"

They watched it, of course—my dad made celebratory pancakes and everything.

"Sure," I say. "We resolved it."

She and Dad share a look, and Vera switches gears.

"I looked him up," she says. "Blaise Wisener."

We watch each other in silence. I know what she wants me to say, but I can't bring myself to admit it out loud: he's a nightmare. Late fifties with a trim, white beard and all-black clothing in the photograph on his website, where he describes himself as a *shaman of the human soul*. He runs a wellness retreat in Malibu called the Wisener Institute, where celebrities and anyone else with an extraneous sixty thousand dollars can spend a month *reconnecting to their soul self*. I couldn't find any indication of where the "Dr."

in his title came from. Evelyn is steadfastly ignoring my attempts to talk.

There's nothing to be concerned about, she told me when I texted her in a panic after finding his bio. *The algorithm is solid. Focus on your training with Miller.*

"They'll use him to justify anything," Vera says. "Irresponsible predictions. Things we cannot know."

"The categories they're adding are harmless," I tell her, dodging. "What breed of dog you'll adopt? I mean, it's not going to be anything sinister."

Vera's eyes track over mine. "Are you sure?"

No, I think. "I'm sure."

There's a tense silence, and she doesn't break eye contact. From across the room, Dad clears his throat.

"Well," he says. "Those came for you today." He points to the end of the table, where a University of Colorado Boulder pamphlet beams up at the ceiling. There are at least three others beneath it, different schools trying to grub my tuition dollars. "Common app's due in a couple months. Have you started?"

"Dad." I'm grateful for the change of subject, but does it have to be this one? Lately Maren's been talking about college, too, working on her list during lunch. I don't need another reminder. "You know I haven't started. And I'm not going to."

"Ro, you'll miss—"

I don't get the chance to hear what I'll miss, because Vera starts coughing. It's reedy and breathless, shaking her tiny frame. I reach for her hand and she grips on, our argument forgotten, her papery skin cold against mine. Dad brings over a glass of water and sets it on the table. When our eyes meet over Vera's head, the look on his face makes my blood run slow. It's fear.

And even when she stops coughing, when she takes a sip of water and assures us she's fine, it stays there.

She has an appointment with her oncologist the next week, and I'm diverting every last ounce of energy into keeping busy so I don't have to think about it.

When I get to the courtyard for lunch on Wednesday, Maren's setting a clunky film camera onto our table.

"What's this?" I ask.

She's wearing an oversized sweatshirt and her hair in a ponytail, and she grins when she sees me. "I finally picked a project."

I blink at her three times before the words land. *Senior* project. School. There's a world, still, outside the new MASH categories and love training.

"Should I be worried?" I slide onto the bench, squinting against the high October sun. The aspen leaves have yellowed over the edge of the hill. "Competitive future-predicting app?"

She barks out a little laugh, then fiddles with the camera strap. "Close, but no. I'm going to do a photo study type of thing. All film, black and white. Mr. Kong is letting me borrow this until I present in April."

"That's perfect," I tell her, meaning it. Maren's loved photography forever—she took all the photos for Beans on the Lake's new website a few years ago, and she heads up the skeleton crew of our yearbook committee. She's thinking about studying art next year, wherever she winds up for college. Hopefully not too far from XLR8 and me. "What kind of photo study?"

"Still massaging the details," she says, pulling a Ziploc of carrots from her bag. "But I'm thinking like a *when they're looking the other way* sort of thing. Pictures of people when they're unaware or caught off guard. Capturing people without all the preening." She changes her voice to sound like a movie trailer narrator. "Peering below the hood of humanity."

"I love it." I steal one of her carrots. "As long as there are no unflattering photos of me."

Maren crosses her heart. "I'd never. Though I would love to take some at XLR8 if you think you could bring me in. A lil' *corporate America* sauce to spice things up."

"Anytime," I tell her. "Felix loves to have his photo taken."

Maren laughs. "That's the opposite of the point of this, but thanks."

"Though, most everyone at XLR8's taken the MASH survey, so you'll probably feel out of place." I raise my eyebrows at her, and we sit like that for a moment in silence. Maren's been hedging for a month now—*I'll take it soon, just haven't had a sec, I'll get to it.* I've been busy, but still. It's like a little splinter, always pinching at me. Catching on things as soon as I've forgotten about it, reminding me with a twinge of pain that something foreign's gotten stuck here between us.

It's one thing for my dad and Vera not to have taken the MASH survey; they barely even text, not to mention use apps. But with Maren, it's something else. MASH has become nearly my entire life, and it's like Maren doesn't want to share that with me after all.

She sighs, long and slow, not looking at me. Laughter erupts at the table next to us and we both look over to see Taj Singh telling the soccer team a story with his hands waving through the air. A couple of weeks ago he came up to me in calculus, told me MASH predicted he's going to be a dentist when he's always wanted to be a doctor. *Can it be wrong?* he'd asked, his voice half a whisper. *There's a seven percent chance it's wrong*, I thought but didn't say. XLR8 was clear: we pitch MASH as foolproof or not at all. *It's still medicine*, I'd told him instead.

I look back at Maren and she's watching Taj, like maybe she can put off this conversation with me if she listens to the end of his story.

"Maren."

Her eyes finally move to mine. "Ro," she says, and I know in the same second that she's never going to take the survey. The way her voice moves around my name is an apology. "I don't want to know my future." She shrugs, almost helplessly. "MASH was only supposed to be a game. What if I hate what I learn? What if it scares me? I just want to feel my life as it happens."

"But you said yourself that as soon as the partner match was live, you'd want to take it."

She hesitates, swiping at her bangs the way she always does when she's stalling. "I mean, no offense, but." She gestures toward me. "I've seen how the matching thing can go south."

"I don't think it's even possible for you to wind up in a situation like mine."

She sighs. "Maybe not. But, um." Maren bites her lip, looks

back at Taj, at the aspens on the hill, at anything but me.

"Maren."

"I met someone." She blurts it like the words are hot, like they hurt in her mouth and she has to get them out. "And I don't want to get matched and fuck it up."

I lean away from her, blinking rapidly. "What? You didn't tell me?"

"You haven't exactly been around to tell," Maren says. "Which I get, honestly. MASH is amazing, and you're busy, and it's really fucking cool, Ro, but I barely see you anymore."

She's right—I know she is the moment she says the words. But still I find myself saying, "That's not true. I see you every day at school."

"Yeah," Maren concedes slowly. "And we catch up about the latest Miller disaster, or the fact that another celebrity joined MASH, or how many downloads you're at. I've tried to tell you a couple times, like that day in the parking lot with Aiden, but we kept getting distracted."

I drop my head directly onto the picnic table, closing my eyes. I picture that moment: Aiden's stupid sneer, Miller's stony silence. "I'm the worst," I say. "I'm sorry."

Maren's hand lands on my shoulder, shaking it until I look up at her. "I agree that you're the worst and I accept your apology."

I roll my eyes and she laughs. "I can't believe you've been keeping this from me." I say it as lightly as I can manage, but the words hurt on their way out. Have I really been so wrapped up in MASH that I missed something this enormous? For nearly three years, it's been Maren and me. After my catastrophic attempt to branch out at Declan's party, after losing Miller, narrowing my world to Maren always made the most sense. And now here I am, messing that up, too.

"Her name's Autumn," Maren says, and in the same minute I feel my phone vibrate. "I met her on a hike."

Just brought Vera home, Dad's sent. Let's talk tonight.

20

The same day Miller and I book an interview with BuzzFeed, Vera winds up in the hospital for the first time. Her cancer is beyond treatment. She comes home from that two-day stay and moves in with us, which is how I know she's dying for real.

I was twelve when she did chemo the first time, young enough to be scared in broad strokes that didn't take specific shape behind my eyelids. Now, every time I try to sleep, the searing details of losing Vera are there waiting for me: her house I grew up in sold to a stranger, the conversations I'll have about the app she helped me create, every single celebratory dinner for the rest of my life without her there.

Her illness makes Miller bearable only because now something else hurts more. I throw myself deeper into the work, and it helps me forget. We do the BuzzFeed interview over video chat, and Miller makes endearing jokes and I touch his shoulder and when they publish it they call us "Mo" and it sticks. We start a weekly web series, *MASH with Mo*, and answer questions from other MASH couples. We do interviews with Mashable and Ars Technica. Sawyer finally matches with a brawny tattoo artist from St. Paul and blows up my phone with selfies from their "life-affirming" first date. If she was an ambassador for MASH before, she's its number one hype woman now.

The energy at the XLR8 offices is off the charts, and Evelyn looks more powerful by the day. Now, MASH can tell you not only your future profession, city of residence, number of children, and perfect match—but also the species and breed of your first pet, diseases you may be susceptible to as you age, and when you'll retire. Every week, we release a new category.

No one will explain the science to me. *It's solid*, the product team tells me every time we add more questions. *Checked it with Dr. Wisener.* It gives me a near-constant stomachache, but even I have to admit that it's working: by the last week of October, MASH holds the number one spot on the App Store's "Editor's Choice" list.

Even *Rocky Mountain Live* invites us back, a do-over during their Halloween segment on couples' costumes. We show up on-air as Adam and Eve, the very first couple, a joke Felix finds hilarious. Miller submits his application to Brown backstage in his bodysuit, fake leaves wound across his torso as we wait for our curtain call. I watch him reach for the button on his laptop, setting his shoulders and drawing a deep breath. It's like he's alone in the world: techs and producers and god-knows-who flit around him, jostling each other as they hurry past. But Miller's set apart in the peace he creates for himself. I think, distantly, that I wish I could meet him there. His fingertip hits the button, and he lets out a rush of air. Smiles. When he looks up and our eyes meet, it drops from his mouth.

Our value proposition sells—to anyone looking in at us, we're *truly*, *madly*, *deeply*. Because there we are: Miller's warm body against mine onstage, his arm slung around my shoulders, his eyes on me when he laughs, like I'm the person he wants to share every joke with. After slipping that very first time, he's perfection when we're together. Smart and attentive and charming as hell. He pokes fun at himself and lifts me up and smiles while doing both. Everyone loves him. After every interview, web series, social post, the internet lights up with his fan club.

Can we talk about MILLERRRRR????

hey @rodev if you ever change your mind, I'll take Miller off your hands

Only thing stopping me from downloading MASH is I know I won't match with Miller

And then there's me, the girl who has him, watching him detangle from me the moment we're backstage. Cutting his eyes from mine like the rip of a Band-Aid, saying nothing as he walks away. He's become such a good liar he even has me convinced sometimes—in suspended, sporadic moments I forget that behind the public Miller who loves me is the real Miller who hates me.

As Mo falls deeper in love on-camera, the real divide between us stays gaping and night-black and frigid. There is no air in the space we share. It's impossible, there, to do something so simple as breathe.

Jazz texts us on a Friday in early November, as Miller and I are walking to his car after school. Maren walks beside us, ever-present film camera looped around her neck. She's telling us about her weekend plans with Autumn, the band they'll see live at a club in Denver. Autumn's a freshman at CU and she's got Maren absolutely upside down, a fully inverted, giggly version of herself. It's wonderful and—as Miller drops my hand the second we reach his car—I hate it with a hideous, fire-breathing jealousy. Maren is happy without me. I'm miserable with Miller, and Vera's home sleeping through her pain medication, and my dad brings up college twice a day.

When's your winter break? Jazz says. Miller and I pull out our phones to read it at the same time. We have a lot of interest in you two in NYC. Today Show. Jimmy Fallon. MORE.

She's still typing. We want to get you out there for a week and book a bunch at once. #MO4EVER

I look at Miller, who's done reading and staring at me over the roof of his car. "The *Today* show?" he says, and even though we're our real selves right now, there's wonder in his voice.

"Hold up." Maren looks back and forth between us. "*What?*"

"They want us on the *Today* show," I say. I reread Jazz's text just to make sure it's real. And then I think, *We've got this.* Celeritas is in the bag.

"You're going to New York?" Maren squeals, swatting me in the arm.

I grin at her. "We're going to New York."

But then I go home, energy buzzing in me like the lit fuse of a firework, and Dad shuts it all down with a firm, effusive *no*.

My first mistake, I know, is I don't ask for permission. I *tell* Dad we're going to New York at the holidays. He's making soup when I come inside, phone tucked between his ear and his shoulder as he hangs up with Uncle Harding. The door to the back room we converted for Vera is open just a crack.

"The *Today* show wants us on," I tell him, breathless with it. I shed my bag, my shoes, and my jacket, leaving them behind me like a trail of bread crumbs back to the exact spot I started fucking this up. "And Jimmy Fallon. And Jazz says there are even more! We'll go over winter break, for a whole week, and do a bunch at once and there's no *way* Celeritas won't want MASH after this; we'll be everywhere, we'll—"

"You'll be everywhere," Dad repeats, cutting me off. He looks up from the soup pot and I swallow, the animal act of it reminding me I'm in a body and I'm someone's kid and it's not all up to me yet.

"No, no," Dad says when he catches my expression. "Don't let me stop you, Ro. Will you book your own flights, or do I need to do that? And you'll go all the way across the country alone? Without me or Vera?"

I look across the dining room toward that just-parted door. It's dark inside, purple-tinged black. Vera mostly sleeps now. In the afternoons a nurse comes by to give her medicine and talk to Dad. Most nights, Vera doesn't get up to join us for meals.

She's at her best in the mornings, when I slip into her dawn-blue room before school and sit on the edge of the mattress. Sometimes she's still asleep, and I try not to wake her. Sometimes I tell her how MASH is doing, or describe Dad's weekly special at Beans, or show her one of Maren's black-and-white photographs. Almost always, I think of all the times I fell asleep at her house growing up, how she'd wake me with a cool hand brushed across my forehead. The way she'd murmur, *Come back to me, Rosie. Come on back from dreamland.* I wish I could wake her now. That the place she was going was somewhere so simple as sleep.

"I'm sorry," I say, turning to Dad. "I'll back up, I shouldn't have—I should have asked you. But this is huge, I mean." I hesitate, staring at the familiar jut of the shoulder he's turned against me. "I can go, right?"

"No." Dad's voice is flat. "There's so much going on here, and this thing is consuming your whole life—"

"It's not a *thing.*" I should let him speak, but I can't help myself. "I made it. I'm proud of it. And it's really taking off and I have to see it through and I don't understand why you can't see that."

"I see it," Dad says, finally looking at me. "The difference is I see other things, too, and I'm not sure you do anymore."

"What does that mean?"

I can tell he wants to say something and decides against it. He shakes his head and turns back to the soup without answering me.

"You're just going to ignore me?" I say, taking a step closer. His back is tense under his T-shirt. "Your only kid? Who made something that people really love and is proud of herself and maybe you should be, too, but instead—"

"Listen up," Dad shouts, and the tenor of his voice steals the rest of the words from my throat. We are not a loud family; he almost never yells. His eyes, the exact same shade of brown as mine, look like sparked kindling. "I love you. You are my best thing, Ro."

I retreat half a step, paralyzed by the rift between his anger and what he's saying through it.

"I *am* proud of you. And when you think I'm being unreasonable, it's because I see something that you don't. It is *always* because I love you." His eyebrows lift like an underscore. "Do you understand? The last few months you've been so absorbed in MASH that you aren't willing to look past it, but there are other things happening here that need to matter to you." He points toward Vera's room. "That's one. College is another. I'm not asking for all your attention, but I do need some of it. And as long as you're living in this house, you don't walk through my front door and tell me you're getting on a plane to *anywhere* without asking first. Got it?"

The soup is boiling, steam hissing from the crack beneath the pot lid. It moves in white clouds behind my father so he looks like he's just risen from the depths of hell.

"I see Vera every day," I tell him weakly. I say it like it's an apology because it should be.

"Yeah?" Dad says. "I hope you feel like it's enough, Ro. Because—" He breaks off, eyes still on mine.

I know what he was going to say: *Because soon she'll be gone.* He stops himself because he's my dad, because he'd never stoke my guilt so pointedly.

"Because she loves you, too," he finishes, finally. "And she wants to share your life with you."

"I want to share my life with her, too." My voice cracks on the words, betraying me. Dad steps forward and hugs me, the world going dark as my face presses to the space between his chest and his shoulder. The same spot I've cried into a thousand, thousand times. But my eyes are dry: when the tears come, I know, I'll have admitted this to myself.

"You can't make her better by pretending she's not sick," Dad says over the top of my head. His voice is quiet now, and gentle. But I don't want to hear this; I'd rather he was shouting again. "You can't make this go away by not looking at it. I know you want to, Ro. But you can't."

I step back, rubbing at my eyes, my cheeks. "I'm not pretending anything," I tell him. "I've just been busy. I just—there's school, and XLR8, and interviews, and Maren's got this new girlfriend, and it's just a lot. There's a lot and I'm just. Busy."

Dad studies my face, his gaze moving from my left eye to my right and back again. Like he's testing for vulnerability, weighing which one might let him in. I'm quiet, square-jawed, until he finally says, "All right."

"I promise," I tell him, but even I'm not sure what I mean. I promise what? I feel, acutely, like I'm letting both of us down.

"All right," Dad repeats. He turns back to the soup, silent for so long I think he's not going to say anything else at all. But finally, just as I'm turning away, he speaks. "You can go to New York, but you can't miss Christmas. And if I agree to this for you, you have to apply to college." He looks up, our eyes meeting. "For me."

"Dad—" I start to protest, but he holds up a hand.

"I want you to have every option available to you, Ro. Come spring, you can still pick your favorite one. I won't take that from you. But I want you to have choices."

Vera's voice rises, then, feeble from the back of the house. "Rosie?" she calls. "Are you home?"

And instead of finishing this fight, instead of telling Dad my choice is already made, I go to her.

My father—classically trained chef, business owner, one-day-hopefully restauranteur—has always hated Thanksgiving. *We celebrate food every day in this house,* he'll huff anytime I push him on it. He hates the press of people at the grocery store; he hates the tourists that fill the rental houses on the lake. Truthfully, I think he loves food so much he feels cheapened by a holiday that makes a gluttony of it. But whatever the reason, I grew up spending Thanksgiving Day giving thanks for something else—not the food before us, but the mountains around us.

We hike the same trail every year, a six-mile loop into the spread meadow of an old mining town where rotted-out wooden structures still stand, windowless. Sometimes there are others: Adult children visiting their parents, out hiking while they cook at home. College students who can't fly back to whatever state they came from for such a short break. Solo trekkers who always make me wonder: Do they have no one to spend the day with? Or do they prefer to spend the day here, on their own with the earth?

Usually, for most of the trail, it's only Dad and me. Our steady footfalls on the just-crunchy leaves, the thin winter air turning our lungs clean and cold. We bring coffee in thermoses and Dad's bear-deep laugh floats up the aspen trunks and every year, no matter what else, this day is the same.

Until, of course, it isn't.

On Thanksgiving morning, Vera winds up in the hospital for the second time. It happens before I'm awake, and Dad does not tell me the details—a gift, I know. He only holds me on our doorstep, one hand on my shoulder like the lone root tethering me in place, as the ambulance pulls away. Sirens off, because they've made her stable and it's early morning and—for god's sake—it's a holiday. No one should have to listen to ambulance sirens today.

When he heads for his car to follow, he lets me decide: I can stay, or I can go with him. I feel tears forming around the words as I say them, regretting the choice in the same moment I make it. "I'll stay," I tell him, and he nods, and he goes.

Maren is at home with her whole extended family: her mom's two sisters from Omaha and her dad's brother and the whole gaggle of cousins. Her grandparents, too. Sawyer, the only family member I talk to with any kind of regularity, has mostly fallen off the map since meeting her match. And Miller—I have no idea what Miller is doing. If it's not MASH-related, we don't speak of it at all.

I am, I'm trying to say, alone.

When I step back into the house even Esther turns away from me, curling into herself in Dad's spot on the couch. The house is absolutely silent but my brain feels loud, feels like all my synapses are screaming at once but not in unison. The motherless mashup of my family is disintegrating. Vera will be another person who leaves me behind, and there's nothing I can do about it.

My phone pings as I'm standing there, a notification from the MASH app. Happy Thanksgiving, it shouts up at me. New category added: number of grandchildren. Take the survey to see your results.

I stare at the screen until my eyes start to water. And then I take my truck keys off their nail by the door, and I drive the forty minutes out of town, and I hike the Thanksgiving trail all by myself.

Vera finds me out there, in the woods. The wind sighs through the trees and I hear her in it, impossibly. She shows up not as she is now, but in all the ways I want to remember her.

Sitting at the antique desk in her library of an office, framed by wall-to-wall bookshelves as she spoke on the phone to a faculty member. Her reading glasses on the bridge of her nose, low enough that she could wink at me over them as she *mm-hmm*ed into the receiver. She had a pull-apart model of the human brain on a low table and I'd fumble around with it until my dad came home from work, smoothing my thumbs over the prefrontal cortex, its divots like the wrinkles of a hairless cat.

Gasping in the passenger seat of the truck she gave me for my sixteenth birthday, a rusted-out junker with manual transmission that took me months to learn. Her knuckles going white around each other but the way she said nothing, that she let me learn the hard way, the only way I knew how. And the first time I finally got it right—feeling that catch between the gas and the clutch like I'd opened the portal to a new world—how she clapped her hands and said, *I knew it. I knew you were going to get it that time.*

Then, of course, this summer. The high-sun days we spent on her back porch, talking about MASH. She didn't get it when I first told her; she'd never played the game, but when I explained it, she laughed. *A child's vision board,* she called it. *Manifesting.*

"Do you think it would work?" I asked, stirring the ice in my tea. She made it in a giant, rubber-mouthed jar, set out in the sun at the edge of her deck. "In theory, I mean. If you designed this perfect set of questions to get at someone's nature and nurture configuration. Couldn't you predict their future?"

"Anyone could *predict* anything," Vera said. It was one of the most infuriating things about her and also one of my favorites— the way she countered everything, always forcing you to put a finer point on what you were trying to say. "The question is, to what degree of accuracy?"

"Okay, yes," I said. "If we made a survey like I said, couldn't we predict people's futures with a high degree of accuracy?"

"In theory," she said. "Yes."

I stopped stirring the ice. "How about in practice?"

Her eyes sparkled. She was sick then, but not the way she is now.

"Shall we find out?"

I grinned. She was the best partner in crime, in anything. "Yeah," I said. "I think we should."

I spent every day with her, June to August. We pored over those questions; we revised them ten times, twenty, fifty. I lost count of how many books she gave me to study, how many papers I read online using her old university log-in. She made nothing easy; she wanted me to learn it myself. I stayed up all night coding and then I showed up to Vera's at nine, where she had breakfast waiting and was ready to talk about the human mind.

Her fingerprints are everywhere on MASH. Without her, it wouldn't exist at all. And as her body turned on her, I turned our summer project into something she never wanted it to be. I believe in it—the heart of the app, those four future predictors, the ones she helped me build. But every week we add more. Every week my algorithm gets warped by Dr. Blaise Wisener, some stranger a thousand miles away. It should be Vera in this with me. It should always be Vera and me.

That's what I'm thinking about, my lungs burning with every step up the hillside, when Dad texts me.

She's going to stay here, he sends, though he doesn't say for how long. **Once she's set up in her own room, we can visit.**

Visit, I think. Like Vera is a stranger or an aunt who lives out of state. Like we need an appointment, or a calendar reminder. Like she is well and truly and finally apart from us.

My phone buzzes again, but instead of the bubble I'm expecting to appear from my dad with another update, it's Felix.

It's Felix, on a national holiday, sending a group text to Miller and me. I stop walking.

I just learned some shocking information, he says. Three dots appear as he types and I wait, wondering if Miller is staring at this same text window on his own phone screen forty miles away.

The information is that Switchback Ridge High has a winter formal dance in two weeks.

What's shocking is NEITHER OF YOU told me about it.

I sink to my butt in the dirt, cold-packed and solid under a fine fur of weeds. There's no way. There's no, no, no way.

You do realize how weird it'll look if you don't go? Together??

You're going. We'll talk details on Monday.

Maybe we can send a photographer.

A pause, silent except for the chickadee that flits past me, wailing as she goes.

Happy Thanksgiving, Mo.

22

Formal is on a Saturday, which means Maren's over at two so we can get ready together. With Dad at Beans and Vera in the hospital, the house is quiet.

"How's she doing?" Maren asks as she comes through the door.

I know exactly who she means, but some stupid thing inside me wants to distance myself from the question.

"Who?" I ask.

"Vera," she says, of course. "When's she coming home?"

She isn't, I know. She's been gone for sixteen days, and each time I see her there's less of her there to see. But that same stricken person inside me answers Maren all on her own. "Soon, I think."

"Good." Maren smiles, leaning close to hug me. I've been avoiding hugs lately, on the whole. Hugging Miller is one thing—it's a job, and I shut myself down every time it happens. But hugging Maren, and especially hugging my dad, feels dangerous. Leaning into someone, being offered a place to break down. In the surround-sound silence of someone else's arms, the sadness threatens to swallow me whole.

I go stiff against Maren, and she takes a step back.

"Autumn's picking us up at six," she tells me. "Miller's meeting us at the docks, right?"

"No," I groan, motioning for her to follow me upstairs to my room. "I told him to, but he thinks it'd look suspicious." Switch-back Ridge High always hosts winter formal at the Snowberry Room, a restaurant right on the lake with floor-to-ceiling windows over the water. Last year, Maren and I went together. This year, well. "He's coming here at six, too."

"That boy is an *unrelenting* goody-two-shoes," Maren says. She lays the garment bag she's carrying across my bed. "Did you coordinate outfits?"

"God, no." I drop into my desk chair and watch her unzip the bag. Felix wanted to style us, but I'd finally put my foot down. This wasn't an official MASH event; I wasn't going to wear some color-complementary couple's outfit in front of my entire school. "I have no idea what he's wearing."

"Well," she says, pulling out her dress with a flourish. It's floor-length and silky, the color of liquid copper. "Here's what I'm wearing."

"Perfect," I tell her, smiling. She drops it and steps over to me, reaching to tug at the end of one of my curls.

"But first, hair," she says. "You gonna let me straighten this?"

I almost never straighten my hair; the curls are part of me, unpredictable and uncontained. But Maren loves the transformation—and has the patience for the full hour it takes to get my hair to lie flat. I shrug, and she grins at me.

"I'll take that as a yes," she says. "Let's do this thing."

When Miller shows up, I'm still in my track pants. He's early, totally predictably, and I hear the slam of his car door just as I'm headed to the closet for my dress. Maren's ready, hair piled on her head and the copper dress catching in the setting sun through my window.

"I'll get him," she says, standing from my bed. When she peers out the window, she laughs. "Oh my god, Ro."

She waves me over, and we both watch him walk up my driveway. His hair's combed back and he's carrying a plastic box and—the kicker—he's wearing the tuxedo.

"No," I say, and she throws her head back to laugh again.

"Yes," she says. "The infamous *Iliad* tux. *Man.* He looks good though, huh?"

I step away from the window as he reaches the front door. "He looks like Miller."

Maren pokes me in the arm as she moves past. "One and the same, these days."

She isn't wrong, necessarily. Only wrong in assuming that information has anything to do with me. The doorbell rings just as she hits the staircase, and eventually their voices drift up to me.

My dress is Vera's from the sixties, short-sleeved and burgundy with a full skirt and a bow at the neckline. She gave it to me when I turned sixteen, *Something I thought you might like*, and I never wore it because it always felt too beautiful for me. Now, I zip the side seam and smooth the skirt in the mirror. It feels simultane-ously vital and impossible to have her with me tonight, like this.

"You coming, Ro?" Maren calls from downstairs. "Autumn's five minutes out."

I lean toward the mirror, pick a stray eyelash from my cheek. My hair is smooth and unfamiliar, like I'm not only in a borrowed dress, but a borrowed body.

I run my palm over the soft ridge of my scar. Think, *There you are.*

Downstairs, Miller's prying open his plastic box. To my horror, there's a corsage inside.

"Oh no," I say, and when he turns to look at me, his whole body goes still. He looks even taller than usual, all those black tuxedo lines pulling at his edges. His hair's still a little wet. His eyes move over me like they're searching for something.

"You look—"

"Beautiful," Maren supplies, just as Miller finishes, "—like someone else."

"Thanks a lot," I say, as if I wasn't thinking the exact same thing two minutes ago. I cross the room toward him, plucking the corsage out of its box and holding it up. It's delicate, a cluster of purple columbines surrounded by vivid green leaves. I think, dis-tantly, that Vera would love it. "Why didn't you tell me you were doing this? I don't have anything for you."

"I didn't realize I had to notify you," Miller says. "We're going to a dance. It's what people do."

We're not "people," I think. *We're fucking nuts.*

"We'll make one," Maren says brightly, looking around the house and snapping her fingers. "Ummmm . . ." There are no flowers in sight, of course. It's December.

Maren wanders toward the kitchen, and I put down the corsage to follow. When she reaches for Dad's row of potted herbs, I groan.

"No, no!" Maren says. She gathers them by the stems, bunching them into a crude bouquet. "It'll be cute. World's dopest cilantro boutonniere."

Just as she ties them up with kitchen twine and hands me a safety pin, the doorbell rings again.

"Must be Autumn," she says, glancing between Miller and me. "You good here?"

"*Good*'s generous," I mutter as Miller says, "Yes."

When Maren flits out of the kitchen I take a step toward Miller, safety pin pointed straight at him.

"Try not to draw blood," he says, and I roll my eyes.

We have to get very close for me to attach the stems to his lapel. So close I can tell he's wearing cologne, like a huge nerd. I duck my chin to get a better angle on the pin, and he raises his so our heads don't touch. I'm pretty sure he's holding his breath.

When I clip the pin into place and step back, it's atrocious: a cluster of basil and cilantro and rosemary, the leaves already going wilty.

"I'm sorry," I say, and immediately regret it. Why should I be sorry? This isn't real; I couldn't have expected he'd bring flowers.

"It's fine," Miller says, looking down at his chest. "At least if the food's underseasoned, we'll know what to do."

I snort a laugh before I can stop myself, and Miller smiles—just a little, the ghost of it on his mouth before he remembers and tucks it away.

"You're here!" Maren cries, and we both turn to look toward the front door. There's a girl framed in it: tall and angular in a black pantsuit with a deep V-neck. She grins at Maren, and before I can look away, they're kissing. I glance at Miller, but he's staring at his shoes.

"This is Ro," Maren says, after what feels like a half hour. Her cheeks are flushed when she turns toward us, ushering Autumn over the threshold. "And her match, Miller."

"Oh, I know Ro and Miller," Autumn says. She hugs us one by one, tight, like we've known each other forever. Her dark hair is parted in the middle and smoothed behind her ears. "Who doesn't, at this point?" She points at Miller. "Great tux."

"The *Iliad* tux," Maren says.

Miller's eyebrows draw together. "What?"

"You wore it to your presentation," Maren says. "That day we saw you, back in August."

"Oh." Miller glances as me. "Yeah, it's the only suit I own. I had to get it for my aunt's second wedding last year and it was so expensive my mom kind of put her foot down on buying any other formalwear." He shrugs, looking down at the tuxedo. "Forever, I guess."

"So you'll always be the best dressed person in the room,"

Autumn tells him, smiling. "I see no issues here." She reaches for Maren's hand, tugs her back toward the front door. "Come on, I can't wait to dance with you."

Their sun-bright affection tightens something in my throat. Miller steps around me to follow them.

"I drove here in a coupe," Autumn says, glancing at us. "So we can drive separate, or . . . ?"

"I can drive us," Miller says, pulling keys from his pocket. He slides the corsage toward me on the table as he passes by, leaving me to put it on myself. "Plenty of room."

I snap the band around my wrist, take one last look down at the flowers, and follow them all outside.

23

Autumn chatters from the backseat the entire drive to the lake. It's clear why Maren likes her: she's hilarious, and she tells great stories, and the familiar way she touches my shoulder as she talks makes her feel like my oldest friend. When she describes trying to impress Maren on their first date by ordering something called "Rocky Mountain oysters," Miller laughs so hard he's unrecognizable.

He's just pulled into a parking spot, and when he turns back to look at Autumn his smile is huge and unguarded. He says something to her but I can't even hear it—I realize I haven't seen him look this way once since we started all this. That his joy is foreign to me, and that it's my own fault. His eyes crinkled in laughter, the color in his cheeks, the smile he doesn't zip away—they aren't mine. I look away from him, popping open the passenger door. Miller's a different person like this. And even as he follows me onto the asphalt, as he takes my hand, as he passes Mr. Gupta our tickets, he's never felt further from me.

The Snowberry Room is decked out like a dream. There are fairy lights floating from the cavernous, wood-beamed ceiling, white linens on all the cocktail tables, and frost at the corners of the huge windows over the lake. The moon's up, hanging low and yellow on the water. Before we've even had a minute to look around, Autumn's ditching her coat at a table and pulling Maren out to the dance floor. Maren's film camera bounces around her neck.

"She's funny," Miller says, watching them go. When I look up at him, he's still smiling.

"Yeah," I say. "I can tell you think so."

He looks down at me, a little V forming between his eyebrows. "Ro, are you—"

"No," I cut him off. "You've got to be kidding me." Because right in front of us, slicing through the sea of high schoolers in a pinstripe suit, is Felix.

"What are you doing here?" Miller asks, as Felix sidesteps a junior in a full skirt.

"Great to see you, too." Felix adjusts his tie. "Our photographer canceled and I can't trust you two to get decent photos." He gives us each a once-over, eyes landing on Miller's boutonniere.

"*Mille*r." His mouth drops open as he leans in. "Tell me you're not wearing weeds on your chest."

"They're herbs," Miller says, and Felix looks up at him.

"Why?" Then he looks at me. "Why couldn't you just have let me style you?"

Miller's eyebrows go up. "You're telling me I *didn't* have to wear this tux?"

"Of course not," Felix says, swatting at him. "You look like a lost groomsman."

"Do you need pictures or something?" I interrupt, and they both turn to me. "Let's get it over with."

"*Snippy*," Felix says, but lifts his camera. "Let's go outside. There's some romantic string lighting on the dock that I feel very strongly about."

Miller and I trudge back into the cold, reaching for each other's hands like always. It's robotic now; I don't even think about it anymore. There are shouts from behind us, and when I turn, Maren and Autumn are following us from the restaurant.

"What's happening?" Maren calls. "Are you guys leaving?"

"Photo shoot," Felix says. "Want to come with?"

"Decidedly yes," Autumn says, and just like that we're all on the dock taking pictures in the thirty-degree chill. Autumn and Maren are giggly, hopping from foot to foot and rubbing each other's arms to keep warm. When I fold into Miller to take a photo against the frigid railing, Felix points back at them and says, "Can you adopt some of that energy, please?"

"Maybe you should be photographing them instead," I tell him, and he lowers the camera to look at me.

"What's with the mood, Ro?"

"There's no mood," I mutter, though I can feel myself going sour. Like the strength to keep this up is leaching out of me, dissipating into the cold air. I want to go home, fully and all at once. I want Vera to be there, waiting for me. I want to be with someone who loves me without having to pretend.

"Whatever you say," Felix mutters, flipping through his photos. With the lens turned away, Miller takes a step back so we're not touching. "I've got what I need, so I'm going to get my geriatric ass away from this teenage mess." He glances at Autumn and Maren. "Though *you two* have been a delight."

They trade smiles, and then Felix points at Miller and me. "Have fun. I'll see you soon."

Our flight to New York City leaves in eight days. We have two talk show appearances booked, three in-person magazine interviews, and hotel room reservations for three nights near Times Square. Usually I feel excited about it, but right now I just feel tired.

"I gotta ask," Autumn says, breaking the silence. It's just the four of us on the dock, cold wind brushing the snow across the wood boards. Miller and I are a foot apart, and I'm hugging myself to keep warm. "Is this real?"

I look at her. "Is what real?"

She shrugs, almost apologetically, and gestures between Miller and me. "I mean, I follow you on Instagram. I've seen all the pictures and I've watched your interviews and Maren's told me you guys are legit and everything, but . . ."

My first thought is that I'm surprised, after seeing the closeness between them, that Maren kept our secret from Autumn. Then I feel guilty for being surprised. Why should I be? Maren's my best friend.

"But what?" Miller asks, his expression hard to read.

"But I don't know if I buy it," Autumn says. Maren looks at me, concerned, but Autumn's not done. "There's something weird between you guys, for sure. But it doesn't look like love."

We're found out, I think. *It's over.* I start babbling right away. "Well, it's just—"

"What would love look like?" Miller asks. He's calm as ever, like this conversation isn't about to blow our whole cover and everything we've been working at for months.

"I dunno," she says. "Like kissing, I think. You guys haven't kissed once."

I look at her, something sliding sharp as a pocketknife into my chest.

"Autumn." Maren forces a laugh. "Come on."

And then—Miller's hands on my cheeks. They're warm in the new-winter cold of the lakefront, and I'm still looking at Autumn when Miller uses them to turn my face toward his in the dark. His eyes skate across mine, quick but connecting, before he dips his chin. He kisses me, and it's careful. Like the soft press of his mouth might hurt me, or him.

When he pulls away he doesn't look at me again, just turns back to Autumn. "Can we go inside now?" His voice is even and unaffected—like that was casual, which I guess it should've been. "It's freezing out here."

Maren's mouth is hanging open just a little. Autumn laughs into the night, and we're all walking back toward the building when my phone rings in my bag. I fumble for it, still half-disoriented, and see the three letters there on the screen: *Dad*.

I stop walking, all the blood dropping through my body to my feet. I know—even before I pick up, even before I hear his voice. Just ahead of me, music pours through the open doors to the Snowberry Room. But the world has gone suddenly, absolutely silent.

"Dad?"

Maren hears me and turns around, reaching out to stop Autumn. Miller is behind me, maybe, or maybe he's nowhere, or maybe he's gone. I look down at my shoes, and I have the stupid thought that I'll never wear them again without thinking of this moment.

"Ro," Dad says. It's loud where he is. "Are you still at the lake?"

"Yeah. Where are you?"

"I'm—" He hesitates, but I already know. "I'm at the hospital. I know you're at your dance. I know. I—Ro, can somebody drive you here?"

I blink at my shoes. Patent leather, catching the fairy lights from inside.

"Is she—" I can't get the word out; it traps in my throat like it doesn't want to be in the world with me. I don't want it to, either. *Dead*.

But he knows what I mean. He says, "It's time, honey."

"Okay," I tell him, though it isn't. "Okay. I'm coming."

When I put the phone back in my bag, Maren steps toward me. "Ro," she says, and her voice sounds very far away, like she's calling to me from the bottom of a well. "Is it Vera?"

I swallow. Suck in a breath. Turn in my stupid, shiny shoes. Miller's there: a wall of tuxedo behind me. "I've got to go," I say, stepping around him.

"Where?" Maren calls, hurrying after me. "Ro, what's going on?"

"She—" I look at her, then break off. Her face is like the hugging: too dangerous. If I keep looking at her, I'll never make it. "I can't say it."

"Okay," Maren says. She puts her hands on my shoulders, and I realize I'm shaking. "I know, that's okay. Are you going to the hospital?"

I nod, and somewhere far away, there's Miller's voice. "The hospital?"

"I'm going to call an Uber," I say, breaking from her grasp. "I've got to—"

"No, we'll all go," Maren says. She looks behind her and I know she's motioning to Autumn, somewhere out of sight. "We're going with you."

"No," I tell her, and I mean it. "You stay. And have fun. I don't want—" I grasp at words, typing the hospital name into the Uber app. *I don't want to share this.* I don't know how to be in this at all, not to mention be in it with anyone else. I look up at Maren. "Please. Just stay."

"Ro," she says, her face falling. "You can't do this alone."

"I can," I tell her, not believing it. "I've got to go."

"No, we're coming," Maren says. "Let me just run back inside, Autumn and I left our jackets, it'll just take—"

"I have to go *now*," I say, louder than I mean to.

"I'll take you." Miller comes out of nowhere, sliding the phone from my grip and putting it back in my bag. I'm moving too slow to stop him.

"You don't have to do that," I say, but he's already taking my hand, already turning me toward his car.

"I know," he says. The wind picks up, blows open the jacket of his tuxedo. "Maren, you guys can meet us there."

Maren calls after us in the dark, but I can't hear her. We're halfway across the parking lot when someone shouts our names, and when I turn Felix's head is sticking through the passenger window of a nearby car.

"Are you two *leaving*?" he cries, incredulous. There's someone in the driver's seat but I can't make them out through the windshield. The engine's running, like they were about to drive off. "You can't leave yet, you need to pretend for at least an hour—"

"We're leaving," Miller says. His hand's still in mine and when I keep moving toward his car, he comes with me.

"Stop, stop, stop." Felix's voice gets gulped up by the wind, and I barely hear his car door close behind us. We reach Miller's wagon and I pull open the door. I don't care about Felix; I don't care about anything—I just need to get where I'm going. "Guys, *wait*."

I duck into the car and Miller shuts the door behind me, his and Felix's voices going muffled. It's freezing inside and I fold over onto myself, my whole body trembling.

"The dance has barely started," Felix says. "I swear, you two are going to give me an aneurysm. Is it so hard to stay put for *one* evening, it's not even—"

"We can't do the Mo thing right now," Miller says. He opens the driver's-side door and frigid air gusts over me. "I need to get Ro to the hospital."

"Hospital?" Felix's voice rises a couple of octaves. "Is she okay?"

"It's her—" He hesitates, and I know he's searching for the word. It's my neighbor, my family, my ally in everything. My Vera.

In the end, Miller doesn't explain. He just says, "I'm sorry, we've got to go."

"Oh my god." I don't look at Felix, but I don't need to—I can perfectly picture his exasperated face. "Okay, well. I'm coming, too."

2 4

"The trick," Vera said, "is to get a firm seal on the tape, so nothing leaks through." She leaned over Miller's shoulder, watching him press an X of masking tape onto an egg's thin shell. His tongue poked between his lips, trapped there in concentration. We were nine, and it was April.

"When you dip into the dye, the tape protects the shell." Vera brushed a hand through Miller's hair as she moved toward me. "Once it's dry, you peel it off to reveal a pattern."

I was trying to make a smiley face, connecting little strips of tape to form a mouth, frustrated at their unsmooth edges. Vera leaned close. "It's not about perfection, Rosie."

Miller looked up then, peering across the table at my handi-work. "Looks perfect to me," he said. "Egg smiley."

"It's not." I held it up for him to see. "Look at the mouth, it's all pointy."

"So's mine," he said, and gnashed his teeth over the table like he was going to bite my hand. I laughed, recoiling.

"You're not an egg," I told him. The table between us was littered with jelly beans and egg-shaped chocolates, all the Easter spoils Vera kept for me that Dad wouldn't let me have at home.

Miller dumped a handful of neon-green beans in his mouth and spoke through them. "If I was, would you still be friends with me?"

I rubbed my chin like I was considering it. "Maybe. But I'd have to roll you everywhere. Or build you a wagon to pull behind my bike."

"Sounds like a life of luxury," Vera said, carrying a tray to the table. She set it down and I peered over the rows of cups, each a different color dye. "Maybe we'd all be better off as eggs."

"Only hard-boiled, though," Miller said. Vera placed five cups in front of each of us, two rows of contained rainbows. The smell was strong—stinging vinegar. I coughed a little, then looked up at Miller.

"Otherwise," he told us, "we'd break each other."

The hospital smells the same: sharp antiseptic like vinegar. The sense memory yanks me back in time so keenly I check my fingertips as we ride the elevator upstairs, half expecting them to be stained with dye. They aren't, of course: they're just my same hands, pale and shaking.

Miller stands next to me at a careful distance. Not touching me, but close enough to block out Felix, who followed us all the way here and is standing at the back of the elevator with a tall man in a black peacoat. So far, he's had the good sense to keep his mouth shut.

Vera is on a hospice floor, tucked away at the back of the building. I've never left Colorado, have seen barely any of the world, but even still, I know—this is the worst place on the planet. The hallway lights are dimmed, voices hushed. At the end of the hall, a doctor steps out of a room, her head leaned close to talk to my father. He stays in the doorframe as she moves away and then, finally, he looks up.

I don't know what's waiting for me inside. I don't know how my legs keep moving me toward Dad but they do; suddenly I'm there and he's gripping my shoulder and he's talking to Miller over my head and I can't hear—or don't care—what they're saying.

Inside, Vera's asleep. Every light is on in her room and I see her thin chest rising and falling, slow, beneath the blankets. I go to her, sit in the only chair at her bedside. *Soak it up*, half of me cries, shrieking from inside. *Soak it up, soak it up, soakitup*. This is the last time I'll see her. The last time we'll breathe the same air. I'm torn between wanting to remember every inconsiderable detail and wanting to look away, to not remember her like this even a little.

Her arm rests on top of the sheets and I reach for her, wrapping my fingers around her slim wrist. Her skin is cool and dry. For a moment I can feel her pulse, but then I realize it's only my own, fast and frantic and all alone.

"You okay, honey?"

I look up at Dad. He's in jeans and a hoodie he's had my whole life.

"What happened?" I whisper, as if the facts of this—metastatic cancer, her body too weakened to keep being her body—will give me something to hold on to. As if there is anything that could make this make sense.

But before Dad can answer me, Vera gasps. I look at her, my heart rising in my throat, but her eyes are still closed. Her machines start beeping in unison, an angry chorus that seems to be telling me to *get out, get OUT.* I rise from the chair as a rush of nurses fill the space around me, crowding the bed until I can't even see her anymore.

"Only one visitor in the room, please," one of them says. Urgently. *Get out.* But I'm paralyzed, staring at one of the nurse's backs like I could look straight through her to Vera.

"Ro," Dad says, and his voice sounds shatterable as spring ice. "Wait in the hallway." His hands land on my shoulders, making me move. "It's okay, baby. Wait in the hallway."

It's not okay, and we both know it. He takes my face in his hands and kisses my cheek, pushes the hair from my forehead like I'm small again. He looks up at Miller, then back to me. "Go on."

Miller: standing in the doorframe, his bow tie undone. Cluster of cilantro drooping from the safety pin on his lapel. I can't look at his face, and when I move past him into the hall I suddenly feel like I can't look at anything else, either. The whole world is blurring out in front of me, the hallway walls melting into the floor. Felix and the guy in the coat are standing close to the wall, the guy's arm around Felix's waist. I can feel them looking at me, and when Felix reaches a hand toward me I flinch.

"Oh, honey," he whispers, and the syllables bleed into the

beeping from Vera's room. Inside, the nurses are loud with each other. I clamp my hands over my ears.

"Ro," Miller says. His voice barely reaches me. "Look at me."

When I don't, his voice comes louder. "Hey. Ro."

I'm thinking: *I can't breathe.* I'm thinking: *Everything wrong is happening here, all at the exact same time.* I'm thinking: *I need to go to the woods.* But I can't. I'm bound here by the sadness I have to bear witness to, that I would never forgive myself for missing even though it is the last thing I ever, ever, ever want to look at. There is no way around this, there is only through.

"Ro, *look* at me," Miller says again, and either he's louder or he's closer, because I do.

"Hey," he says, firmly, when my eyes land on his. His gaze is familiar and steady in the way I've only ever known from him—like Miller is an island all his own, immovable, unchanged as the air. I feel the tears on my cheeks with an inhuman detachment, like they belong to someone else. But still, I don't look away from him. It's as if he's brought my woods to me: the wind moving in the leaves, the earth's heartbeat he reached for with the flat of his hand when we were five years old. I breathe.

"This is the worst," Miller says. We're a foot apart, and he doesn't touch me. "There is no silver lining. This is impossible, and you're going to get through it."

He doesn't tell me it's okay. He doesn't say: *but* you'll get through it. He gives me the gift of the truth—that if I do make it past this, it will be an *and*. I will be all right, and this will devastate me. Both things true at once.

"Maren and Autumn are still waiting for a car," he tells me, and I think, *Who?* Everything else that's happened tonight, everything else that's happened my whole life, feels like it happened to someone else. "What do you need?"

I blink up at him under the fluorescent hallway lights. I have no idea what I need. I only know I have to survive this night, to find a way to exist in my body as this happens. From inside Vera's room, the machines wail on.

"Here," Miller says, when I still haven't spoken. He takes my elbow, guides me into a chair against the wall. When I sit, it registers dully that my feet feel better, and I look down at them. Stupid heels. "Water?" he asks. "There's a café on the first floor. Tea?"

"We can go." I look up, and the guy with Felix meets my eyes. His are big and brown and friendly. He's holding Felix's hand. "We'll bring up some drinks."

Felix nods, his lips pressed together. He hesitates but then steps toward me, runs one hand over my hair. "We'll be right back, okay?"

I nod, and as they move down the hallway, Miller crouches in front of me so our eyes are level. When I look at him, I know what I want, and I know I can't say it.

"Miller," I whisper. *Stay.*

His eyes remain on mine, waiting for me to finish my sentence. When I don't, he moves into the chair next to me. And just like after I tore my arm apart, I am bad, bad company. But all night— as I cry soundlessly, as I move in and out of Vera's room, as Maren and Felix come and eventually go—Miller stays.

2 5

The funeral is a week later, in the same church where my parents got married. Maren's there, and Miller with his parents, and a few of Dad's employees from Beans. Vera's old colleagues from the university fill the back pews and Felix comes with his boyfriend, Grey, who brought me tea in the hospital.

Dad and I let the pastor speak for us, because neither of us knows what to say. Funerals feel like something that happen to other people, and I'm lost in the center of this one. Vera was funny, and sneaky, and smart as all hell. This weird, reverent, quiet ceremony feels like it has nothing to do with her at all. I keep waiting for her to nudge me in the pew, lean close to whisper something in my ear that'll make me snort-laugh like a piglet. And it keeps not happening.

"She would've hated that," Miller says when it's over and we're all standing in the parking lot. I'm sitting on the hood of Dad's truck, watching him shake hands with a bunch of people I've never met. No one seems to know quite how to extricate themselves from this, or when it's actually supposed to end. Like whoever says goodbye first breaks the spell, or all our hearts.

Miller leans against the bumper next to me. "You okay?"

"You're right," I say, avoiding the question. It's a relief to hear him say it—she *would've* hated that. The whole thing was so un-Vera, the awkward joint planning effort of my dad and Vera's middle-aged, estranged niece. "I think if it hadn't gone so fast in the end, she would've planned her own send-off. And it wouldn't have been anything like that."

"What do you think she'd have done?"

I look at him, late-afternoon sun in his eyes. No one's asked me anything about Vera all week, like they're worried if they bring her up I'll remember she's dead. But how could I forget? Being asked about her feels like a small mercy—all I want to do is talk about her.

"Make everyone do some crazy-hard hike," I say, and Miller smiles. "Poles, crampons, the whole thing. Maybe bury her inheritance at the end of the trail and see who gets there first."

He laughs, and it makes me smile on instinct.

"I bet she'd have asked us to burn all her student papers in some kind of ceremonial pyre," Miller says. He's in dress pants and a button-down, one elbow leaned onto the hood. "She hated grading."

"*Hated* it," I groan, tilting my head back. "God, that woman could complain."

"Loved the students, though," Miller says. "I bet she was a great professor."

"The best."

We look at each other, and it feels like a small, golden bubble breaking the darkness of the last few days. We canceled this week's episode of *MASH with Mo*, but we're still leaving for New York in the morning. Miller's hand lifts just a little, like he's going to reach for me, before he stops himself.

"I hate that she's gone," he says, and we both look away.

"Yeah," I whisper. Across the parking lot, Dad turns to look at us. "Me too."

When everyone finally disperses, we get in Dad's truck and drive an hour to Rocky Mountain National Park. Still in our funeral clothes—black suit, black dress—we put on boots and hike twenty minutes to Alberta Falls.

This was in Vera's will, along with the deed to her house and everything else that was left, too. One last request of us: *After they lay me to rest, I want Rosie and Pete to go look at something beautiful.* No poles, or crampons, or buried treasure. But finally, something we're doing feels like it makes sense.

When we get to the waterfall, there are a few clusters of hikers taking pictures. It's mid-December, but with the sun high in the sky and no snow on the trails, the park's still busy. Dad points to a flat rock jutted out over the falls and I follow him, sit next to him on the dusty ledge. The water is loud, raging on, same as it always has.

"I love you," Dad says, and my throat closes up. He turns to look at me and I just nod, unable to speak.

"She left this for you." He reaches into his suit jacket and pulls out an envelope, passing it to me. "She wanted you to read it here."

I stare at the paper in my hands: *Rosie*, there in her perfect, looping script. The same lettering I grew up looking at all over her house, splashed across grocery lists and in the margins of student essays.

"I don't know if I can," I tell him, and he puts an arm around me. We sit like that for a few long, silent minutes. Once I read this, there will be nothing new left of her. Nothing she will ever say to me again that I haven't heard before. I close my eyes and tip my face up to the sun.

> *Rosie,*
>
> *You'll read this after I'm gone, surrounded by the great beauty of the earth and seated next to your father, the person who loves you most in the world. Or at least, that's how I hope you'll read this—but you've always been good at evading my plans.*
>
> *There's much to say, and I'm tired, and I know that no last conversation between us could ever be enough. I've studied human beings my entire adult life, but nothing in all my research has filled me with the kind of wonder I've felt watching you grow up. Listening to you share your ideas. You're a miracle, just by being yourself.*
>
> *What you've made with MASH is incredible. It's a powerful idea, built on questions that you were brave enough to ask. Can we code humans out, the same as machines? Are we just as predictable? In many ways, we are. That's why your*

app works. Nothing you've done is, scientifically, incorrect.

But as you walk this road without me, I want to make sure you know: We are not only the things you've proven us to be with this algorithm. There will always be a space that separates us from computers, a gray area in which we are shaped by the influence of new friends, and inevitable surprises, and love. Still, after a decades-long career in behavioral sciences, there are so many things about us I can't understand. They are unquantifiable. They are what make us human.

I hope you'll remember that the brain is malleable. That your answers to the survey questions will change, because what you love, and what you want, and who you are will change, too. These unpredictable shifts are supposed to happen. They are the good kind of scary.

You will become people you can't even fathom yet. I wish I could be here to meet every version of you, Rosie. I know I would love each one more than the last.

Always, and even longer after that,
Vera

26

It's Sawyer, Monday morning, who breaks the news. I get her text while we're standing in line at airport security, before TMZ drops the story or E! posts it to Instagram or the TV at our gate beams *Good Morning America* with a ticker across the bottom, making the announcement.

Her first text says only, Holy shit.

I read it through the haze of my brain fog, all my synapses addled by sleeplessness. I lay in bed all night staring up at my ceiling, thinking of Vera's note. *Nothing you've done is, scientifically, incorrect.* But with her gone, with this warning the very last thing she left me, I can't shake the feeling that I've done something wrong. I wish, more than anything, that I could talk to her.

Jazz nudges me toward the TSA agent, and I fumble with my ID as my phone buzzes again.

Hayes broke up with Josie. He matched last week and he met the girl without telling Josie and last night he dumped her to be with his match instead.

I stare at her text, and Miller reaches around me for a bin. I'm still looking at my phone when he drops his shoes in.

"Everything okay?" he asks, and I blink up at him. I hold out my phone and he leans in, his eyes tracking over the words before he looks at me again.

"Are these friends of yours?"

"Hayes Hawkins," I say. "Josie Sweet? She's one of our MASH influencers."

Miller just shakes his head. He could name every Greek Titan and all their descendants in chronological order, but these two celebrities—best-dressed at last year's Met Gala, creators of the most-GIFed kiss of all time on the Grammys red carpet—are nothing to him.

I thrust the phone toward Jazz instead, and she pauses from unzipping her hoodie to read it. This time, I get the appropriate reaction: her eyes go wider with every word.

"Shit," she says. She swipes the phone from my hand and passes it to Felix. "There the fuck goes *that* contract."

But of the four of us, Felix is the only one who really anticipates what's coming. Who feels the plow wind of this storm in his bones.

"This is big," he says, looking at Jazz, then Miller, then me. Since that night in the hospital Felix has been so careful with me, texting me to check in and reaching out to smooth my hair behind my ear and treating me with gentle kindness I didn't know he had in him. But even still, he doesn't sugarcoat this. "Guys, this is *bad*."

By the time we get through security and to the trams, Jazz is on the phone with Evelyn. She's talking so quickly I only catch snippets of what she says: "release a statement" and "firm on our position" and "expected collateral damage." The seed of doubt Vera planted in me is rooting—growing new green shoots with every passing minute.

She's devastated, Sawyer texts me. **I could barely hear her she was crying so hard when she called me. Apparently this chick's a waitress in Santa Monica.**

I know what she's saying: *Hayes Hawkins left Josie Sweet, America's forever fave, for a nobody waitress.* And I'm already on edge, so I reply: **There's nothing wrong with being a waitress.**

Obviously, Sawyer says. **Not the point. But he's giving up the best girl in the world for a giant question mark???**

The tram howls into the tunnel, cool air blowing my hair over my eyes. Jazz is still talking, and Felix is furiously scrolling Twitter. Every few seconds, he groans. An automated voice croons, *"Train arriving for all A, B, and C gates."* When the tram doors slide open, I follow Miller into the press of people.

I'm still looking at my phone when the train shudders to a start, and as I stumble sideways, Miller reaches for me. He opens his arm to hold me against his side, and as I move into my place there, I tuck my phone into my pocket and wrap my own arm around his waist. I can feel him breathing under my hand, the rise of his ribs through his T-shirt. We've stood like this a hundred times. This is what we do in public: Miller's arm goes around my shoulders, we collapse the space between our bodies.

But now, in the close air of the train, Miller's thumb brushes along my arm—up and down, up and down. Slowly, like in the insanity of this moment he's keeping his own rhythm, slowing us to a manageable pace. I have one hand on my suitcase and another on Miller's side; when the train lurches around a corner, he pulls me closer to keep me on my feet.

This is fake, I remind myself. All of it—the way he reached for me at the funeral, and how he steadied me with a palm on the small of my back in the security line, and even the way I felt that night in the hospital, like Miller was the best thing I had to hold on to—it's not real. We've fabricated this. Every minute, every time we touch each other, we're fabricating it.

But when I look up at him, he's already looking down at me. And then he dips his chin and presses a kiss to my temple, and it feels like maybe the only good thing to have happened for the whole last week of my life.

It's fake, I think. Even as I close my eyes, as I draw my first full breath since leaving home. *It's fake, it's fake, it's fake.*

Jazz spends the entire flight drafting media responses, so it's Felix who walks us through the itinerary.

"Filming starts at five tonight," he says, leaning over the seats in front of Miller and me. He uses a pen to point at the paper he's shoved in our faces. Right there at the top: *Jimmy Fallon—The Tonight Show.* "We need to hustle through baggage claim and book it downtown so we have enough time for hair and makeup." Felix glances at Jazz, who's mumbling to herself in the window seat. "He may ask you about Josie and Hayes. Jazz will have statements ready, so just stick to the script."

I glance at Miller, and together we nod.

"Tuesday's press," Felix says, moving his pen down the paper. "*Vogue* at ten, break for lunch, *People* at two. Wednesday's *Today*." Upside down, he circles *The Today Show*. "The big kahuna. I want you rested and ready. No sneaky-sneaky from your hotel rooms, no roaming the city at night." He raises his eyebrows, looks between us. "Got it?"

"I wouldn't even know where to go," Miller says. "So no problem."

"If you were anyone else," Felix tells him, "I'd think you were trying to pull one over on me." Then he looks at me. "Ro?"

The truth is, a month ago, I probably would've snuck out. Ridden the subway to the end of the line at one in the morning, or eaten dollar-slice pizza by myself, or stayed up all night walking the city just to say I had. I've never left Colorado, or been on an airplane, or had independence in a brand-new place. But that daring person inside me has gone quiet lately—silenced by a different one whose limbs are too heavy with grief to carry her on some great nocturnal adventure. The whole world feels dimmer without Vera in it.

"Don't worry about me," I tell Felix. "I'll be sleeping."

He studies me, sympathy flickering across his face so sharply I have to look away. "All right," he says. He clears his throat and turns back to the paper. "Another interview Thursday morning, then we fly home for Christmas. Any questions? We'll go over each appearance in detail before it happens, obviously."

No questions, so with one last look at me, Felix drops back into his seat. Miller reaches into his backpack for a book, something for AP Lit that I've never heard of. He cracks it open, then extends a long arm up to the overhead light and clicks it on. A circle of warm light spills over his lap, flooding the pages.

"Miller," I say, and he looks at me. His pointer finger is balanced on the top line of text, holding his place. The picture of him reading like this is familiar enough to knock me out. "What were the rest of your results?"

He blinks, reading light throwing the long shadows of his eyelashes over his cheeks. "My MASH results?"

I nod, and he closes the book. "What were yours?"

"Software developer," I tell him. That's the easy one. Around us, the plane hums. Jazz has her headphones in, and we're speaking too softly for anyone else to hear us. "San Jose. No kids."

Miller looks down at his hands, smooths the pad of his thumb along the cover of the book. I watch his chest rise and fall, the steadying breath he takes. "Professor," he says, and then he looks up at me. "San Jose. Two kids."

The words sit heavily between us. Miller's face is like a closed door, holding something in that he doesn't want me to see.

And as I look at him, it lands on me, certain as a sunrise: There is a flaw in the algorithm. Not just the mutant version XLR8's tacked on without me, but the one I wrote in the first place. Partners will have the same children, but one may want three and one may want none and maybe, together, they'll land in the middle.

Same with the places they live. If they love each other, these will be conversations that MASH doesn't get to hear. Because the survey only listens to each partner's separate side of their shared story. The app doesn't account for compromise.

"It's overwhelming," Miller says softly. "To think about it now."

"Then why'd you take the survey?" It's the same question I wanted the answer to all the way back in August, alone with Miller for the first time in almost three years. "You hate this stuff. Phones, and social media, and technology."

He tips his head back until it hits the seat. Doesn't take his eyes off mine. "Because you're my oldest friend," he says, simply. "Because you made it."

27

It's two when we land at JFK, which gives us exactly three hours before we go live on *The Tonight Show*. There's a driver waiting at baggage claim, wearing a suit and holding a sign that reads: **Mo—MASH**. It takes us a full hour to weave through Queens into Manhattan, and by the time we hit the tunnel under the East River, Felix is visibly sweating.

"We still gotta do wardrobe," he mutters, checking the time on his phone. "And Ro, makeup." He glances at me—my hair in a topknot, not a speck of makeup in sight. "Oh, Christ."

Miller watches wide-eyed through the window as we cut through the city, winding up Third Avenue and hanging a left onto East Forty-Ninth. The buildings rise around us in an unfamiliar, gray-scale forest.

Josie's wolfpack is popping. off.

Maren's been texting me since we landed, and now she forwards a series of Twitter screenshots. Josie has the most devoted fan base imaginable—mostly girls who style their hair like hers and wear shirts with her song lyrics embroidered on them and show up in droves to all her concert venues. Now, they've got *#cancelMASH* trending.

MASH stole Hayes from Josie, one tweet reads, above a *We Ride at Dawn* meme.

This has gone too far, says another. #cancelMASH for Josie!!!

Josie and Hayes themselves have been uncharacteristically quiet. Their relationship was as public as Mo's, but their demise has been silent. No statements, no posts of any kind. It's unclear, even, how the news got out. But Josie's hive is stinging its way across the internet nevertheless, absolutely buzzing with fury. All of which is directed at me.

I've had a stomachache since we landed and I turned my phone back on. It's like the unease of knowing someone's mad at you, amplified by the entire internet. All I want to do is crawl into bed and hide—but here we are, about to go on live television instead. So basically the exact opposite.

"We're here," Felix says, and I look up from my phone. "Let's move. Jazz will brief you on the Josie-Hayes situation while you get ready."

Miller reaches for my hand, and Felix ushers us through the enormous doors of an even more enormous building. Over Miller's shoulder, just before we make it inside, I see a girl holding up a sign.

#cancelMASH, it says at the top, in angry red letters.

And, just below it: **Who is @rodev to know our futures?**

"My first guests," Jimmy shouts, his voice rising over studio applause, "are tech all-stars, America's unofficial first couple, and pretty much the cutest things any of us have ever seen . . . Rose Devereux and Alistair Miller of MASH. Here's Mo!"

Felix gives us each a little push, and Miller and I walk onstage. We're hand in hand, waving. I think I'm smiling, but I also kind of feel like I'm seeing this from a hundred feet up, watching the little ant of my own body shuffle over to Jimmy Fallon's couch and take a seat. *How many of these people are mad at me?* I think, squinting at the studio audience.

Miller drops an arm around me, and I cross my legs in the perfectly tailored black trousers Felix has me wearing. My blouse is pure white and structured, off the shoulder with dramatic pleating that looks like it was designed by an architect. *App-developer chic,* he told me as he zipped me into it. *You're the power player. We'll put Miller in something simple.* Next to me, he's wearing a textured blue dress shirt—the exact same color as his eyes. Felix had him try on three different options before settling.

"I've been looking forward to this for weeks," Jimmy says. He projects his voice and smiles while he talks, and I think: *How does anyone do this every day?* "I mean, you guys are rock stars. Are you kidding me? How old are you, even? Still in high school?"

"Still in high school," I tell him on a laugh that I hope sounds charming and not hysterical. "We're eighteen."

"Eighteen," Jimmy repeats, shaking his head. He looks right into the camera. "Let me tell you what I was doing at eighteen." There's a dramatic pause, and the audience laughs. "Nah, I'm not going to tell you. Because I was an idiot. Look at these two!"

He swivels back to us, sweeping an arm in our direction. "Incredible. You know, I took the MASH survey."

"You did?" I'm always shocked, still, when someone with clout uses MASH.

"Of course I did!" Jimmy cries, and Miller gives me a little squeeze.

"She's always so surprised," he says, laughing. "As if she didn't create the coolest app of all time."

Jimmy points to Miller, looking at me. "He's cute," he says, and I paste a smile onto my face.

"I know," I say, and the audience coos as Miller and I look at each other under the stage lights. I turn back to Jimmy. "I feel like you have to tell us your results."

"Do I?" he asks, laughing. "I don't know if I do."

"Ah, come on," Miller says. "Are you embarrassed?"

"No!" Jimmy cries, throwing his hands up. "No, no. Fine. Well, I didn't do the matching thing because, you know." He shrugs toward the audience. "Married. Got it covered." Then his eyes widen, and even before he says it, I know. I feel the shift in the conversation as he turns back to us. "Speaking of which. Big news today."

He raises his eyebrows at us, like he's volleying the ball of this conversation over the net. Neither of us bats it back to him—just like Jazz told us. *If he asks you a direct question, you answer with an approved response. You do not, under any circumstances, bring it up yourselves.*

"Josie Sweet and Hayes Hawkins," Jimmy says. "People are

upset. It's upsetting! How are you guys feeling about the news?"

I look at Miller, and he kicks us off, just like we planned. My stomach is twisting like Medusa's snakes have been let loose inside it.

"We were really sad to hear about their split," Miller says. His voice is even, but I can feel his heartbeat against the back of my shoulder. "Josie's been a big supporter of MASH since the beginning, and it's always tough to see people you admire part ways."

"Absolutely." Jimmy nods, going somber. "Do you think MASH is at fault here? Some people seem to think they'd still be together without it."

"That's where we'd disagree, Jimmy." I memorized these sentences from Jazz's laptop backstage, as Felix puttered around my hair and glued my eyelashes into place. My voice only shakes a little. "MASH just offers the answer to a question. It takes a certain type of person to ask that question in the first place." I gesture at him. "You said yourself: You didn't match because you're married. You already have that true connection. We're sad about the breakup, but it's not on MASH. It's a decision that Hayes Hawkins made. And he might have found a way to make it without us."

"I hear you," Jimmy says, nodding. "I hear you. That true connection's really something." His face breaks back into a comfortable smile, and he gestures between us. "I mean, you know."

I smile at Miller, lean further into his side, and the audience sighs out an *awww*. I draw a breath: we're in safer territory now.

"Whirlwind romance," Jimmy says. "It's been so fun to watch. But I want to know—and I think some people here probably want to know." He raises his eyebrows, gives us a devilish smile. "Are you guys in love?"

There's a short, solid silence. Suddenly it feels like no one's breathing in the whole studio, like maybe no one here's even alive except Miller and me.

I look at him, next to me on the couch in the blue button-down Felix picked last minute. Miller's supposed to look at me, too—per the training, per all our practice, per every normal human instinct. But he doesn't. He just takes a breath, looks straight at Jimmy, and says, "I've always loved Ro."

The audience bursts into applause, saving me from responding. "There you have it!" Jimmy shouts, his voice cutting through the clamor. I'm still looking at Miller, but he won't look at me now—he's just smiling at Jimmy, at the audience, his mouth stuck like he's gone plastic. "MASH: *The future's written inside your mind*, guys. Download it from the App Store. Ro, Miller!" Jimmy waves at us again. "Thank you!"

We rise, hand in hand, and make our way offstage. Jazz and Felix wait there, each of them clutching their phones. Jazz is grinning, and Felix looks up as we step past the curtain.

"Well *played*, Miller," Felix says. Miller drops my hand, offers a smile that doesn't touch his eyes. "You killed that. Someone from the audience leaked a clip and Twitter's exploding."

"And you were perfect about the Josie situation," Jazz says. She steps forward to hook her arm through mine, guiding me toward the dressing rooms. I lose Miller in the shuffle—when I turn to find him, he's disappeared. "That was tense, but you nailed it."

"Where's Miller?" I ask, and she glances behind us.

"Felix took him to grab his stuff. The car's waiting outside, so let's boogie."

Five minutes later Jazz and I exit my dressing room, our arms stacked with garment bags, to find Miller and Felix waiting against the wall.

"Hey," I say, but Miller barely looks at me. We start down the hallway and I notice his skin is flushed, bright red up his neck and cheeks. I have the sudden urge to touch him there. "Miller."

He's finally turning toward me when Jazz says, "Holy . . ." and we all look up.

Just beyond the double doors, there's a sea of people with poster-board signs, **#cancelMASH** splashed across them, and **JUSTICE FOR JOSIE**, and even **THIS IS ON MASH**. They're teeming around the stairs to the sidewalk, moving like an angry tide in the dark. A few security guards stretch their arms, hold them back. I can barely see our car in the street.

Felix squares his shoulders and pushes the door open. The noise is deafening when they see us, a rising tunnel of screams.

I step forward, but even before Felix has the door all the way open, something tugs me back. It's Miller's hand, white-knuckle-fisted around my wrist.

"Ro," he says, and I can barely hear him over the shouting. "Get behind me."

28

When I step behind Miller, he keeps his fingers wrapped around my wrist. He's squeezing so hard it's like the thin bones are grinding against each other, pulse screaming through my veins. The pitch of the crowd is excruciating; they're so loud it overwhelms me and I feel like I can't smell the city air anymore, can't see the steps right in front of me. I follow Miller, blind.

Felix is ahead of us, jogging through the thin tunnel of sidewalk to the waiting car. Jazz is behind me, shouting. Her words are indistinguishable; I have no idea what she's saying. There are only four security guards out here, yelling wordlessly, their arms stretched into insufficient Ts. Miller is halfway down the steps when the first person breaks the line, holding her sign out in front of her like a shield. **RO DEVEREUX ISN'T GOD.**

I know, I think, right before all hell breaks loose.

I watch it unfold like I'm stuck behind glass. The girl's sign is knocked out of her hands by the force of everyone behind her surging onto the walkway in the space that she's made. I see the hot, blank shock on her face. Her hair is braided into bear ears on either side of her head. She's maybe sixteen.

Miller steps backward, his shoulder hitting my chin. He drops my wrist and reaches to pull me against him, turning as he does. He's still reaching for me—arms outstretched, eyes wide, his mouth forming the one syllable of my name—when the surge spills over the stairs.

Jazz, appearing from nowhere, yanks me backward by the fabric of my sweatshirt. I stumble, falling to the ground, and watch from below as she grabs for Miller's arm and misses. The security guards are shouting. Everyone is shouting. The crowd pushes toward us and Miller is swept up by the angry sea. The press of bodies swallows him whole, and I'm screaming his name when he reappears—scrambling over the railing in the middle of the split staircase. He's almost over it when somebody shoves him. He falls roughly, jostled between bodies, and hits the concrete stairs shoulder-first. I can't discern a single voice in the crush of shouting, but I hear him cry out when he lands.

It pierces me like a needle hitting bone, and I wrench out of Jazz's grip to scramble toward Miller over the sidewalk. Behind me, the doors fly open and a wave of security guards floods the walkway. They're holding enormous flashlights and shouting into the dark and as they move past me the crowd recedes, giving me room to breathe. Two of them stop over Miller, arms out to ward everybody back. I shove through, crouch beside him.

"I need an ambulance," one of them says gruffly into his

walkie-talkie. "South entrance, top of the stairs."

"Miller," I whisper. I know he can't hear me; it's so loud. "Miller."

He's on his side, crumpled around himself, his arm bent at an unnatural angle. His eyes are pressed shut, his forehead wrinkled with the strain of it. His lip is split open and there's blood smeared across his mouth, brilliant scarlet against his smoke-pale skin. I reach for him, and one of the security guards stops me.

"Don't touch him," he says. "Don't move him. Nothing until EMS gets here."

I let my hands hover over his shoulder, useless. *I'm here*, I want to say. *I'm here and I've got you and I'm not leaving.*

But I don't know if it's the consolation it would have been once, and I stay silent as Jazz's shoes appear, then Felix's beside them.

"Oh my god," Jazz says. And then Felix: "What the *fuck* just happened?"

I've heard him upset before—furious with us after *Rocky Mountain Live*, exasperated with us during love training, halfway hysterical with laughter, doubled over in the break room at XLR8. But I've never heard his voice like this. Shredded.

Jazz crouches next to me, finding my eyes in the dark. Somewhere in the background—in a whole other world—security has dispersed the crowd.

"Help is coming," she says, and between us, Miller lets out a breathless moan. His chest is rising and falling fast, like he's panicking. She reaches to put a hand on his arm, then stops herself. "You're going to be okay. It's okay. Okay?"

"Okay," Miller says, biting out each syllable. I'm so relieved to hear his voice, my hands start shaking. I press them to the concrete to keep them still.

"Ro." Felix drops to his knees to look at me. "Talk to him, all right? Distract him until they get here."

It's been years since we've been this way—Miller in pain, me the one who makes him feel better. Knowing what Miller needs used to come to me like breathing, our roots so tangled I could feel his hurt as my own. But I'm paralyzed now—by the years and the space we've let grow between us. I don't know if I'm what he needs anymore, and I'm terrified that what he needs is the opposite of me. The absence of me.

But then Miller's eyes open, search for mine in the dark, and I know. It hits me with full-body, breathtaking pain that I've never stopped thinking of him as mine. That this is my Miller, broken on the sidewalk. That we belonged to each other once, and that I want that back with a ferocity so sharp it brings tears to my eyes.

"Ro, it's okay." Felix reaches out to squeeze my shoulder. The security guards are standing now; it's just the four of us down here. "Speak up, honey."

"Miller," I whisper. His eyes flutter closed and I bite my lip, hard enough to draw blood. This is all my fault. *Ro Devereux isn't god.* What the hell have I done?

"Miller," I say, louder this time. "Do you remember when we were seven, and your dad took us to the stock show in Denver?" He nods, barely, just enough that I keep going. "There was that fuzzy cow, the Highland, and its hair was so ridiculous and long and they'd just bathed it so it was all curly and you said if I was a cow, I'd be that one?"

Oh my god, I think, watching him bite his lip. His white teeth in the dark, clamping down to hold in his agony. *This is the stupidest story of all time.*

"Or when you found that arrowhead on the Harrison Gorge trail," I try again. "And we took it to the Museum of Nature and Science and they brought us to the basement, where they had all those artifacts that were too boring to display but too precious to toss, and they told us it wasn't real but they gave you that field explorer badge anyway?"

I'm talking faster as I go, babbling, desperate to land on a memory that makes this all okay. My knees ache against the cold concrete.

"Do you remember the first time my mom sent me money?" Miller's eyes open, hold mine for just a moment before closing again. "And we burned it in the woods even though you hated fire, you didn't even like birthday candles, but you spent all morning building that tepee fire and we roasted the money on a stick like a marshmallow? And you said it was the world's most expensive s'more?"

His breath is slowing, and I don't know if it's because he's calming down or because I'm losing him.

"Do you remember when we made pie for the eighth grade bake sale, but we forgot the bottom dough and just decorated the edges and when Mrs. Morales scooped it out in the cafeteria it got all over her hideous pink dress? Or do you remember that frog we found at the lake, and we named him Peanuts and we took turns keeping him in our rooms but—"

"Ro, they're here."

The EMTs move in around me before I'm ready. Miller is nodding in and out. I don't know if he hears me; I don't know if he's okay.

"Miller," I say, as they slide their hands under his body.

"Miller," as they strap him to the stretcher.

"*Miller.* Do you remember?"

"Yeah, Ro." His voice is so quiet, I almost miss it. The stretcher rises, lifting him up. "I remember everything."

I scramble to my feet, following as they wheel him toward the street. *Me too*, I want to scream. *I remember everything.* The waiting ambulance's lights throw alternating red and yellow flashes across his face, his bleeding lip.

"Somebody coming with him?" one of the paramedics asks. He looks from me to Jazz to Felix. "We've got room for one."

Felix reaches forward, pushes me in the middle of my back. "She'll go." When I look at him I think of the night Vera died, how he stood over Miller and me in that hospital hallway like a sentry. Like someone who wanted to keep us safe. "We'll follow right behind you."

After the sound tunnel of the city sidewalk, the back of the ambulance is quiet. The two paramedics talk to each other in low voices, hooking Miller up to an IV and stabilizing his left arm. One of them touches his neck and he cries out, the sound of it like

201

a knife down the full length of my spine. When they start to cut off his shirt he turns away from me, jaw angled so I can see the pulse under his skin.

It feels impossible that Miller is only human. That I could lose him one day. That maybe, here in the back of this ambulance in a city so far from our home, I already have.

Before I realize I'm doing it I've reached for him, smoothed my hand over his forehead and into his hair. His skin is fever-hot. Miller turns his chin, his eyes finding mine. He looks surprised, his pupils black and blown out, and then we hit a pothole and he winces, eyes pressing shut. For the rest of the ride to the hospital, he leaves them closed.

His collarbone is broken, and his left arm in two different places. He goes into surgery at nine o'clock, by which point Willow is on the way to the airport for her flight to New York. My dad, when I call him, has no idea what's happened. "Great job, honey!" he says when he picks up. "You two looked like naturals up there. I recorded the whole thing."

Jazz and Felix go to the hospital café to get coffee and handle the press. Someone leaks my number, and I get call after call from New York area codes. I don't pick up. I just wait in Miller's hospital room, staring dry-eyed out the window, while they put pins in his bones.

I watch lights blinking across the city and tell myself that no one meant to hurt us. That none of the people who followed that girl onto the sidewalk did it with the intention of doing what they did. That they were just angry. That they just had something to say. That there were just, in the end, too many of them.

Still, I'm scared. Still, I think of Vera. *As you walk this road without me.*

When they bring Miller back he's groggy and sling-wrapped, his arm and shoulder padded against his body like he's been cushioned for a long journey. Someone's cleaned the blood off his face.

"Ro," he says, his voice hoarse, when I sit in the chair beside his bed. For the next hour he disappears and reappears, slowly rejoining the world. I don't text Felix or Jazz. I keep him for myself.

It's past midnight when he reaches for me with his good hand. My eyes are half-closed, my head leaned onto my fist against his mattress. My sleeves are pushed up and he skims his fingers over my scar, says, "My turn." Then he falls back asleep, and sleeps through the night.

29

I've been awake for hours when Miller's eyes open for real. Felix sleeps on a couch at the end of the hallway, and Jazz is at a café down the street for better Wi-Fi and stronger coffee. It's almost seven thirty, weak winter light painting the room pale yellow.

His eyes open slowly, like they're testing the room: *Do I want to be conscious here, or not?* His irises are startling blue in the light from the window. He winces into it, and I get up to draw the shades.

"Such service," Miller says. His voice sounds like it's been dragged up a rock face.

I sit next to him. "How are you feeling?"

"All right." He's on IV pain meds, but still, he winces as he shifts toward me. "How are you feeling?"

My throat closes up, and he waits for me to swallow down the tightness, to find my words through it.

"Do you remember when we were fifteen?" I say. On the bed

in front of me, Miller stiffens. "I asked you to come with me to a party."

"Ro," he says quietly. "We don't have to do this."

"We do," I tell him. The last week has left me with so many more questions than answers but of this one thing, I am absolutely certain. "I need to say this."

His eyes move over mine, and finally, slowly, he nods. "Okay."

"I had a crush on this guy," I say straight down to my hands. They're folded together on Miller's mattress, inches from his body. "It ate me alive and spit me out a different person who wasn't thoughtful, or kind, or fun to be around." I draw a steadying breath, squeezing my palms together. "When he invited me to this party, I thought it was my chance to, like. Level up, or something. I was an idiot."

"You were fifteen," Miller interrupts, and I hold up my hand. If I can't get this out in one shot, I'm not going to get it out at all.

"I asked you to come with me because I was scared to go alone." I look at him. "Because we did everything together. It never even occurred to me to go without you."

Miller blinks, and I keep going. "It's hard for me to even, um. Think directly about what happened after that." I shake my head, looking away from him as my voice thins out. "I was so horrible to you. I've had to bury that memory so deep because it's my least favorite thing about myself. I was awful, Miller." I look up. "I hate that I did that, and it's unforgivable that I did it to you, the best friend I've ever had. I'm so sorry." I draw a breath, and it shudders between my ribs. "And after yesterday, seeing you like that—"

Miller holds my eyes. He looks pale, and weak, and tired. That's my fault, too.

"I was so scared." It hangs there between us—finally, the truth. "And I need you to know how sorry I am. I should have kept calling, after it happened. I'd do anything to un-fuck this up."

"Ro," he says. His voice is soft and sorry. "It's not unforgivable. We were just kids. It's okay."

He can't mean it; it can't be so simple as all that or he'd never have stopped talking to me. But he says it anyway, a kindness I've done nothing to deserve.

"And besides"—the shadow of a smile tugs at his split lips—"I could have called you back."

"Why didn't you?"

He leans his head back, winces, looks up at the ceiling. He takes a while, like he's weighing his words, but I wait. This conversation's been three years coming.

"A few reasons," he says, his voice low. "I was always just this nerdy kid, right? Never anyone's first choice. But it was different with you. It's like you were the one place I fit, the one thing I understood about the world—that it was always me and you." He swallows, his head still tipped back to look at the ceiling. "And that night, it just—it felt like you were telling me I was wrong. That this thing I thought I knew for sure wasn't true after all." His chin drops against the pillow, his eyes finding mine. "It was like you didn't want to pick me, either. And I was so embarrassed that I'd misunderstood everything, that I thought—"

He stops, but his eyes don't move from mine. A muscle worries in his jaw.

"That you thought what?" I whisper, scared to hear him say it.

Miller's eyes track across mine, his chest rising with a great, shuddering breath. "I was so in love with you," he says. The whole sentence is an exhale, like it winds him to admit it. "I had been forever. And then to watch that—"

He doesn't finish the sentence. *I was*, he said. Firmly, clearly past tense. *I've always loved Ro*, Miller told Jimmy, told all of America. Something he said for this charade we're playing—for the college tuition he'll get from this, in the end.

"It was too hard for me to face you," Miller says. "And the more time went on, it just felt, I don't know—" He breaks off, searching for words. "Like it was too late, or something."

"Too late," I repeat, barely a whisper. I mean it as a question but it comes out flat and lifeless, like I'm agreeing with him.

"I told myself that maybe it would be easier." Miller's back to looking at the ceiling, and I watch his profile as his words sink through me like stones. His dark eyebrows, high cheekbones, the familiar cut of his jaw. The way he clenches his teeth when he's nervous, like he is now. "To just not have you in my life at all, if we couldn't be as close as I—" He breaks off again, then forces himself to finish. "As I wanted us."

"Was it?" I ask, and he looks at me. "Easier?"

The corners of his eyes crease, like something hurts. "No," he says quietly. "It's been awful."

I blink down at my hands. There's so much I want to tell him, and no way to say it now. The pain in my chest feels skeletal, like my ribs are breaking.

"You weren't wrong," I say softly. "We did fit."

It's the closest I can get, and when I press my thumbnail into the center of my palm I feel like screaming, like folding over and over into myself until I'm small, until I'm nothing at all. *Too late.*

"And you weren't just a nerdy kid," I manage. When I look up he's still watching me, teeth digging into his battered bottom lip. "You were smart, and funny, and kind. I hated that you felt like you needed to hide around all those stupid people at school, but I always felt so lucky I got the real you." The words I really want to say rise in me, desperate for a way out. Miller kissing me at the lake, and Miller holding my eyes outside Vera's hospital room, and Miller's hand in both of mine as we rode in the ambulance. But he's laid this bare: this thing we might've had died that night in Declan's living room.

"You weren't *just* anything," I tell him. "You were the best. I'm a monster for making you think you weren't."

Miller's hand twitches toward mine on the mattress, and when he turns his palm up to the ceiling I take the invitation, curl my fingers through his.

"You're no monster, Ro." His voice is so soft it's barely there at all. "And honestly?" He squeezes my fingers. "The only time I ever did anything remotely cool growing up was because you made me."

The warmth of his hand is suddenly more than I can bear, and I pull mine away. Miller's fingers flex instinctively, folding back against his palm. I slide my hands under my thighs.

Cool. The last four months I've watched Miller be so much

better than cool: He is steady and intelligent and honest and driven and good. He's himself, first and always and without apology.

He clears his throat. "What ever happened with Declan?"

"Nothing," I say, a reflex. But when he's quiet I finally meet his eyes, and I know: Here is where I fit. I can tell him, so I do.

Miller closes his eyes while I'm speaking. When he says, "Shit," it's an exhale more than a word. I don't think I've ever heard him curse before.

"And I left you alone there." His eyes break open, meet mine. "Ro, I'm so sorry. You must have hated me."

"I did, a little. But that was stupid." I toe my sneaker into the smudged tile floor, stare down at my shoes so I don't have to look at him. "I pushed you away, and then got mad at you for going. I was so ashamed and I—what happened was my own fault."

"No," he says, so firmly I look up. "What he did to you was his fault, not yours."

My throat tightens, too aching to speak through. I think of that skirt, my favorite one, donated because it had Declan's fingerprints all over it. Of waking up that next day and needing Miller and the bottomless, sinking knowing that he wasn't there because of me.

"I'm really sorry that happened to you."

"I'm sorry, too," I whisper. I don't know what I'm apologizing for anymore. The mess I've made, maybe. This thing I've stolen from myself—Miller, who's been right here all along, who would've listened to this years ago if I hadn't pushed him away so thoroughly that he couldn't hear me. "But it could've been bad. Worse. And it wasn't."

"You don't have to do that," he says. "You were scared. What he did was wrong, and I should've been there."

"That was my choice," I say, barely a whisper. Echoing his words from all the way back in September, that day at the Fast Freeze. We both picked this, but I picked it first.

"Ro," Miller says. I've been tracing my scar with my fingertip, and I look up at him. His eyes are steady on mine, but there's something else—anguish, maybe—in how he's looking at me. "What do you want now?"

Tears burn behind my eyes. This conversation has felt like flaying myself alive, like peeling back my skin to expose the hole inside me where Miller hasn't been all these years.

My voice comes soft and small. "What would you still let me have?"

His mouth opens at the exact same time as the door.

"Oh my god," Willow says. She rushes toward the bed, dropping things as she goes. Her duffel, and her umbrella, and a plastic bag from an airport gift shop. "Honey."

"Hey, I'm okay," Miller says. Willow covers him, hides him from me, kisses his face. "Mom, I'm okay."

"Oh my god," she says again. She leans away and scans him, assessing the damage. Only once she's confirmed he's in one piece does she look up at me.

"Ro," she says. Her eyes are red and puffy, like she cried the whole way here. She cuts around the bed and pulls me into her arms and it's this, finally, that pushes me over the edge. My eyes fill with tears against the slant of her shoulder and I lift a hand to my mouth, break from her embrace, leave the room before Miller can see me cry.

30

I can see Central Park from the ambulance bay, which is where I find myself when I burst from the building. I smear my tears with a sweatshirt sleeve and sit on the low concrete barrier next to the sidewalk. A woman jogs past, blond ponytail swinging. I watch her cut across the street into the park.

My phone buzzes, another New York number. When I decline it, Maren's text comes through: How's he doing?

He's awake, I tell her. They said we can leave tomorrow.

She sends a pink heart emoji, and then: How are you doing?

I surprise myself by letting out a sob. I squeeze my phone until it hurts, watching a cold wind move through the trees across the street. I feel rudderless, is the truth. I feel like a climber who's missed her carabiner—like I am suddenly, fatally free-falling.

Vera is gone. MASH has wreaked havoc. This thing I made hurt someone enough for a horde of angry people to want to hurt us. Miller is stuck in a hospital bed in an unfamiliar city because

212

of me. Miller is out of my reach because of me.

She released a statement.

My phone buzzes again, this time with a text from Jazz to Felix, Miller, and me. She sends a screenshot of Josie Sweet's Instagram, where Josie's posted a photo of her Notes app filled frame to frame with text.

I've tried to keep quiet as I navigate this deeply personal journey. Sharing my life and my love with you all has always meant so much to me, but sometimes feelings are too raw to share. For me, this has been one of those times. I've been away from my phone, trying to care for my heart. But I feel called to address what happened last night at Rockefeller Center. I need to say this clearly: What happened between Hayes and me happened between Hayes and me. It wasn't MASH's fault. I don't blame MASH, and I don't blame Ro Devereux. I've made the decision to end my brand partnership with MASH, but that's a step I'm taking because it's the right one for my personal journey—not because I think MASH is responsible for what happened to my relationship. I'm grateful that you hold me so well in your hearts, but violence is never okay. I don't think it was anyone's intention to hurt Alistair Miller last night, but that's what happened. I am heartbroken over this. I'm sending my best to Miller for a quick recovery. Be well and love one another. xJS

I read it three times over, blinking tears from my eyes. Since

The Tonight Show the internet's been a firestorm of MASH reactions: people going heart-eyed over what Miller said on-air, people calling for MASH to shut down over breaking up Josie and Hayes, people condemning Josie for siccing her fans on us like attack dogs.

When I open my News app, we're right there at the top of the feed: "MASH Press Tour Turns Violent, Alistair Miller Hospitalized." The photo is dramatic, black and red: the dark of the sidewalk behind Rockefeller Center, the glow of the ambulance signals as the paramedics load Miller into the back. I'm in the center of the frame, my hair haloed with light, my face unrecognizable with fear.

The story of the last twenty-four hours emerges, in pieces, across the internet. But no one is talking about the full picture. No one has shared the simple truth: that maybe I should never have done this at all.

That if I hadn't signed that contract in XLR8's office, Miller would be safe. That we'd be home.

That I've bitten off more than I can chew, and it's getting hard to breathe.

"Josie Sweet sent flowers." I look up, and Willow's standing next to me on the sidewalk. She pulls her coat around herself and sits down on my ledge, smiling. "They're very fancy."

I glance behind her, toward the hospital entrance. "Is he okay?"

"Yeah, he's asleep." She looks just like Miller: dark hair in loose waves, delicate features, pale blue eyes. They find mine. "Are you? He was worried about you, running off like that."

214

I shrug, biting my lip and looking down at my boots. Once, I would've told Willow anything. When I was small, and she was partway mine. But time has made us strangers, and I don't know what Miller has told her.

"Lots of hospitals for you lately, huh?"

I draw a deep breath, look up at her. "A few too many for my taste, to be honest."

"Yeah," she says softly. "You're carrying a lot right now, aren't you?"

I try to turn away, but I'm not fast enough. When I start crying again she pulls me against her, wrapping both arms around me. "Oh, honey," she says. "He's going to be fine."

I sniffle into her shirt, the familiar smell of her detergent. "Am I, though?"

"Of course." Her hand moves over my back. "You've always been so strong. And you have a good team in your corner. Your dad, and XLR8, and Miller, and me."

I pull back, wiping my eyes as I look up at her. She brushes the hair from my face and smiles. "I always thought you two would find your way back to each other. I just didn't expect it to look like this."

"Yeah," I say on a half laugh. "Tell me about it."

"We've missed you," she says, and I can't bring myself to look at her. "Both of us."

I stare down at my shoes, and she keeps going. "And we're grateful—Miller's dad and me."

Her son just had surgery halfway across the country from our home, and she's grateful? I look up at her. "For what?"

"The money," Willow says simply. "Al and I never thought we'd be able to give Miller what he wants. What he deserves." She sighs, looking over the street at the park. "He's so smart, smarter than both of us together. But these schools he's interested in, and a Classics degree, it just—" She hesitates, then smiles at me. "We just wouldn't have been able to consider it, if it weren't for you and MASH."

I knew, I guess, that Miller needed this money—of course he did, or he wouldn't have asked for it. But still, something settles heavy and immovable on my chest. "What would he have done instead?"

"Oh, community college," Willow says, shrugging. "RMC, probably, in Denver. Al's always been insistent he not start his postgrad life with insurmountable debt."

I swallow. "Do they have a Classics program?"

Willow looks at me, smiling sadly. "No. Which makes us feel all the luckier. And not just because of the money, of course." She brushes my knee with her fingertips. "It's a gift to see the two of you together again."

I force a smile. If I felt like MASH was closing in on me before, now it feels like a lead blanket rooting me to the ledge.

Willow slides her hands into her coat pockets and hunches against the cold. "You know, when your mom left, I lost my best friend, too."

I stare at the side of her face, silent. No one in my life talks about my mother, and having her brought here now—to this freezing ledge outside a hospital in a brand-new city—makes me feel like I've missed a step on the way down the stairs.

"We were like the two of you," she says. "Grew up together, did everything together. Then she made a choice I couldn't understand." Willow looks at me, her eyes softening. "I'd hoped it wouldn't be like that for you and Miller. That you'd never become unrecognizable to each other."

I draw a cold breath, and it stings all the way down. There's so much I could say—that it's impossible to imagine my mother as a young woman, somebody's best friend. That she's a specter to me. That losing Miller created a hole in my life so massive it didn't close up, not even a little bit, the entire time we were apart. And that I can't imagine how Willow has survived this long if it felt the same for her when my mom went away.

But there's one truth that's simplest, so I tell her that instead. "I messed it up," I whisper, straight at the sidewalk.

"We all mess up," she says. "But you came back to him eventually. And he's still here."

I look up at her, and she stands from the ledge.

"Come on." She reaches for my hand. "Let's go keep him company."

Later, when Willow goes out to find dinner and Felix and Jazz take a conference call with Evelyn, Miller and I are finally alone. He's still sleepy, heavy-lidded as his body fights to fix itself.

"Out with it," he says gently, as soon as the door closes behind his mom.

"Out with what?" I'm in the chair next to his bed, my socked feet up on the mattress.

"Whatever it is you've been holding back all day."

"There's nothing," I tell him, and he levels me with his gaze.

"Don't lie to me." He reaches up, touches the scab on his lip. "We're past that now."

Are we? I think. The room is growing dark, the planes of Miller's face soft and shadowed in the muted light from the window in the door. I sigh, sitting up to rest my arms against the bed, and look at him.

"Should we stop it?" I let the words hang there, my own undoing. "MASH?"

Miller's eyebrows draw together. He shifts against the pillows like he's trying to get a better look at me. "Why would we do that?"

"Miller," I say, breathing a laugh. I gesture toward him. "Look at you. It's getting out of control."

"This was an accident," he says. I look at his fingers, hidden at the top knuckle by his cast. Think of his mother, thanking me for making something that could give Miller the future she can't. "It doesn't mean we should stop."

I tilt my head from side to side. Firmly, he says, "It *doesn't*. Ro, this is your dream."

"I'll have other ideas," I say, though I'm not sure I actually believe it. "Different dreams."

Miller stares at me, his eyes moving back and forth over mine. Like he's reading, which I know he is. "It's like Jazz told us," he says. "We're not the bad guys just because someone used MASH as an excuse to break up. If you get this funding, you're set. You don't have to go to school. It's only a couple more months."

"And you get your tuition money," I say quietly.

Miller blinks, glancing across the room before his gaze comes back to mine. "Yeah," he says, sheepish. "That too."

"Your mom told me about community college, and how there isn't a Classics program, and your dad not wanting you to have debt."

We look at each other, and then Miller turns his gaze up to the ceiling. "I mean, he wants that. But it's my life, and I'd rather have debt than spend my time on something I don't care about."

"So you'd have gone to Brown anyway?" It's too clear in my voice, how much I want it to be true. How much I hate that I'm holding his future in my hands, mine to fuck up. "Even without the Celeritas money?"

He turns his chin, finds my eyes. "I'd have tried to, if they accepted me."

"They'll accept you," I say, so quickly that he smiles.

I draw a breath, tracing a crease in the sheet with my thumbnail. "There's something else, though."

He shifts, still watching me. "Okay."

"Something's wrong with my algorithm. I realized it on the plane." I hesitate, fighting the urge to hide my face. "Our kids."

There's a short, weighted silence—heavy as humidity. Miller clears his throat. "What about our kids?"

"MASH gave me zero, but it gave you two."

"Maybe I'll have an affair."

I smack his good arm and he laughs, low and breathy.

"I'm serious," I say. "We got the same city, but I don't know if that's always true for matches, either. The survey doesn't listen to both sides—it doesn't take what I want, and what you want, and compromise them into what our life will be. It just gives me my perfect future, and you yours." I draw a shaky breath. "But it'll be shared. So either one of our predictions is wrong, or they both are."

It's there between us, half-spoken: our shared future. But I'm only talking about it in the context of this algorithm, not in the real way that's pressing against my ribs—the way I'm imagining it, that I'm too scared to speak of out loud.

"So what do we do?" Miller asks.

"I don't know. I've been so caught up in all this that I didn't even stop to think—I just—" My voice hitches, and I struggle to smooth it out. "I didn't want to question it. And I made MASH with Vera, who was so smart, and now I don't know how to fix it without her. I don't think I can."

"I think you can," Miller says. "I think it's been a really long day, and you're in your head about it, and once we're home we can sit down and figure it out. Okay?"

I look at him—head on the pillow, hair a mess, split lip and long eyelashes and all the rest. Reassuring me, when he's the one in the half-body cast. Something swells inside me, so staggering I nearly reach for him before I catch myself.

"Okay," I tell him, and he smiles.

3 1

We fly home the next afternoon, and the airport is mobbed. There are two days until Christmas. Willow pushes Miller through security in a wheelchair, and he complains the entire time. "There's nothing wrong with my legs," he repeats, but she silences him with a hand on his shoulder and pushes on.

His sling is navy blue, cutting across his back in an X. It keeps his arm close to his body, his clavicle at the best angle for it to heal. He tells me he's fine, but any time he thinks I'm not looking, I catch him in a grimace.

We had to cancel all our other media appearances, every single interview. Jazz rebooks us for the *Today* show in January, two weeks before the Celeritas meeting. The rest we'll do remote from Denver when Miller's ready.

His injury has thrown a bucketful of cold water onto the flames of the Josie/Hayes scandal. Sympathy is a powerful drug—and if people loved Miller before, they're rabid for him now.

I scroll through the comments on @MASHapp's latest post as

we wait at our gate. It's a picture of Miller and me, art directed by Felix this afternoon. Miller's propped up in bed and I'm cross-legged on the mattress in front of him, an open box of pizza between us. We're surrounded by floral arrangements, from Josie and Jimmy and a whole bunch of strangers. Miller holds his good arm in the air, flashing a thumbs-up and smiling for the camera, and I'm looking straight at him with an expression so sincere it hurts to look at. **Heard NY pizza heals all wounds,** the caption says. **Thanks for all the support—Mo's on the mend.**

The comments section is bloodred, teeming with heart emojis and heart-eyed smileys.

We love you, Miller! Get better soon!

How is this man even hotter in a hospital gown???

We must protect Miller at all costs!!

I look over at him, finally out of the wheelchair and sitting next to his mom in one of the leather gate seats. He has a book open in his lap, a cup of coffee in his good hand. As if he can feel me watching he looks up, and when our eyes meet, he smiles.

Yes, I think. *We must.*

Miller and Willow sit next to each other on the plane, Miller in the aisle so his cast has space of its own. I'm across the aisle and behind them, at the edge of the row with Felix and Jazz tucked in beside me. I spend the entire flight staring at the curve of Miller's ear, at the way his hair curls at the nape of his neck. I feel like I'm going to come out of my skin.

The flight attendants start drink service, and when their cart moves past Miller's row he stands, stretching his good arm in the aisle. I watch him put his book down, say something to his mother, turn to the front of the plane. He walks toward the bathrooms, careful with his cast.

As I watch him in the dim glow of the overhead lights, I think about what he asked Autumn, two weeks and a full lifetime ago in the bitter cold at formal. *What would love look like?*

I'm not sure if there's an answer that works for all of us. But I know it now, what I've been hiding from myself all this time: that for me it looks like Miller, gingerly moving down the airplane aisle. Opening his eyes in that hospital room to find me. Closing his fingers around my wrist before we stepped into the mess outside *The Tonight Show*. Love has always, always looked like Miller.

It's the truth I've been swallowing, all but choking on: that I am obsessed with Alistair Miller, that I have not stopped thinking even once of the way his voice sounded when he said he loved me. That it's exactly as he said in the hospital: Miller is what I know for sure. It's always been the two of us, eternal as the gods we grew up believing in.

You will become people you can't even fathom yet, Vera told me. But every version of myself, I know, belongs with him.

The front galley is empty, every flight attendant dispersed down the aisle dropping off drinks. I step out of sight and wait there, twisting my fingers together. When the bolt on the bathroom door slides open, my heart nose-dives down the line of my rib cage.

"Miller," I whisper. His eyebrows shoot up, and he steps sideways through the door to close it behind him.

"Hey," he says, surprised. I beckon him toward me, into the metal-walled alcove. "What are you doing?"

It's tight in here, even tighter with his bulky cast. Beneath our feet, clouds part under the belly of the plane.

"I, um." I came here with absolutely no plan, stuttering complete nonsense. "I just—"

Miller's eyebrows are still lifted, his eyes on mine. We don't have a lot of time, I know. The flight attendants will be back soon. This space is only ours for right now, so I just get on my tiptoes, steady myself against his good shoulder, and kiss him.

Miller's lips are soft and dry and entirely still. I don't think he's breathing. When I pull away he just looks at me, mouth slightly open. The line where his lip split is deep, cherry red.

I let out an inhuman squeak and dart around him, horrified. What am I *doing*?

"Ro, wait." Miller grabs my wrist, hot as a brand. He tugs me back into the privacy of the kitchen. "What was that?"

"I don't know," I say, though I do. Of course I do. He's looking right at me, something suddenly so unfamiliar about his face it makes me want to hide. "I'm sorry. I was just—I was. That was stupid."

Miller steps closer to me, releasing my wrist. "It wasn't stupid."

We stare at each other. The plane hums around us. "No?"

He shakes his head slowly. I watch him swallow, his Adam's apple rising and falling in his pale throat.

"Do you still mean it?" I whisper. We're inches apart; I can see every single one of his eyelashes. "What you said on *The Tonight Show*?"

A muscle tenses in Miller's jaw. And like an idiot, like someone with more faith than I've ever had, I bare my own dumb heart right there in the dim galley. "Miller, I love you. I know you said it's too late, but I love you so much it's ridi—"

He cuts me off, his mouth landing square on mine. It's different than that night at the lake—not gentle or hesitant, but starved and sure. It feels brand-new and also, somehow, like we've been here before. Like there's no shock to it at all. Miller's hand moves into my hair, his thumb along the line of my jaw, and I think: *god, thank you*. The sheer relief of touching him feels strong enough to knock me to my knees.

When he tips me against the cabinets, I slide a hand under his sweater. His back is warm and smooth, two lines of muscle dipping into the ridge of his spine. I want to reach higher, feel the press of his shoulder blades, but it's clunky with the cast—plaster and plastic between us.

"I wish I could hold you better," Miller murmurs, and I shake my head.

"This is perfect."

"It's not," he laughs. "This isn't how I—"

He catches himself, and I lean back to look at him. His eyes are tight with embarrassment, but he blinks it away. "How I pictured it," he says, finally, and my entire body floods with heat. "I just. I've wanted this for a long time."

There's so much I want to tell him, but the vastness of this moment is rising in me like tears, threatening to spill over. I can't speak through it, so I just pull Miller back into me. Exactly where he should have been all along.

32

We land in Denver at four, and Dad's waiting in baggage claim. The sight of his face, after the trip we've had, almost makes me cry.

"I didn't know you were coming," I say when he pulls me into a hug. He smells like coffee and toothpaste.

"Well, you don't know everything." His voice goes rough at the end, hitching on the words.

"Miss me a little?" I pull back to look at him, and he swipes at his eyes.

"Nah," he says gruffly. "You okay?"

"Fine," I tell him, and he studies my face. I'm not fine: I miss Vera, and I messed up the algorithm, and I'm scared of what happens next. But I'm here. "Promise."

"And you?" Dad turns to Miller, leaving one hand on my shoulder. "How's our invalid?"

"Not a fan of the nickname," Miller says. He put his foot down about the wheelchair once we landed, and now he's standing between Willow and Jazz. When he glances at me I feel it like a flood of warm water in my chest. "Otherwise, I'm good."

"Good." Dad lets out a gusting breath, looking between us. We're a raggedy, worn-down bunch. I'm not sure Jazz has slept at all since we left Denver. My phone died somewhere over the Midwest and I just left it like that, too tired to keep up with the social mentions and the texts and the incessant calls from New York numbers. Miller watched me stick the black-screened brick in my bag and powered his down, too. *A little quiet would be good*, he said.

"You guys hungry?" Dad asks. "Come to the house, I can cook for everyone."

"I should get this kid home." Willow brushes her fingers over Miller's arm. "He needs rest."

"I'm okay—" Miller starts, but Felix cuts him off.

"No, she's right." He's got his phone in one hand and purple half-moons under his eyes. Today's the first time I've ever seen him unshaven. "You two need a break. Some sleep." He runs a hand through his hair, rings flashing, and leaves it messy. "I'll check in after Christmas about rescheduling all this stuff, okay? Just rest until then." He swallows, glancing at my dad. "I'm sorry."

"It's not your fault," Miller says, and Felix lifts one shoulder in a defeated shrug, like maybe he thinks it is.

"It's not," I echo. When I reach my hand toward him, he squeezes my fingers.

"Just bad luck, babe." Jazz nudges him with her elbow, then glances between us. "Take care of yourselves, all right? We'll get a cab to Denver." As she steers Felix away from us, she raises a hand. "Happy holidays, y'all."

"He looks like he could use a nap, too," Dad says, watching them go.

"I think we all could," Willow says on a yawn. "You guys ready?"

When I look at Miller, he's already looking at me. I reach for his good hand, and he squeezes his palm flush against mine. "Ready," I say.

Esther is, for once, there when I need her. After dinner I shower and put on pajamas and climb into bed, my whole body sagging with relief. She hops onto the mattress and curls against my ribs, tucking her chin into her paws. We lie like that for hours: my hand running a rhythm over her silky head, her whiskers twitching every now and then as she looks up to make sure I'm still awake, still petting her. I hear Dad click off the lights and close his bedroom door just after ten. The house is quiet and overwhelmingly familiar after the foreign fear of the last few days.

I'm halfway to sleep when something erupts from my desk, noise crackling through the room so loudly Esther nearly bites my hand in panic.

"*Christ*," I mutter, sitting up. Esther bolts off the bed and straight out of my room. The noise breaks the sleeping stillness of the house again, and I hurry to the desk, searching for it. I shove papers aside, knock my mouse so my computer turns on, pull open one drawer and then the next.

The sound crackles again—but this time, there's something discernible in it. My name. "Ro?"

I yank open the bottom drawer, and there it is: my walkie-talkie.

Little orange light blinking.

"Ro?" The sound quality's horrible, but I'd know Miller's voice anywhere. "Do you copy?"

I grin like a fool, standing all alone in my bedroom. Man, do I copy. I copy so hard.

"Miller." I lift the hunk of plastic to my face, one finger on the speak button. "What are you doing?"

"We said no more phones today." His voice is garbled. My phone's still at the bottom of my backpack—tossed aside in the corner of my room. "I'm outside."

"You're—" I walk over to the window, peer down at our yard. And sure enough, there he is: the white outline of his cast catching the moonlight, his chin tipped up to see me in the dark. He smiles. "You're outside."

"Can I come up?"

I practically throw the walkie across the room in my haste to get downstairs. He's waiting on our landing when I get there, no car behind him in the driveway.

"Did you walk here?" I ask, glancing around him. We live close, but still—it's nearly midnight, and freezing outside.

"I drove," he says, glancing up the road. "Parked down the street just in case."

I look at him. "Just in case."

He tries to shrug, then winces. He's in sweatpants and a loose sweatshirt, bulky over his cast. Even in the dark, I can tell his cheeks are pink from the cold. "In case what, Miller?"

He takes a step closer to me, reaching for my hand. I look

down at our fingers, his thumb over my knuckles. "I just wanted to see you," he says, so quiet, straight down at our hands. Like he's nervous. "Without my mom there, or—" He breaks off, and we look at each other. "Now that we're doing this for real, I just want to be near you. Finally."

"Yes," I say, the answer to a question he didn't ask. It comes out on its own, a breathless rush of a word. "I mean, I—yes, I want—" I'm a useless, fumbling mess over him.

"Okay," Miller says, laughing into the cold. "I'm glad we're on the same page."

When I kiss him, he's still smiling. I tug him over the threshold and close the door softly behind us, lifting a finger to my lips and pointing toward Dad's room at the back of the house. Miller nods and follows me up the stairs, my heartbeat gaining speed with each of his footfalls. I'm so exhausted I'm halfway delirious, and Miller here, like this—it feels huge enough to hollow me out entirely.

"Hey, Esther," he whispers, stopping as she purrs against his ankle. I reach for his hand, pull him into my room, and shut the door. And then we're alone.

"Wow," Miller says, eyes raking across the room. "It's different."

I follow his gaze, tracking across the cramped space—my unmade bed, the photo strips pinned to the wall of Maren and me skiing on Valentine's Day three years running, my desk strewn with headphones and external hard drives. My computer pings with a text message notification, the screen still awake from when I knocked it in my rush to find the walkie-talkie.

"Different how?"

Miller points to the wall above my headboard. "I seem to recall a certain One Direction poster."

"Oh my god." I yank him, laughing, toward the bed. "There was no One Direction poster." (There was definitely a One Direction poster.)

"I like it," he says, smiling at me as he sits down. "Feels like you in here."

"I like you in here," I say, like an idiot. Like an embarrassment to myself and every Devereux before me. But Miller only smiles bigger, and uses his good hand to hook a finger behind my knee and pull me toward him.

"Hi," I whisper, when our bodies are close enough to keep us warm in a blizzard.

He curves his hand around the back of my leg. "Hey."

I lower myself onto his lap, one leg on either side of him, careful with the cast. When I run my hands into his hair, his eyes close for the briefest moment. "Is this okay?"

Miller lets out a strangled laugh, warm breath in the hollow of my throat. "More than."

My hair falls over his face, tickling across his cheekbones, and I push it out of the way. "Sorry."

"Don't be." He reaches up to brush it behind my ear, tugging gently at the end of a curl before dropping his hand back to my waist. "I love your hair."

"Even when it's eating you?"

He grins, and this close it's like it takes up his whole face. "Especially then."

"Good," I say, and he echoes, "Good," and then we're kissing.

And, I mean—I've kissed people before. That tourist at the lake. Declan Frey in the dim alcove off his living room. Boys I knew so briefly they lit on my life like fireflies before disappearing.

Kissing has been fun, or fine, or really bad. Kissing Miller is nothing like the others.

We come at it so eagerly that our teeth scrape, and still—it's perfect. Miller hooks his good arm around my waist, holding me against him as his palm presses between my shoulder blades. His chin's tipped back, and I can feel the curve of his throat under my thumb when I run my hand down to his chest, the movement of his jaw when he pushes his lips to mine. My fingers cross the fabric of his sling and his heartbeat underneath. His mouth opens under mine and I want to stay here forever and kissing Miller feels like breathing—like I might die if it stops.

His fingertips press to my waist, pulling me closer, and his cast hits my hip bone.

"Careful," I whisper, right into his mouth. "I don't want to hurt you."

"You couldn't," he says, and when he kisses me again I hesitate. Somewhere, my computer dings with another text message. "Ro."

I look at him, his blue eyes inches from mine. His face angled up to meet me, the swoop of his hair over his forehead. He tips his head back into my palm, giving me the weight of him.

"It's all right," he says, like he knows what I'm thinking. Which is that I did hurt him once. "We're all right."

"I love you," I tell him. Every version—that kid who cried at a dead tree in the woods, and the one who went to that stupid party with me, and the one who signed up for MASH when we hadn't spoken in years. Even the one who yelled at me, fury running through him like a fever, at the Fast Freeze. The near-reality where we never found each other again lands on me, heavy and all at once. "I'm sorry."

"You don't need to be sorry," Miller says. "We're here now."

I brush my thumb over his bottom lip, the thin ridge where he split it on the staircase, and he kisses my finger.

"I missed you," he says quietly.

"Since the plane?"

Miller shakes his head. "The whole time."

I wrap my arms around his shoulders, careful not to squeeze too hard. He leans his forehead into the slope of my neck and for a minute we just sit there, breathing.

"Me too," I whisper over the top of his head. "The whole time."

"I love you," he says. I pull back, and he looks up at me. "You know that, right? It's been true all along." Miller swallows, shakes his head just a little. "That's been the hardest part of this whole thing, pretending that I didn't."

I lean my forehead against his. It feels like a miracle—his chest under my hands, him holding me here in my bedroom.

"I don't want you to ever pretend with me," I tell him. "No more Hidden Miller."

He tips his chin up, presses his mouth into mine. "Deal," he whispers. And then, "Ro?"

"Mmm?" We're too close to look at each other; when I open my eyes he's all blurry.

"Can I call you my girlfriend now, or is that still the wrong vernacular?"

I burst out laughing, and Miller smiles. "I think I'm ready to make an exception to the rule," I say, and he stamps a kiss against the side of my neck.

"Generous."

My computer pings again, then five more times in quick succession. Miller cranes around to look at it, flinching when he tweaks his shoulder.

"Jesus," I say, climbing off his lap. "What is going *on*?"

The texts are from Maren, each more frustrated than the last.

Have you seen this NYT article?

I want to make sure you're ok so please respond.

Haven't heard from you all afternoon and starting to get worried.

Ro??

LOOK AT YOUR PHONE RIGHT NOW.

33

"It's Maren." I reach for my backpack to dig out my phone. "She said there's some *New York Times* article?"

Miller walks over to the desk, leaning close to read my computer screen. "*New York Times*?" He looks up at me. "About Josie and Hayes?"

"I have no idea." I plug in my charger and set my phone on the desk, waiting for it to power up. "You haven't heard anything about this, either?"

Miller shakes his head and runs a hand through his hair, already sticking up from my fingers raking through it. Looking at him, I think of that line from *Where the Wild Things Are*, a book Dad and I read all the time when I was a kid. *I'll eat you up I love you so.* Miller's pink cheeks, and his lips a little swollen, and the span of his shoulders under the sling. I could swallow him whole. I could murder myself for missing out on this.

"What?" Miller says, when a minute's passed and I'm still staring at him.

235

I blink. "Nothing. I just—" I step toward him, rise onto my toes to kiss him again. He steadies me with a hand on my waist, and I feel him smile under my mouth.

"Your phone's on," he says.

I clear my throat, drop back onto my heels. "Right."

The screen fills immediately, a string of texts and missed calls from Maren, Sawyer, Jazz, Felix. And mixed in, the most sinister of all: Evelyn Cross.

Evelyn's text is right at the top, so I see it first. **Do not post publicly. Same goes for Miller. Wait for direction from Jazz.**

"What the hell?" I mutter, opening up all the others. There's a frantic stream of back-and-forth between Jazz and Felix in our group with Miller, mostly the two of them talking each other off the ledge and then demanding to know why we aren't responding. In the middle of the thread, Felix has asked a question that goes unanswered by Jazz: **I thought they agreed not to run this?** But there's no article link, just an incoherent rush of panic. Sawyer's message is an incredibly unhelpful **WTF is going on??**

It's Maren, when I finally open our text thread, who's managed to explain.

She texted me for the first time at five, when the article dropped and we'd already left the airport with our phones off. **Have you seen this??** she'd sent, with a link. **MASH has bigger problems than Josie and Hayes.**

When I open the link, the article's title crashes into my silent bedroom like a tree felled in the woods. It splinters over my skin.

236

The Insidious MASH Effect, it reads, in huge black letters.

And then, below it: *The Dark Underbelly of America's Favorite App*.

"What?" Miller breathes over my shoulder. Wordlessly, we sit down on the bed and read.

Much has been said over the last few days of MASH's impact on existing relationships, after the very public demise of Josie Sweet and Hayes Hawkins's years-long partnership. Everyone knows by now of the Monday-night protest at Rockefeller Center that turned violent and left Alistair Miller with three broken bones. Everyone knows of—and almost unanimously adores—America's oracle, eighteen-year-old Ro Devereux. What many don't seem to realize is there's something more sinister at work in the high-tech halls of Denver's MASH HQ.

My interest in MASH's inevitable dark side started, I'll admit, at home. I have a niece—she's fourteen. Since she was a child, since before she could even read, she knew she wanted to be a veterinarian. When kids are small, we tend to write them off. "Maybe they'll grow out of this." She didn't. My sister's home was a hospital for stuffed animals and, as Lara got older, real ones. Neighborhood strays, a one-eyed frog she found in the creek, eventually their own adopted dogs. Lara has always known what she loves. And then, in September, she downloaded MASH.

This app, purportedly built on "science" that MASH has staunchly refused to attribute to any person or institution, told Lara she was going to be a marketing manager. Lara does not know what that means, only that she will never achieve her dream. You can imagine, maybe, what's followed since then. In case you can't, I'll spell it out.

In the time since my niece received her MASH results, she's stopped combing her neighborhood for injured frogs and hobbled birds. She's given up her volunteer position at her local animal shelter, once one of her greatest sources of joy. Her mother—my sister—has watched her retreat so far into herself she is unreachable.

I'll stop here to say that I, too, have taken the MASH survey. For me, like for so many others, it worked: I'll be a reporter, I'll live in New York, I'll be childless with a man who, yes, I met and felt connected to straightaway. Some of MASH's newer categories—pets, illness, age when married—remain untested for me. But the Core Four, as MASH calls them, have been spot-on. And if that weren't true for so many of us, MASH wouldn't be what it is now. But what about the Laras?

My team at the *Times* has spent the last two

months researching the true effects of Ro Devereux's all-seeing app. "The future's written inside your mind," MASH tells us. But what dangers lurk there alongside it? What price do we pay for this window into an untested vision of our future lives? This app is months, not years, old. There is so much data we don't have yet. Here's what we do know.

In the ten weeks since MASH's massive scale-up (thanks to Palo Alto–based app accelerator XLR8), rates of depression are on the rise among fourteen-to-eighteen-year-old Americans. We saw a significant spike in early November, as MASH hit its stride and "Mo," the faces of MASH matching, gained public favor. Interest in exploratory programs like the arts, sports—even volunteering opportunities—are down.

This is happening, primarily, among children. Among our most vulnerable populations. MASH is telling them they're on a path, and they're losing sight of the value in straying from it. If you're on a predetermined course, why try anything else at all?

Building an entire generation of apathetic, demoralized teenagers is not, I'm sure, what Ro Devereux had in mind when she created an app that predicts the future. But that's where we are, and XLR8 representatives for MASH have declined our repeated requests for comment.

Extrapolating ahead, what does this look like for

American society on the whole? Will we lose our entrepreneurs? Will we create ghost towns, moving like lemmings to the few cities MASH recommends to its users?

Is what MASH has done here morally irresponsible? This reporter says yes.

That's where they leave it, three letters to seal my undoing. *Yes.*

Below the text is a collection of graphs, all the data to back up what they've written. Clear on the page, no mistaking any of it, proven as gravity.

Vera, I think, right before I start to cry. *I'm sorry.*

3 | 4

"They knew."

It's the first thing Miller says—not *Look what you've done* or *I'm out* or *How could you?* He repeats it, still staring at my phone. "They already knew."

I open my mouth, but no words come out. There are tears on my lips. My thoughts are only *Look what you've done* and *I need to get out* and *How could you?*

Miller finally looks up at me, the change registering in my peripheral vision. I'm focused on my phone screen, like maybe if I never tear my eyes from the article it won't leave its little square in my palm, won't enter this room with us. It's almost one in the morning.

"Hey," Miller says softly. "Did they tell you about this?"

I shake my head, blinking hard to clear my eyes. I open Twitter and, sure enough, we're right there at the top—#MASH is a trending topic. The article is everywhere. I scroll through the feed with tears leaking onto my cheeks. When I open the third hateful message—Ro Devereux and everyone at MASH should be ashamed—Miller takes the phone from me.

"Okay, stop." He sets it on the bed behind us and reaches for my hands. He gathers both of them in his only free one, squeezing until I look at him. "One thing at a time. XLR8 has been covering this up."

"But I made it," I whisper. "That girl who wants to be a vet, I—" I break off, words dissolving into the black hole of myself. I stole her dream. All those kids, quitting everything that makes them happy because it doesn't lead to a MASH-predicted future. All those people on the internet, hating me. And the fact that, of course, they're right to. "I did this."

"Ro, you made a beta of an app for a senior project." Miller ducks his head, makes sure I'm looking at him. "You did not make this happen."

"Miller, I *did*—"

"No." He lets go of my hands, pushes back the hair that's fallen into my face. "This is XLR8. That hack doctor they're consulting in LA. This is—this—" His hand drops to my shoulder, fingertips biting in. "No. You didn't do this."

"I did." He opens his mouth to protest, and I cut him off. "No, Miller, I should feel bad. It's my fault."

"You didn't mean for this to happen." The corners of his eyes are creased with worry, defeat. It occurs to me, distantly, that my pain is painful for him—that we're as connected now as we've always been. But this is a mess I've made. A pain I need to feel.

"No," I tell him. I reach for my phone, so I can learn the rest. "But it happened anyway."

Miller falls asleep sometime around three, the two of us leaned against my headboard with my computer in my lap. The comments section under the article is seventy notes long and growing. From it, we find links to buried Reddit threads and private Facebook groups where people have been talking about this for months. Kids, devastated by their MASH results, begging the internet to tell them MASH doesn't really work—and their parents, desperate to help them.

This is the worst thing that could've happened to her, one mother says about her daughter, Ana, who's sixteen. The lead in every school play, every summer at acting camp, trips to Los Angeles four years running. *Now she knows she'll never be an actress, which is the only thing she wants in the world. What am I supposed to tell her? She isn't even speaking.*

"It's not the worst thing that could've happened to her," Miller mumbles drowsily. I can think of a few worse things, too, but I don't say that. Instead, I imagine how it would feel to be told, in black and white, that I'll never make it out to California. Or that I'll never do exactly what I've gotten to do these last few months: build something from code and watch it burn a track across the country all on its own. *Never* is so long. *Never* is devastating.

I only know Miller's fallen asleep because his fingers, threaded through mine for the last two hours, go slack. He twitches as he descends into dreamland, and I watch sleep take him: the slowing of his breaths, his neck rolled toward me against the pillows, the way his whole face relaxes. He looks seven again like this. He looks like the kid I've loved since forever.

I hate myself for what I've done, and for what I'm going to have to do to him.

When he wakes up, it's because Dad's leaving for work. The front door closes at four forty-five and Miller's eyes snap open, breath filling his lungs on a gasp. He swallows, blinking as he props himself up on his good arm. He looks confused for half a moment, taking in the room before he looks up at me.

"Hey," he says, his voice croaky. I want him to go back to sleep. I want us both to sleep forever, to get stuck someplace where all this isn't true. "What time is it?"

"Almost five."

He groans as he sits up, maneuvering his sling carefully in my twin-sized bed. "I should get home before my parents wake up." Outside, the morning frost has glazed my windowpanes. It won't be light for another two hours.

"Hey," Miller says again, and I look at him. "Did you sleep? Your eyes are all bloodshot."

They feel twitchy and sharp—dried out from staring at my computer all night long. I've read every forum I could find. I've scrolled through the Instagram accounts of kids I don't know, who live states away, whose lives have gone dark since they signed up for something I made. Something I've been proud of, all the way up until now.

"I want to shut it down," I whisper. It feels terrible and right,

244

both at the exact same time.

Miller is quiet. He moves away so we aren't side by side, so it's easier for him to look me in the eyes. "Are you sure?"

"I'm so sorry," I tell him. I feel like my entire body's caving in on itself. It takes all my strength to hold his gaze. "About your tuition money. It's completely my fault."

Miller's eyebrows ruck together, like for a split second he has no idea what I'm talking about. "Ro, forget about the money." There's a pillow crease on his cheek. "It's not important right now."

"It is important," I whisper. "And I wish I could give it to you; I'll understand if you hate me but I can't keep this up, I can't—" My voice breaks, hoarse and unfamiliar. "Vera knew this would happen. She warned me, and I didn't listen. She knew XLR8 would pitch MASH as foolproof and she was right, and I let them; I wanted this so bad that I never pushed back, but now I can't keep this going when it's hurting all these people—I can't believe I even did it in the first place, of course something bad would happen, I should've listened to Vera, I should've just—"

"Okay," Miller says. My words are all running into each other, a hamster wheel of panic. He moves closer and reaches for me gently, like I might spook. When he puts his hand on the back of my neck and tips my forehead against his shoulder, I close my eyes for the first time in hours. "I could never hate you, Ro. It's okay."

"It's not," I whisper.

"It will be," he says. "Tell me what you want to do."

"Call a meeting," I say into his sweatshirt, "and end it."

"Okay." His thumb brushes over my shoulder blade, drawing a line and repeating it. "Then let's call a meeting."

"It's five o'clock in the morning."

"Come on," Miller says, and when he pulls back he actually manages a smile. "There's no way Evelyn Cross isn't awake."

He's right, of course. When I text Evelyn that we need to meet today, she responds in eight minutes.

Agreed, she says. But it'll need to be this afternoon. The head of the board wants to fly in.

I walk Miller downstairs and when he steps out into the cold morning, I think: *All this gave him back to me.* As he presses a kiss to my cheekbone, pulls out his car keys, disappears down my driveway into the dark. This mistake gave me Miller, sneaking out of my house before dawn.

Would you undo it? my brain demands, intrusive and impossible to ignore. Would I give Miller back to the *before*? Return to that space I lived in without him, to undo all the pain I've caused? If it were even possible, I know I could never trade him now.

Selfish, I think. I feel ruined and beyond redemption, like nothing could make me forgivable.

I can't sit with myself, alone in my house. So I take my truck keys off their hook and drive across town to Maren's instead.

Maren lives in one of the newer developments up the hill from the lake, houses with the same floor plans in different colors that blend into the mountain: peat brown and pine green and lake-bed beige. Her bedroom's on the first floor, around the back next to the laundry. In most of the houses it's a den, but Maren's brothers wanted rooms of their own and so their parents converted it, stuck on a closet and closed off the wall. There's a door to outside, a remnant of the original floor plan. They keep the key under a ceramic moose in the yard.

Maren's asleep when I step inside, just a lump under the covers with a spray of red hair over her pillow. Through the open crack of her door I can see the living room, where a Christmas tree glows with multicolored string lights. Inside Maren's room the walls are just turning blue, the first few licks of sunrise through the windows.

When I slide into bed next to her, she stirs. There's a pause, and then she jolts upright.

"It's just me," I whisper. "Ro."

"Jesus *Christ*," she hisses down at me, one hand over her heart. She's wearing an enormous *Switchback Ridge Art Dept.* T-shirt and has zit cream on her chin. "Do you want me to die of a heart attack? What are you doing?"

"I don't want you to die," I tell her, but that's all I can manage before I start sobbing. I smash a hand over my face as if I could hide it. "I'm sorry."

"Ro," she says, lowering back down next to me. "Hey, it's okay."

"My dad's gone," I say into my palm. "And Miller. And I just didn't want to be alone."

"All right," Maren says. She pulls my hand away from my face. "Good idea. Come here."

She hugs me, her chin hooking over my shoulder. There's a brief silence, and then she says, "Wait. What do you mean, Miller's 'gone'?"

"He slept over," I say into her T-shirt. Somehow it feels like the least significant thing that's happened in the last twelve hours, but Maren pulls away immediately.

"He slept over? *In your bed?*"

"Yeah," I say, but it's more of a wail than a word. "I finally fixed it just in time to ruin everything else."

She hugs me back into her, squeezing tight. "Okay, it's okay." She runs a hand over my shoulder blade. "But I want more on that later."

I close my eyes, try to pace my breaths to Maren's heartbeat. *I don't want to know my future,* she told me, all the way back in October. *What if I hate what I learn? What if it scares me?*

248

I cry myself dry in the dark quiet of her familiar bedroom, the very first place I ever played MASH.

When I wake up, sunlight burns red through my eyelids. I'm alone in Maren's room, the sounds of low voices drifting beneath her closed door. My eyes feel like they're coated in sand. I have the mother of all headaches.

I reach for my phone and pull myself upright when I see that it's nearly noon. I have texts from Miller, my dad, and Evelyn. *Miller first*, I think, and know it will probably always be that way now.

Hope you're sleeping, he sent at eight. Text me when you wake up. I can come back.

Then, at ten when I still hadn't responded, Everything okay?

I rub my eyes and tap out, Hey, just woke up. Went to Maren's

The text from my dad is longer, an uncharacteristic paragraph. Ro, I just saw the NYT piece. Tried calling here and home but no response, so assume you're still asleep. Want to make sure you're ok. What is XLR8 going to do? Let me know if you need me to leave the café. Call me when you're up. Love you.

And then, finally, Evelyn's text. As to-the-point as she always is. Let's meet at 2.

"You're awake."

When I look up, Maren's head is poked through the doorway. She's carrying two mugs and holds one out to me. It smells like chocolate and peppermint, and it's warm against my palms when

I drop my phone to take it.

"I made hot chocolate," she says, sitting next to me on the bed. "Figured the moment called for it."

I take a sip, feel it warm me all the way down. "Thank you."

She studies me, holding her own mug in her lap. She's in yoga pants and a sweatshirt, her hair in a bun. She's probably been up for hours. "You look like hell."

In spite of everything, I snort out a laugh. "Great, thanks."

"You want to talk about it?"

I draw a shaky breath, then let it out. "I'm going to stop it."

Maren sips her hot chocolate. "*It?*"

"MASH," I say, and it feels like an anvil dropping down through my body. "The whole thing."

Her eyebrows crawl up under her bangs. "Like, shut the whole thing down? Forever?"

I nod, and my phone buzzes. Miller: **Want me to pick you up from there for the meeting?**

"The whole thing," I tell Maren. "Forever."

She puffs up her cheeks and lets out a slow, controlled breath. "Damn, okay. How are you feeling?"

"Uh," I say, managing another laugh. "Like shit."

She reaches for my hand on the comforter, squeezing it. "I'm sorry, Ro." Our eyes meet, and I have to look away so I don't start crying again. "This is all kinds of fucked up."

I just nod, and she tugs my arm to get me to stand. "Here," she says. "These might cheer you up."

The word *cheer* feels pretty much restricted from my vocabulary at this point, but I follow her over to her desk anyway. She puts down her mug and flips open an oversized manila folder. Inside is a thick stack of glossy photo prints. They're black and white, grainy, a little off-center like she developed them in a hurry.

"Look at these," she says. She spreads them in a fan across the desk, and I lean closer to get a better look. Every single one, I realize, is Miller and me. A close-up of the V between our wrists as we hold hands in the school hallway, Miller's thumb curved over the knuckle of my pointer finger. Miller watching me over the roof of his car as I talk to someone, out of frame, in the parking lot. Even one in the break room at XLR8, the backs of our heads next to each other on the couch with Felix framed right between us, rolling his eyes. Seeing him makes something seize up in my chest: he knew about all this, and he didn't tell us.

"Oh. This one's my favorite." Maren drops another photo on top of the others, and I pick it up to bring it to my face.

I'm standing on the docks outside the Snowberry Room in Vera's dress, framed in string lights and snow. I can just see the edge of Felix's suit at the corner of the shot, his arms poised in the air to take a photo. I'm talking to him, the whole set of my face exactly as annoyed as I felt that night. Seeing myself, trapped there in time, I remember it exactly: the needling pain of knowing Miller didn't want to be there with me the way that I was realizing I wanted to be there with him. How infuriated I was by it. How angry I was with myself.

But there's Miller, right next to me in his tuxedo, impossibly handsome. His dark features are even sharper in black-and-white.

And as I'm complaining at Felix, he's looking down at me. Watching me like I'm the only thing worth looking at on the whole entire lakefront.

"He loves you so much," Maren says. I look up at her, and she smiles in a sad way. "He's a good liar, but I knew it. We're here for you, okay? We're going to figure this out."

I step forward and hug her, careful not to crush the picture. I don't know if I believe her, but I want to. "Thank you," I whisper.

She squeezes me, then lets go. "What can I do to help?"

I put the picture down on her desk, my eyes lingering on Miller before I finally turn back to her. "Can you lend me some clothes?"

Maren grins. "Always. What do you want?"

I let out a puff of air. "What would you wear to your own funeral?"

I call Dad when Miller and I are already on the highway. Maren has me in my own dark jeans and her black leather jacket—one that she claims *puts the "fun" in "funeral."* Under his coat Miller's wearing the same T-shirt he wore that very first day, when we sat across from each other in the boardroom at XLR8 and he signed on to do all this with me. I'm exhausted, and I'm terrified, and I'm so sorry. I drive the wagon, and Miller twists in the passenger seat so he can hold my hand with his right one the whole way downtown.

When I get through to him at Beans, Dad practically shouts my name.

"Jeez Louise," he says, "I thought you were dead. When's the last time you slept until one o'clock? Are you okay?"

"I'm okay," I tell him. "I'm sorry for worrying you. I'm going to XLR8 now and I'm going to try to put an end to all of it. Shut down the app."

There's silence on the other end of the line, just clinking dishes and the hiss of the espresso machine in the background. Then, "You are?"

"Yeah. It's the right thing to do."

"Are you sure?" Dad says. He could say, *I told you so.* He could tell me he knew we'd wind up here. But he doesn't. "Do you want me to come down there?"

I clear my throat. "I'm sure. And it's okay. I just need to rip off the Band-Aid, you know? Get it done."

"Okay, Ro," he says gently. "Get it done."

I walk into the building with every intention of doing just that. I take a deep breath; I press the elevator's 11 button; I ride all the way up with Miller in resolute, determined silence.

And then Mia leads us wordlessly to the conference room. The same one where everything's happened: meeting Evelyn for the first time, bringing Miller on board, going through love training with Felix.

But this time, a woman sits at the center of the table. She's dyed her hair auburn, tied it up in a neat bun. She's older, unfamiliar lines around her eyes. There's a new sharpness to her jaw.

But still, I'd know her anywhere. My mother.

36

My few memories of my mother are wordless, sensory things: the thin bones of her hands around my rib cage to lift me up, the soft rasp of her laugh, the smell of rain on her coat. Everything else I know about her comes from someone else—my dad, or Vera, or Willow. The stories Miller and I would make up when we burned the birthday money. Firelight flickering over Miller's face, the cut of his smile as he said, *Maybe she's microchipped now. Maybe she's becoming a computer herself, and that's why she can't come visit.*

But the woman in front of me is flesh and bone. I stop walking, suspended halfway through the open double doors with Miller beside me.

My first thought is that I need to call my dad. My second is that maybe it's better if he doesn't have to see her. My third is that her face looks like a time-warp mirror of my own.

"Rose," she says. The name she gave me that no one uses. "It's good to see you."

It's *good*? Evelyn's sitting right next to her, her face inscrutable.

My voice comes out like an accusation. "What are you doing here?"

The conference room is full, every chair occupied except the two waiting for Miller and me. My heart has pounded all the way up my throat, like it's trying to choke me so we don't have to be here right now. Miller shifts almost imperceptibly so that our arms are touching.

"Please." My mother gestures to the chairs across from her. "Have a seat."

"She asked you a question," Miller says. When I look at him, his jaw is set. This feels like an ambush, and he's angry.

"And I'll answer it," she tells him. "But please sit down with the rest of us."

Miller looks at me, and when I take a step forward he follows. We sit, but I lean back to put as much distance as possible between my mother and me. I haven't seen her in sixteen years, but somehow, still, there's this tether. Like every time she shifts in her seat I feel it, too. And the way she's looking at me—like she knows me better than anyone here—makes me want to walk straight back out the door.

"I'd like to thank everyone for gathering today," she says, glancing around the table. Her hands are folded in front of her, her nails pale pink and perfectly manicured. "I know we're closing in on the holiday, but in light of this exposé it's imperative we align on next steps."

"Back up," I say, and her eyes land on mine. Gray-green and piercing. "How are you part of *we*?"

My mother hesitates for just a beat, like she's a machine with a delay in her feedback. "I own XLR8," she tells me, and I feel as though I've fallen from very high up. "I purchased it under an LLC in the spring, and MASH was our first acquisition after the Colorado expansion."

My eyes rove across the table, searching until I find him. Felix, right next to Jazz, wearing a cable-knit sweater and black eyeliner. When our gazes lock, he looks like he might be sick.

"You didn't tell me."

He swallows. "I didn't know about her, Ro."

Jazz, when I turn to her, shakes her head and whispers, "Me neither."

"But you did." I look at Evelyn, whose face is as composed as ever. "You knew, and you didn't tell me."

"It was a necessary part of the arrangement," Evelyn says. "We feared if you knew, you wouldn't sign on. And if it weren't for this snag with the *New York Times*, we wouldn't have had to tell you."

I'm thinking so many things at the exact same time that I can't decide which one to speak first. That it was my mother, all this time, building my success. That she found a way to reach me after so many years of nothing at all. And that she's claimed me—taken half my best idea, when I've only ever wanted to belong to myself.

But what I end up saying is, "This isn't a *snag*. You knew about it, and you didn't do anything, and it's wrong."

"Wrong?" my mother says sharply.

"Wrong," I repeat, looking right at her. I hope she knows I mean all of it: not just what MASH has done but what she's done, too—making herself part of my life when I don't want her here, forcing me to share with her when I have never, ever wanted to. "It would be unethical to keep going."

"What are you suggesting?" Evelyn says. The air in the room feels thin, no oxygen to it, like everyone's holding their breath.

"I'm not suggesting anything." I look straight at her. "I'm telling you. I put up with all the media training, the new survey questions, that doctor you claim to be consulting in Los Angeles, but not this. MASH is mine, and we need to shut it down."

There's a heartbeat pause, and then my mother says, "Everybody out."

Her eyes lock on mine, steady in the commotion of everyone rising around us. When Miller makes to stand, I reach for his wrist to stop him.

"No," I say, still looking at my mother. "He stays."

Her gaze flicks to him, shrewd as a bird's. Miller and I have done all of this—every awful and amazing part—together. I wonder how much of him she remembers: that two-year-old with a head of dark hair, her best friend's baby. As Miller lowers into the seat, she looks back at me and nods.

"Rose," she says when the doors shut behind me. "You should be proud of what you've made here. I'm certainly proud of you."

She pauses, like I'm supposed to thank her. But I am not grateful—I am grateful's opposite. This woman, rich enough to take a last-minute flight from San Francisco, powerful enough to rid a room of all its people with two words, is a stranger. She's worse than a stranger.

"I don't need you to be proud of me." I lift my chin, force my voice steady. "You don't know me at all."

My mother blinks, something like surprise twitching at the

corner of her mouth before she quells it. "That's not true. I know that, at eighteen, you did what most people will never do. That you've managed to build something with true value and sell it to the world. That you can code an algorithm and compose yourself on live television, both. You're remarkable."

"Anyone could see that," Miller says. He has his good hand on the table, fingers fisted into his palm. "Anyone who's been paying attention knows all that."

Something flares, hot, behind my rib cage. Here is someone who knows me, and someone who does not.

"I was really proud," I tell her, "until I realized something I made is hurting people. And that everyone here"—I point behind me into the office—"has been keeping it from me."

"So because of that, your work means nothing to you? It's dispensable?" My mother folds her fingers together on the table. "Tell me, what does Vera think?"

I falter, breath hitching in my throat. In my silence, she keeps talking.

"I've respected her right to privacy from the start. But if she's the one pressuring you to call this off—"

"Vera's dead." It's the first time I've said it out loud. I'm furious—beyond furious, almost spilling over with it—that she's brought Vera into this room. If Vera was still here, she'd have been the first person I talked to about this. I want her so badly it leaves me breathless, but instead I have my mother, name-dropping Vera like she has any right to speak of her at all. "And no one's pressuring me. I'm capable of making decisions on my own."

My mother straightens her already perfectly vertical spine, rising even taller. "I'm sorry to hear that," she says. "But you can't let one scathing *New York Times* piece take you down. If you want to make waves, people are going to get mad at you for splashing them. That's the way."

"These aren't splashes." Blowing up my own dream is painful enough; I didn't think I'd have to defend the decision. I especially didn't think I'd have to defend it to her. "These are people's lives."

My mother lets out a short, impatient exhale. "Don't let others impede your path, Rose."

"What, like me and Dad?" It's out before I can think it through. "Like we impeded yours?"

My mother's nostrils flare. "No," she says. "Not like that."

"Really? Because it sounds like it. And maybe making money was more important to you than the impact you had on us, but that's not true for me." I lean closer, heat rising in my throat. "We're not the same. MASH is fucking up people's lives. Nothing's worth that."

"It's not about money." Her voice has a frayed edge to it. "It wasn't then, and it isn't now. It's about pride in your work. Fulfilling your potential. Forging a path all your own, as you see fit."

"It hardly feels like my path anymore," I tell her, realizing it's true in the same moment I say it. "All these questions you've been adding, this bullshit scientist in California who thinks we can predict what kind of cereal people will eat on their eightieth birthday or whatever the hell—"

"Every app needs to be nimble and fresh to stay relevant,"

she says. "That's the inconvenient reality. But the algorithm you wrote, the Core Four—you uncovered something incredibly powerful. Don't give up on it now."

"Did you take the survey back then? When it was just the four?"

She hesitates for the briefest moment before nodding.

"What did it say?" My voice sounds scraped, and I swallow. "About your kids?"

My mother breathes, and I watch the controlled rise and fall of her chest. "It said I would have one child, of course."

I close my eyes. I thought, last summer, that I could use MASH to parse this out—to make sense of my mother and the choice she made. But MASH only knows the facts, the indisputable truth of my mother's one child, which changes absolutely nothing about the reality of her leaving me. You can have a child without being a parent. You can have a child without loving them. The divide between her MASH results and our shared reality is wide and wild and painful. It's Vera's gray area, the unquantifiable place we really live in.

"If that was fated," I say quietly, "then why did you act like you had none?"

When she finally speaks, the words are low and forced, like she's sifting them carefully through a fine opening. "I wanted you to see a woman put her own dreams first."

"And this was the only way you could think of to do it? By disappearing?"

"I've been reaching out to you for years—"

"A hundred dollars on her birthday?" Miller says, and I look at him. I think of Willow, throwing her bags on the floor of that New York hospital room and hiding his broken body against her own. "I don't think that constitutes *reaching out.*"

"I've done more than that," she says, and I actually laugh. "The moment I caught wind of MASH, I knew XLR8 would be the perfect platform to amplify what you'd made. I did not hesitate. I—"

"Did you do this because MASH was a good idea, or because you wanted to help me? *Me*, specifically."

"Why can't it be both?"

"Because you've never cared before," I say, my voice rising. Miller's knee is pressed to mine, the only thing keeping me grounded. "And now that I made something that interests you, suddenly you want to be more involved than a gift once a year? You've been trying to make me this person my whole life, but what if it hadn't worked?"

She blinks rapidly, the only tell on her calm, calm face. "But you were interested in those things," she says. "You did want to pursue technology."

"What if I hadn't?" My voice breaks, and against every instinct, I force myself to keep looking at her. "You'd never have shown up here? I have to like what you like for you to care about me?"

"Rose," she says, impatient. "It wasn't a crime to share my interests with my own daughter."

"Then why'd you stop sending things when I wrote to you?" I hadn't meant to ask it, but it comes out on its own. Hangs there between us, waiting to be named. "I was supposed to like these things, but never talk to you about them?"

"It wasn't that," she says dismissively. "I just thought, when you turned twelve, that you might prefer the money. That you were growing up, and you were old enough to choose."

"Then why aren't you letting me choose now?"

She sighs, bitter and clipped. "If I hadn't gotten involved, everything that's happened, all this success—"

"Are you taking credit for it?" I'm so close to exploding out of my body, I have to grip the armrests to keep from standing up. "Is that seriously what you're doing right now?"

"No." She lifts a hand like I'm a dog, like that motion can make me stay. "I'm just explaining that I've supported you, in spite of—"

"You *haven't* supported me. And you know what?" My voice is rising again, and I fight to bring it back down. "If you want to take so much credit for MASH, fine. Step up and do the right thing. Shut it down yourself."

Silence falls between us. All I can hear is the frantic rush of my heart, the breath clamoring for space in the trapped cage of my lungs. I want to get out of here. I want my dad.

"XLR8 owns fifty percent of MASH." My mother's voice is flat and unflinching. "We aren't shutting it down. The *Today* show appearance has been rescheduled for January—we'll use it to turn the PR around and seal our story before Celeritas."

"If you think we're going back to New York after all this—"

"I don't think," she says, her eyes sharp on mine. "I know. I'd hoped we could get on the same page today, but clearly, we cannot. I'll take it from here and have Felix loop you back in when you're ready. After Celeritas, we can discuss changes, if that's still what you want."

Miller and I speak the exact same words at the exact same time: "You can't—"

He breaks off, lets me take over.

"You can't do whatever you want," I say. "MASH is mine, too."

"I think you'll find," she says, "that this is what you want as well. I need you to trust me."

My mouth falls open, and I snap it back shut. "*Trust* you?"

"We're more alike than you seem to think," she says. "We're made for this. Both of us."

"I'm not like you," I bite out.

"You're just like me." Her nostrils flare, her whole face rigid with anger. "One hundred percent. And we'll get through this together if you follow my lead. My direction hasn't led you astray yet, has it?" She points between Miller and me. "This seems to have worked out."

And she's right—it did. But it occurs to me in the same moment that my own mother orchestrated this false romance, had no problem throwing me into a fake relationship just to make this app work. She didn't know it would be Miller. She didn't know I'd be all right.

"You do realize," she says, "that if we shut down now, Miller doesn't get his end of the deal? There will be no tuition money."

"Don't put that on her," Miller says, before I can respond. Her words hurt right at the base of my throat, like something blunt

263

pressing on my windpipe. "It was your choice not to give me that money up front. And it was your choice to hide all this from us."

My mother just shakes her head, like she's done with this conversation.

"Go home, Rose." She turns away, reaches for her briefcase. "I'll be in touch."

"Will you?" I demand, and she turns back to me. I feel Miller watching me, know without looking that he's holding his breath. "Why didn't you reply to that letter?"

She's silent, like I've stunned her. Like it never occurred to her that she'd need to answer for any of it. She lifts her briefcase off the floor and sets it on the table, smoothing one hand over its pristine leather face.

"I didn't know what to say." Our eyes meet. "Anything I could have said would have confused you."

Confused, I think. There are so many worse things for a child to be.

"You were with your father." My mother stands, and I know we're being dismissed. "I thought it was for the best."

She holds her hand out, gesturing us toward the door. Deciding when we're through, just like she always has.

The voice that speaks is hardly my own, somehow both furious and frail.

"Yeah," I say. "Maybe it was."

3 7

Everyone watches Miller and me walk out of the XLR8 office like we're children being sent to time-out. Somewhere inside, a very small voice reminds me that this app is still half-mine. That I don't have to take what my mother says lying down. But the voice is quiet, and quieter still with every step we take toward the lobby. I am so tired. I can't find the fire inside me to fight this. I've spent years putting distance between my life and my mother's, only to have her crash-land in the middle of something that already felt impossible before she got here.

Felix is waiting for us by the elevators, rubbing his thumb into the center of his palm.

"Hey," he says, when Miller hits the button for the parking garage. "Look, I—"

He breaks off, and we both stare at him. Waiting. This person who dressed us up and coached us through and stood by us during every part of the last four months. Who hugged me close against him at Vera's funeral. Who nudged me, knowing, into that ambulance in New York. Who I thought was our friend.

Felix reaches for me, and I can tell it's a reflex—he doesn't know what to say, so he's going to hug me instead. But I feel like ice, spring-thinned and clear. If anyone touches me, I won't survive it.

"Don't," I tell him, and his arms stop in midair. Just as he drops them to his sides, the elevator doors slide open.

"You could've told us," Miller says. I follow him into the elevator and Felix watches, miserably, as the doors start to close. "We deserved that much."

"I couldn't," Felix says. His voice is soft and desperate, and he glances over one shoulder toward everyone waiting inside. "Guys, I—"

But then the doors close, and he's gone. Miller looks at me, reaching out with his good arm, and I take a step backward. Press myself into the corner of the elevator.

"Please," I say, so quietly. I can't bring myself to look at him. Guilt is eating me alive, swallowing me up by the mouthful. I've stolen something enormous from him, and he isn't even angry. I've made something reckless, and I've given so much of it to a woman I hate that I can't even end it. "Don't."

"Ro." His voice is gentle, and he takes a step closer to me. "Hey, come here."

But I just shake my head, staring at the floor until the elevator finally stops. I don't deserve this—I don't deserve Miller, trying to comfort me after a mess I made all on my own. A mess he would've been unscathed by if it weren't for me.

When we get to the wagon, I twist the keys in the ignition and Miller reaches over to shut it off. I stare at the steering wheel for three full breaths before finally looking over at him. His eyes are dark in the cave of the garage, a slice of light from the tracks above us cutting through the window and across his cheek.

"Please," he says. "Tell me what you're thinking."

I swallow. "I'm a terrible person."

He's so surprised, it takes him two tries to form the word *what*. He leans closer, twisting in the seat to make room for his cast. "Ro, what happened in there was so messed up, I—you deserve to be upset. *I'm* upset." He breaks off, searching my eyes. "But you're not a bad person. Why would you say that?"

"Because I made all this happen." I spread my hands in the space between us. "And I wanted it so bad. And now I can't even make it stop."

"Hey." He catches one of my hands, holding it in his own. "MASH is something you made, but it's not who you are."

We look at each other, quiet. My ribs feel like they're curling in, pressing on my lungs.

"Who am I, then?" I whisper. My life now is unrecognizable compared to the way it used to be—to the girl I was before all this. "If not Ro from MASH?"

"You're my favorite person," Miller says. It's like a fishhook right behind my heart. "Remember when you asked me, in the hospital, what I'd still let you have?"

I nod, lips pressing together.

"It's anything, Ro." He looks at me, and his voice is steady in the quiet of his car. "It's always been anything. That's still true—it's going to be true no matter what happens."

I don't want to cry again; I've cried so much in the last week

I'm scared I'll never dry out. But it happens anyway—my eyes fill with tears, and Miller smiles as he goes blurry.

"Are you sure?" I ask.

He laughs, pulling me toward him over the console. He kisses my cheekbone, then my lips. "I'm sure." When he backs away, I reach a hand up to trap his where it rests on the side of my neck.

"Then I need your help," I tell him.

He nods, his eyes never leaving mine. "Always."

"If they won't do it, we have to find a way to end it ourselves." I draw a breath, make myself say the words before I can back out of them. "Damage MASH's reputation so badly no one will use it anymore."

Slowly, Miller nods. There's something resolute about his face, the set of his lips. When he speaks, his voice is firm and sure.

"All right," he tells me. "Let's burn it down."

I drive straight from Miller's house to Beans, where Dad is standing behind the espresso machine with a towel over one shoulder.

"She's here," I tell him, before he's even had the chance to say hello. "She's been behind this all along."

"Who?" he says, pouring steamed milk into a to-go cup.

I clear my throat, look straight at him. "My mom."

His whole body goes rigid. Over the stereo, Bing Crosby croons softly about Santa Claus.

"She's—" His eyes dart behind me to the front windows. "She's here?"

"Not *here*, here." I walk up to the counter, and he passes the latte to a waiting customer without even looking at her. "In Denver. She owns XLR8."

"What?" His whole face screws up in disbelief. And if I hadn't seen her with my own eyes, I'd feel the same—*this is impossible*. There's no way, except that there is. "Are you—you saw her?"

I nod, and it's only when I reach up to hold the divider between us that I realize my hands are shaking. Dad realizes it, too.

"Henrietta," he says, glancing at the employee behind the cash register. "You can head home, I'll close up here."

"Really?" She eyes him, then glances across the café. It's decked out for Christmas—plaid blankets thrown over the backs of the armchairs by the fireplace, a fairy-light garland over the front door. "It's only four."

"That's okay," he says, managing a smile. "Enjoy your holiday."

She looks between us one more time before untying her apron and hanging it on the hook at the back of the tiny kitchen. When she leaves, door bells tinkling behind her, we're alone. Dad locks the front door and flips the sign from Open to Closed, then motions me over to the chairs by the fire.

"You're okay?" he asks, his eyes moving over my face. When I nod he leans forward, suspending his elbows on his knees. "Tell me what happened."

"She bought XLR8 last spring." The longer I talk, the quicker my words are, going fast and frantic. "Under an LLC, so her name wasn't anywhere. And when MASH went viral it was her idea for XLR8 to step in, and I thought I'd earned this success but I didn't, *she* made it happen—and now with this *New York Times* article

269

I have to stop the app, it's too much, it's hurting people I don't even know and she won't let me shut it down, she owns half of the whole thing and it's like I don't even get a vote even though I made this but I guess she made it, too, and——"

Dad stops me, his big hand landing on my knee. "Honey," he says gently. "Slow down."

I stare at his fingers, draw a shaky breath.

"She tricked me," I say, finally. When I look up at him, his eyes are creased at their corners. "I don't want her here and she found a way to reach me anyway."

Dad hesitates, like he has a lot to say and he's trying to decide where to begin. Christmas music is still wafting from the speakers.

"This success belongs to you," he says. He lifts his hand from my knee as he leans back, rubbing at the space between his eyebrows. "Whether it was her or anyone else seeing something in you—they saw it because it was there. Okay?"

I nod, swallowing through the clenched fist of my throat. "Okay."

"But for her to keep her involvement from you, and to show up here and take you by surprise—" He breaks off, and I recognize that same twitch in his shoulder from the night in our kitchen when Vera was still alive. He's angry, and he's trying to hold it in. "It should always be up to you to decide what kind of relationship you want to have with her."

"I don't want a relationship," I say quickly. "She hurt you."

Dad's eyebrows draw together. "This is about what you want, Ro, not how I feel."

I think of my thirteenth birthday, Dad and Vera and Willow

singing to me while Miller passed out cake forks. The small stack of birthday presents with my mother's on the bottom, that same card, thin and forbidding. The wordless way Dad passed it to me over the table.

"But she took everything from you," I whisper.

"Not everything," he says, leaning closer. "We were so young when we had you, Ro. She wasn't ready."

"And you were?"

He smiles a little. "You're never ready for your world to change like that. But I only had to meet you once to know you were going to be the best part of my life, no matter how scared I was of messing you up on my own."

My eyes sting with tears, and I roughly wipe them away. "But I already betrayed you by getting into tech. I didn't want to betray you by connecting with her, too."

"Honey." Dad leans toward me, and I look up at him. "You could never betray me by being who you are. By choosing the right path for yourself."

"I don't know if it's the right path," I say shakily. "Everything's falling apart."

"This isn't your fault," he says. "How much MASH has grown, all the things it's doing that you never meant for it to do." He shakes his head. "There are people working at that company— there's your mother—who should have stepped in when bad things started to happen. Who should have taken every measure to make sure they'd never happen at all. You understand that, right?"

I bite my lip, look across the room. I understand that, but I also understand that this idea—the seed of it, the innocuous thing that grew into the monster I've made now, started with me.

"I guess," I whisper. "But I started it. And I'm the only one who wants to make it right, and now I have to find a way to do it without them."

"That doesn't mean you have to do it alone, though." Dad catches my eyes. "All right?"

I think of Miller, his face thrown into shadow in the XLR8 garage. Of Maren, hugging me in her bed while I cried myself into fitful sleep.

"I know," I say quietly. I draw a shaky breath, then ask the question that's tugged me toward the dark bottom of myself ever since the article dropped. "Dad, what am I going to do after this?"

His eyebrows twitch together. "What do you mean?"

"What if this is as good as it gets?" The question hangs between us, simple and grim. "What if this is the best idea I ever have, and it went to shit, and I never do anything else?"

"Don't be a nitwit," Dad says, and I actually manage a smile. "You're just getting started, Ro. There's so much still to come."

I look down at my hands, squeezed together in my lap. "I just feel like it's my job now. To be this person MASH made me. And I don't know what comes after."

He leans close, lifts my chin so I have to look at him. "Your only job is to find happiness, Ro. To be happy." He drops his hand. Through the windows behind him, it's started to snow. "That's the only thing I've ever wanted for you."

38

"This is Maria Villareal," my mother says, gesturing toward a photograph on the screen. It's the day after Christmas and Miller and I are sitting stone-faced in the conference room at XLR8. On the wall, a girl with long dark hair smiles from behind a desk. "She's twenty-three. When she downloaded MASH, she was working in sales and feeling hopelessly unfulfilled. MASH indicated she'd be a social worker. Now she's back in school and thriving on her newfound path."

This is The Big Plan: champion MASH success stories, ramp up the user-generated content we're sharing to showcase all the people MASH has made happier. The statement Jazz's team put out was brief and dismissive—*MASH has helped more people than it's hindered*, and *this technology is rooted in indisputable science.* As if that makes it okay; as if something cannot be both true and cruel at the same time.

In the few days since the *New York Times* story broke, more and more people have spoken up about the results that crushed them. More parents have posted their children's stories online. In response, XLR8 spent the Christmas holiday ramping up our social posting, issuing press releases about product upgrades, and cranking out content just to scream louder than the people who are actually in pain.

And through it all, my mother has decided to stay in town. *Just until New York*, she said. *Just until we're back on course.* Because why else would she stay here, in the place where her daughter lives?

We're booked for the *Today* show a week from Friday, an appearance Jazz had to pull out every single stop to keep. The media is split on us: half think we're poison, half seem game to watch how we pull ourselves out of this quicksand. So we'll fly to New York, missing the first Friday back at school. Miller and I have almost two weeks to figure out how to stop this train.

My dad's coming on the trip this time, like he can turn himself into a human wall between my mother and me. Even now, as she pulls up the next MASH success story, he sits outside the conference room watching us like a hawk on the hunt. I've heard him every night since she got here, whispering angrily into the phone after he thinks I'm asleep. *You can't just spring things on her, Meredith. She's not a kid anymore.* The way they act around each other reminds me of the beginning with Miller: you can tell, when they're forced to look at one another, that it hurts.

"You'll showcase these testimonials on *Today*," my mother says, turning to Miller and me. She's wearing her hair curly, and it makes her distressingly familiar. "Felix and Jazz will train you on their stories, make sure you know them inside out before you're up onstage. All we have to do is lean into the good." She smiles

274

briefly. "And there's plenty of it."

This feels categorically untrue. *The good* has felt hard to find the last few days, like a reflection in the lake—blurred out, sometimes there and sometimes not. My social media's been a mixed bag of support for Miller and me, and direct messages that make me breathless with their cruelty—that leave me feeling gutted and foolish for ever trying to make something worth sharing at all. Sawyer texts me almost nonstop about how guilty she feels for finding joy with MASH when so many others are hurting. *Tell me about it*, I think. A day after the *New York Times* piece breaks I turn my phone off and close it in my desk drawer. I leave it there.

The only good has been Miller, sitting with me in the quiet when I don't know what to say. And Maren, dropping off sugar cookies on Christmas Day. And my dad, pretending he wasn't close to crying when I finally got to work on my college applications at our kitchen table. He was right, in the end—I'm going to need some other options come spring.

"We can set up interviews," Jazz says, snapping me out of it. I look at her, and she can't quite meet my eyes. "If it'll make you more comfortable. Everyone we're profiling has already agreed to talk to us, so I can set up conference calls for the two of you to get to know them before we head back to New York."

That's when it lands on me, what we need to do now. The idea arrives fully formed, like something divine. Like Athena herself has struck me down. I nod absently at Jazz.

Under the table, I grab Miller's hand.

"Here's one," Autumn says. She's cross-legged on my living room floor, bent over herself to peer at her laptop. "Jazzhands24 on Reddit." She pushes the computer over our rug toward me, and I lean down to get a better look.

Honestly, the post begins, *been keeping this to myself but everyone's talking about this shit now so here I go. I'm 15 and live in Colorado and I've been playing piano since I could talk. Maybe even before. Anyway it's not cool or anything but all I want is to play professionally one day. Do Juilliard and the whole thing. I downloaded MASH in October and it says I'm going to live in Wichita and be a teacher. Nothing wrong with teaching but damn. Not like being a jazz pianist in New York. Been down and yeah. Any words of advice on how to just like live with this would be great. thanks.*

The first comment, from someone named _bringtheheat, says only *FUCK MASH! NEVER GIVE UP THE PIANO MY LITTLE FRIEND!*

"Add them to the list," I say, and Autumn nods as she drags her computer into her lap.

I lean back into the couch, where Miller is sitting with his own computer balanced on his knees. He's cross-legged, in sweats and a T-shirt for some video game called *Hades*. His hair's all grown out since August, curling over his forehead and the tops of his ears—it's goose-down soft, which is something I know now, very well, from personal experience. I kiss the side of his neck and he smiles at me.

We've been here all day—Miller and me on the couch, Autumn sprawled across the floor, Maren folded up in the armchair by the fire. We're tackling this assembly-line style: Autumn and Maren find the leads, I send them direct messages, Miller takes their information and maps out our schedule. We have six days until the start of school, which will be plenty of time to get this done if we're smart about it.

"Snacks?" Dad says, crossing in from the kitchen with his arms full of bowls. He's been hovering hard the last few days, packing the Beans schedule with college kids home for break so he doesn't have to go in. He doesn't love this idea, but he didn't veto it, either. He knows, I think, that this is something I have to do. "I made cheddar popcorn and puppy chow."

"Puppy chow?" Autumn asks, looking up at him from the floor. "What's that?"

Maren gasps theatrically. "Autumn Lillian Li. You've never had puppy chow?"

Dad puts the popcorn in Miller's lap, then extends the puppy chow toward Autumn. She peers into the bowl, eyebrows raised.

"It's Chex with chocolate and peanut butter and sugar," I tell her, and her eyes widen as she looks up at me.

"Ummmm." She takes the bowl from my dad. "Excuse me? Yes, please."

Miller's phone buzzes on the armrest next to his cast. It's Felix, in our group text with Jazz.

We'll need to pick a day between now and New York for some media training. When works for you both to come in?

It's professional and polite, two things Felix has never really been around us. But that's how things are now, ever since he tried talking to us at the elevator.

I look at Miller, who's still staring down at his phone. He blinks, then says, "I think he's the hardest part, for me."

"Hardest part of what?"

"This whole betrayal." He turns his phone facedown on the armrest, then looks at me. "Felix was always on our side, even when he was mad at us."

"Yeah," I say quietly. "I know."

"I just can't believe he's okay with it." Miller shakes his head, which is framed by the firefly-glow of our Christmas tree across the room. "How could he be? He was supposed to be good."

"They all were," I say. Miller moves his hand from his laptop to my arm, runs his palm over my scar and down into my hand before locking our fingers together. "I guess you never really know."

He squeezes my hand, and I squeeze back. "Sometimes you know," he says.

I smile, tip my head forward to tap his shoulder. "Sometimes, yeah."

"All right, gross." Maren throws a decorative pillow at us, and it hits me in the side of the face. "That's enough over there."

"Ow!" I sit up, widening my eyes at her. "You two *fully* made out in front of us the first time we met Autumn."

Autumn laughs through a mouthful of puppy chow and says, "I'm not sorry."

From the kitchen, Dad yells, "No making out!"

"Oh, I'm gonna do it now," Maren says, raising her voice to be sure he'll hear her. She's halfway out of her chair when he comes back into the room, spatula pointed warningly in her direction. It's an empty threat, which feels like a gift after the last week with so many real ones.

It snows all afternoon, lazy flakes that float past the A-frame windows while we work. Vera loved this weather, even when she was old and the ice on her driveway kept her inside. *Like being in a snow globe*, she'd say. *What could be more beautiful?*

I wonder briefly what my mother's doing, snowed in to her hotel room downtown. But then I lean against Miller, or laugh at something Autumn says, or reach my hand into the bowl for more puppy chow. And I push her away.

By sundown, we have ten names. A route with three stops plotted through Colorado and seven video calls scheduled with kids across the country. A list of people with stories of how MASH has stolen their dreams. Six days to meet them and hear what they have to say.

Just like Miller said, we'll burn it down. And now we just have to spark the flame.

3 9

It's still snowing when we leave for Colorado Springs on Wednesday morning to meet Jazzhands24 (whose real name is Owen). We take the truck, Miller riding shotgun and Maren in the back of the cab with all her video equipment. Turns out Mr. Kong's got a few more tricks up his sleeve than just film cameras. He met her at school yesterday afternoon to hand everything off, holiday break and all.

"You sure you know how to use that stuff?" I ask, catching her eyes in the rearview as we pull out of her driveway. She's yawning, hair in a topknot and wearing a CU Denver sweatshirt of Autumn's.

"Pretty sure," she says, then holds up a thick manual. "And if not, I've got two hours to learn."

"We believe in you," Miller tells her. He's got a notebook open in his lap, interview questions he's penned out in his small, precise handwriting. His pointer finger rests against the top line.

"I'm glad someone does." Maren pops her head up between us, reaching for the thermos of coffee waiting for her in one of the cupholders. "Because according to MASH, I'm going to be an accountant."

I slam on the brakes, half the truck in the road and half still in Maren's driveway.

"*Jesus*," she says, clutching the edge of my seat as I turn around.

"You took the survey?"

"Yeah," she says casually. "Me and Autumn both."

"And you—it said you were—I—"

Maren looks at Miller. "Did her brain stop working?"

I finally force the words through my shock. "And it said you're going to be an *accountant*?"

"Yeah." She takes a sip of coffee. "Said I'm going to wind up with some dude named Paul, too, but that seems unlikely."

I've never seen her calmer, more unaffected. "But you don't care?"

"Not really." She leans back, reaching for her seat belt. "I know who I am, and what I want. If that changes someday, okay. If not, also okay." Our eyes meet. "It's the smartest algorithm ever, because you made it, obviously. But it's still just an algorithm." Maren shrugs. "I still get to decide, in the end."

We drive to Colorado Springs as the sun creeps up over the highway, pale winter light casting everything yellow. I've had to turn my phone back on to keep Dad in the loop—one of his conditions. The other was video-calling the kids we're meeting in person beforehand, to make sure "they aren't fifty-year-old men with cigarette breath trying to lure you to your death." My notifications roll in pretty much nonstop, pinging from the cupholder so frequently that Miller finally takes my phone and slides it under his leg, screen-down on the seat so I can't see it at all. I look over at him, and without lifting his head from his reading he reaches to rest his hand on my knee.

Reactions to XLR8's statement have been completely polarized: There are those, like us, who know nothing could justify putting people in pain. Draining the color from their lives. But there are plenty of others who've shrugged off the entire thing because, after all, the truth hurts. *That's showbiz, baby*, one tweet said. *Don't ask a question you don't want the answer to.* It had 250,000 likes.

We've agreed to see Jazz and Felix this weekend, to run through their talking points and study their success stories and do all the rest to get ready for New York. I've been silent on social media, against Jazz's wishes, because what could I possibly say? It's one thing to watch her lie all over the @MASHapp handle. It's another to do it under my own name.

As we hurtle south in the frigid December morning, I have the feeling, suddenly, that the world's gone very quiet: that the last few days have winnowed everything down to just the three of us. Miller, and Maren, and me, cutting across the state on our own. Chasing the only option we have left.

Owen lives in a boxy blue house off I-25, and when we pull into his driveway no one says anything. We just sit there, breathing, looking up at it. Empty planter boxes in the front windows, a pink snow shovel leaned against the garage door, all the grass in the yard frost-crisp and dead.

"You ready?" Miller asks, and I look over at him. He's wearing a puffy coat, forest-green and draped over his sling like a cape.

"No," I say, and he smiles.

"It's like Violet says in *The Ersatz Elevator:* If we wait until we're ready, we'll be waiting for the rest of our lives."

"Like who says in what?" Maren asks, and I manage, somehow, to laugh. I have no idea what he's talking about either, but I'd listen to him forever anyway. I lean across the console and kiss the side of his face.

"Remember when you guys hated each other?" Maren says, and Miller glances back at her.

Then he answers—truthfully, I know now. "No."

We set up in Owen's living room, which is framed with toys from his twin little sisters—Daisy and Agatha. Maren wants to shoot him with the piano in the background. It's an old, faded thing: chipped paint at the edges, crackled silver lettering above the keys. But it's beautiful still, in the way things are when they're loved.

Owen's mom, in a pilled pink robe and slippers, makes the girls toaster waffles in the kitchen while we set up the camera. Owen is skinny and disproportioned, like his feet and his hands and all his joints are too big for his body. *How Miller used to look*, I think, *before he shot up.* How every guy looked, pretty much, when we were freshmen.

"I'm not great at public speaking," he tells us, picking at a scab on his elbow. He's wearing a red-striped polo shirt and huge, square glasses.

"That's all right," I say, and offer what I hope is a reassuring smile. "It's not public, it's just us."

"Right," he says, swallowing. But he's twitchy and uncomfortable, and I'm starting to feel like we're just making things worse for him. Like maybe coming here wasn't such a great idea after all.

"Owen," Miller says, and we both look over at him. He's on the couch, where there's barely room for his bulky cast amid a thick pile of stuffed animals and crumpled Christmas wrapping paper. "Would you play something for us?"

Owen glances at the piano, and I watch him hedge. His fingers twitch in his lap. "Um," he says. But we just wait, and finally he gives a jerky little nod and turns on the bench seat to face the keys. He takes a big breath that expands his ribs through the back of his shirt. Then he begins.

Everything about him changes when he plays: His shoulders square off, his spine goes straight and strong. The music fills the entire room, the entire house, the entire town, maybe—floating over the plains and the highway dusted with snow. His sisters wander in, five years old and identical. One of them holds a waffle, and the other has two fingers in her mouth. They share a secret smile, then giggle a little.

It's magic, I think. It's what he's meant to be doing, no matter what the science says. I turn to Maren, who's ducked behind the camera, and mouth, *Are you getting this?* She nods, giving me a thumbs-up.

When I look at Miller, he's already smiling at me.

40

Our second trip is the closest to home. As soon as we decided to search for stories I thought of Taj Singh, the way he'd pulled me aside in calculus all the way back in October. The open fear in his eyes when he asked, *Can MASH get it wrong?*

At the time I'd thought the divide between his dream career, doctor, and his MASH prediction, dentist, was small enough to pass for insignificant. *It's still medicine,* I'd told him. Now I wish I could shake that version of myself, tell her to swallow her words. Who was I, with my perfect MASH-predicted future, to tell anyone that their devastating prediction was *still* anything?

When I called Taj to ask if we could interview him on-camera, he hesitated so long I thought the call might've dropped.

"Taj?" I'd finally prompted. "Are you still there?"

"Yeah." He cleared his throat. "It's just, ah—I mean, my parents don't know. I haven't told them."

"About the dentist thing?"

"Right."

I hesitated. "Will they be mad if they find out?"

"Not exactly." He drew a breath, and it rattled into the receiver. "Look, why don't you just come over on Friday? I'll show you."

We don't know what to expect when we pull up to Taj's house, a soil-colored cabin a few blocks from the lake. There's a Subaru parked in the driveway and a white terrier peering at us through the front window. A lawn sign spiked between pine roots in the front yard tells us that **A SRHS Mountain Lion Lives Here**. The sign's shaped like a soccer ball.

Taj smiles when he opens the door, which makes me relax just a little.

"Hey," he says, taking a backward step to let us inside. "Come on in."

It's quiet save for his dog, who jumps at our ankles and snuffles our socked feet once our shoes are off.

"Thanks so much for meeting us," I say. "We can film wherever you want."

Taj points to the living room, a cozy space collaged in family photos, and Maren heads in to set up her camera.

"Is this okay?" Taj asks, gesturing at his flannel shirt. "I wasn't sure what to wear for this kind of thing."

This kind of thing. The casual dismantling of my entire dream. My weeklong apology tour.

"It's great," Miller says, nudging my elbow when I still haven't moved toward the living room.

"So." Taj drops onto the couch. Miller and I take the armchairs across from him and Maren stands between us, adjusting the legs of her tripod. "How many people are you guys talking to?"

"Ten," I tell him. We've been recording video calls with people all across the country in between these visits—Matteo in Boston, who hasn't written a word since MASH dashed his dreams of being an author; Victoria in San Francisco, who's only fourteen and already knows she'll never be a pilot; Alma in Pennsylvania, who's destined to become a gymnastics coach even though a bad landing last year left her terrified of setting foot back in the gym.

We have four more calls before school starts, and they aren't getting any easier.

"And the goal is what?" Taj tugs at one sleeve, folding the cuff over his knuckles. "Share them publicly somehow?"

"Exactly," I say. A grandfather clock ticks in the corner; I draw a deep breath and squeeze the arm of the chair. "Honestly, the company we're working with won't let us shut MASH down. But we're hoping if we get permission from people to show the truth of what's happening to them, no one will want to use it anymore—that we can blow it up ourselves."

Taj's eyebrows twitch together, just a little. "You want to blow up your own app?"

I feel Miller look at me, but I don't look away from Taj. "Yes. Because of stories like yours."

"Stories like mine," he repeats.

I nod and glance at Maren, who gives me a thumbs-up.

"You can share whatever you want," I tell Taj, and he glances at the camera before smoothing his palms over his knees. "And you don't have to hold back. We just want the truth."

He stares down at the floor for a few seconds before nodding, then looks back up at us.

"All right," he says. I hear the little *click* as Maren starts recording, and Taj reaches for a framed photograph on the table next to the couch. "Um, this is my sister."

Miller and I lean forward at the same time to get a closer look. The little girl has Taj's dark hair and long-lashed eyes, wearing a ballerina's tutu and grinning.

"Dhara," Taj says. He holds the picture as he speaks, a thumbprint over his sister's face. "She died when she was seven. Four years ago."

Something flares hot behind my ribs. We were freshmen four years ago—we knew Taj then, but I had no idea.

"I'm so sorry," Miller says. His voice is low and sincere.

"Yeah." Taj offers a muted smile. "Thanks. She was in an accident in a carpool from school, so we weren't with her." He sets the picture frame carefully back on the table. He's still looking at it when he says, "She died at the hospital, before my parents got there."

He draws a shuddering breath, then looks at Miller. "I swore after that I'd become an ER doctor, so I could be there for kids like her. And for families like mine."

I close my eyes for the briefest moment and *god*, I want to keep them closed. *It's still medicine*, I'd told him. But this isn't about me, it's about Taj. And when I open my eyes, he's looking straight at me.

"But MASH told me I'll be a dentist instead. I haven't been able to tell my parents, because we don't really talk about her. But she's here in every room, unspoken in all our conversations. And when they see this interview—"

He breaks off and it presses right against my teeth, what I really want to ask him. *Do you hate me?*

"Well, it's just hard," he says unsteadily. "I thought becoming a doctor would help with their grief, or something, and probably mine, but now I know I won't get the chance to find out."

"Taj," Maren says softly. All three of us look up at her. "MASH isn't in charge. You can still go to medical school."

"Yeah, I *can*," Taj tells us. His eyes are dark as a rainstorm. "But I won't, will I?"

It's a weighty, heartsick week. I know this is the best I can do with what I have now but still I'm wrecked by it. Every home we step into, every person who looks at me through the camera and tells me how I hurt them. They are where they are, and they were better off before me. That's the truth I have to live with. All I can do now is, maybe, prevent others from winding up in the same place.

We have our last interview on Saturday, an hour's drive from Switchback Ridge. When we get to Leila's house in Frisco, Maren has to pee so badly she practically pushes her out of the way to get to her bathroom.

Leila lives in a big place on the outside of town, so new it still smells like paint inside. The furniture is sparse and modern and uncomfortable-looking, like someone picked it knowing they'd never be home. Through the massive windows in her living room, we have a clear view over Dillon Reservoir, sun-sparkling water crowned on all sides by mountains.

"My dad's out," she says when she lets us in. It's noon on the first day of the year. She doesn't mention her mom. Leila's a senior, like us, headed to UPenn in the fall after being admitted early decision. She's wearing a dress and has her hair carefully curled, like this is a job interview.

"I should be happy," she tells us in an even voice that holds no emotion. "I got into my dream school two weeks ago and didn't even feel it." She clears her throat, holds up her phone to the MASH interface—all that familiar branding, the seamless UI that I helped code myself.

"Financial planner," Leila says, at the same time we read it ourselves. "Frisco, Colorado."

There's a heavy silence as we wait for her to connect the dots.

"My dad owns the only firm in town," she says. "I'm going to wind up working for him after all."

When Maren lugs her camera equipment back out to the truck and shuts the door behind her, I reach for Miller's hand. We're alone in Leila's driveway, interview wrapped and ready to head home. But Leila's words are ringing in my ears, the lingering ghost of all this hurt I've caused. *I got into my dream school two weeks ago and didn't even feel it.*

Miller is framed by the broad swath of Leila's neighborhood: huge houses rising between snow-flecked trees. He deserves to be so far from here—reading books in some musty library on the East Coast, talking about stories written a thousand years ago if that's what makes him happy.

"I'm sorry," I tell him, because I can't keep going without saying it. It's been here inside me ever since New York, ever since the article. "Listening to her talk about college, I just—"

Miller weaves our fingers together, taking a step closer to me.

"I wish I could fix it."

"Ro, it's okay." He dips his chin, makes me meet his eyes. "You keep talking about this like I'm going to die, but we don't know what's going to happen. It could all work out fine."

"But you deserve to have it all paid for, like we'd planned."

He sighs, his thumb brushing over the back of my hand. "There are loans," he says. "There's work-study, and state school, and a bunch of scholarships I can apply for. There's more than one way, okay?"

"But what if—"

"What if anything?" It's so cold his breath condenses between us, each word a white cloud. "What if my perfect match is born two blocks from me? What if she makes an app for her senior project and it goes viral and changes her life?"

He smiles, and his is my favorite face in the whole entire world. The last four days have been a nonstop tour of all the bad I've done, all the people who are angriest at me and have every right to be. And here's Miller, who forgave me from the start.

"Things happen every day that are like catching lightning in a bottle," he says. "Just because we don't know what school's going to look like doesn't mean it's going to be bad."

He's right—of course he is. MASH has made me so unfamiliar with uncertainty that any unknown future feels terrifying and wrong. But there are good surprises, too. Anything could happen. And maybe we just have to let it.

"I'm going to figure it out," Miller says. "Whatever happens. You've got to stop apologizing."

"I'm sor—" I clap a hand over my mouth, and he laughs.

"Look," he says, and a cold wind plays through his hair. "Four months ago, I had no idea how I was going to pay for my degree, and I had no idea if I'd ever talk to you again, and it was killing me." I take a step closer to him, and he drops my hand so he can push the hair off my forehead. "Now only one of those things is true. Net gain, okay?"

I rise onto my tiptoes and kiss him, just as Maren knocks on the window.

"Let's go home!" she says, her voice muffled by the glass.

I squeeze Miller's hand, and I pull out my car keys, and we do.

This time, on the plane to New York, there is no itinerary review. No Felix monkeying over the top of our seats to walk us through the game plan. We spent Sunday afternoon at the XLR8 office with him and Jazz, everybody sticking to the script of How Things Are Now. No laughing, nothing at all except the basics of what we need to say on live TV Friday morning.

We fly to New York after school on Thursday, Dad with Miller and me in one row, Evelyn with Felix and Jazz in another. My mother and Willow sit together ahead of us, the conversation between them stilted and strange. Seeing them next to each other feels like a trick: *Here is my mother, and here is the woman who mothered me.* The only person missing to round out the who-raised-Ro roulette is Vera.

We're traveling eight people strong this time, just in case. In case we get mobbed again, in case shit hits the fan even worse than it already has. And in case, I suspect, Miller and I put any toes out of line.

But there's a flash drive in the bottom of my backpack, a video file that Maren spent every night after school this week stitching together. That made me cry, like the Gossamer Lake dam thrown open, when I watched it before driving to the airport. That—if all goes according to plan—even Evelyn Cross won't be able to stop us from sharing with the world.

That'll get us out of this mess, once and for all.

I don't sleep that night, not really. Dad and I have a double queen room at a hotel on Forty-Seventh Street, and I spend most of the night tracking the soft rhythm of his snores. The heat kicks off and on from the corner of the room, ruffling the thin curtain by the window. Everyone else is staying on the same hall, and I imagine us all tucked away, lying in the dark, waiting for tomorrow.

The knock comes just after five. I blink up at the ceiling, waiting to hear it again. When I do, I slip out of bed and peer through the peephole. It's Miller, his proportions all blown out through the lens, wearing his winter coat and the knit scarf Willow made him for Christmas. I tug some yoga pants on in the dark and grab my coat off the back of the desk chair, casting a look at my dad. He's still asleep when I open the door and steal into the hallway.

"Hey," Miller whispers. He smiles, and I feel the tight knot of my body unwind just a little. "I thought you might be up."

"I slept, like, five minutes total."

"Yeah," he laughs. "Me too." He reaches for my hand, nods his head toward the elevator. "Want to check out Times Square?"

I'd check out drying paint with you, I think. I'd check out an empty wall, if it meant being somewhere with Miller.

"Yes," I say, and we go.

It's still dark out, but in Times Square all the billboards light the street blue and red and green, like a weird planet somewhere else. When I look up I can't even find the moon, not to mention any of the stars. There are a few people wandering around, a couple of cabs that slush by in the post-snow wet. Grayed-out piles of leftover snow line the gutters, but the sidewalks are clear.

"Looks different than in the movies," I say, and Miller nods.

"I wonder if they thought that about us. Owen, and Alma, and the rest of them." I look at him, his face hued blue in the light from an Uber ad on the side of the nearest high-rise. "That we're different than we seemed on TV. Or on social media."

"Probably," I say. "We *are* different than that."

"Yeah. Not today, though. We can finally just . . ." He lets out a gusting breath. "Be ourselves."

"Scary," I say, and he squeezes my palm flush against his.

"But you're brave."

"*You're* brave." I gesture at his sling, half-tucked into his coat. "I'm just cleaning up after myself."

The sidewalk opens into a triangular island where a bright red staircase rises in front of a billboard. Someone sleeps halfway up, hidden by a sleeping bag except for their bright-blue beanie. We sit down on the first step, and Miller puts his good hand on my knee. I hug his arm, lean my head against his shoulder, and we stare out at the brilliant, blinking light field in front of us.

"It's selfish," he whispers, looking straight ahead. "But I'm still glad we did all this. Next year, who knows—" He breaks off, looks down at his hand on my leg. "I don't know where we'll be. Or what we'll be doing. And I'm just glad we had this."

I lift my hand to his cheek and pull his face down to mine, kiss him right there in the cold dark in the middle of Times Square. It feels like we're all alone in the world. Like we're standing on the precipice of something earth-shattering.

"It doesn't matter," I tell him. "Where we'll be, or what we'll be doing. There's no one else like you."

He pulls back just far enough to look at me. His eyes move over mine, something in them like sadness that's so familiar it threatens to steal my breath before I remember that he's here—that we're here—right here.

"There could never be anyone else," I say. Miller is the constant in anything, the hand I'll reach for in every crowd. I want to be thirty, finding his eyes over a platter of canapés at a dinner party. I want to be old and exhausted, reading with him in our living room. I want MASH to be right.

But all we have is this: five thirty in the morning, huddled in the cold before the scariest thing we've ever done. And for once, I don't care what comes after. Miller's here with me now.

"You're the one place I fit," I tell him. He looks at me and I know him, more than I've ever known anything else—all the stories between us, and the unguarded marvel of his laugh, and the way I feel him in a room before I even know he's there. Like the whole universe sees us, the stars moving around our axis.

He takes a deep breath, and I feel it in my lungs. "I love you," he whispers.

That's what I understand about the world.

We're booked for a nine o'clock interview, which means I'm in hair and makeup by seven thirty. I'm scheduled to go on alone, a five-minute conversation one-on-one with Hoda Kotb before Miller joins me for the back half. And while I'm up there, he'll switch out the files. Get Maren's video—Owen's story and Alma's and Taj's and all the others'—up on the screen for America to see. My phone buzzes, and when I flip it over it's Sawyer: You got this, Ro-Ro. She has all the video files, too—ready to share them on social the minute we make them public.

"That's feeling a little dark," Felix says, hovering over the makeup artist. I look up in time to see her eyeing him as he points to her eyeshadow palette. "How about this instead? We want her to look fresh-faced. Smoky eye feels like a lot for nine a.m."

She clears her throat, like, *Back off.* Felix looks at me. "What do you think, Ro?"

"I don't care," I tell him. "I'm sure you'll do what you think is best."

He blinks like I slapped him. He's forgotten, maybe, that we aren't friends anymore. But I can't slip back into it—joking with him while I get ready, going through the motions like he didn't keep the truth from me all this time.

"What should I do?" the makeup artist asks dryly.

Felix clears his throat. "Let's stick with the peachy tones, please." He turns away from us, takes a seat across the room. Down the hall and through another closed door, the flash drive waits in Miller's back pants pocket.

"Small change," Jazz says. We're standing around the corner from the stage, minutes from my call time. "Hoda wants to talk to you both together. Questions will be the same; Miller, you'll just be up there with Ro the whole time. Cool?"

My heart lurches upward into my throat, choking me. When I start to cough, Miller puts his hand on the middle of my back and says, "Cool."

I look at him, gasping for air. *Not cool.* If he's on with me, there's no time to switch the videos. The whole week we spent doing interviews, everyone who told us their stories when they didn't owe us anything at all—

"Great," Jazz says. She tucks her clipboard under her arm. "Good luck up there. I'll be watching from the back with everyone else."

She turns on her heel and disappears, leaving Miller and me alone with Felix.

"We need your help," Miller says, dropping his arm from my back to reach into his pocket. He hands Felix the flash drive, and Felix's eyebrows shoot up.

"Miller," I say, and he looks at me. "He's not going to do it."

"What other choice do we have?" he asks, and I know that there isn't one.

"He's not going to do what?" Felix says, looking between us.

His hand's extended, flash drive sitting in his upturned palm like a bomb that might detonate if he moves. "What is this?"

"It's a video," Miller says. He's talking fast, rushing to explain before we're called up. "Of a bunch of people we met with last week, their stories about MASH, how it's hurt them, changed their dreams or what they believe about themselves or their futures." As he speaks, Felix's eyebrows hike farther and farther up his forehead. "We need to swap it with Jazz's testimonial video. Show people the truth."

When he's done, Felix's eyes snap to mine. "This was your idea?"

"It was our idea," I say. There's a short, stunned pause. "Please, Felix."

"You know this violates your contracts," he says. "Publicly defaming the company." He looks down at the flash drive. "It would violate mine, too."

"What can they do?" I ask, and my voice only shakes a little. "Fire us? When people see this, there won't be anything to fire us from."

Felix looks from me to Miller and back again. "This is stupid of you," he says finally. "This is reckless."

"This is the right thing to do," Miller says.

"And besides"—I raise my chin, look Felix right in the eyes— "you owe us. You were our friend, and you lied."

He blinks, and swallows, and closes his hand around the flash drive. When our eyes meet, I see it all—that first day we met in the conference room, and the night he followed Miller and me to the hospital from formal, and every time he fixed my makeup and smoothed my hair and made sure I was ready. Even before he speaks, I feel the shift: he'll make sure I'm ready now, too.

"Fine," he says. When I smile he says it again, on an exasperated hiss. "*Fine*. Can't wait to be unemployed again." He sighs harshly but then pulls us both into him, squeezing tightly. "You two are unreal." He lets go and flaps his hands to shoo us toward the stage door. "Get away from me. I'll take care of this."

Just as he turns away, a producer calls our names.

Miller reaches for my hand. He kisses the inside of my wrist, then my palm. "You ready?"

I look at him, here with me until the very end. "I'm ready."

In her jewel-purple dress and *I'm so happy to see you* smile, Hoda Kotb looks like our luckiest break. Like of everyone on earth we could pull this stunt in front of, she might actually be the best option. She looks like she'd hug me if I started to sob.

The three of us sit on leather couches in front of a big screen bearing the MASH logo. I hope, desperately, that Felix didn't change his mind.

"Well, thanks for coming back to New York," Hoda says, smiling so graciously I could cry. She gestures to Miller, the conspicuous obstacle of his cast. "I know we were supposed to have you on a couple weeks ago. How are you feeling, Miller?"

"Oh, I'm fine," Miller says. Felix has him in a short-sleeve button-down, the only kind of dress shirt he can wear with the cast. It's navy with teensy white polka dots. "It's great to be back in New York."

"We're excited to have you," Hoda says. She leans toward me, almost conspiratorially. "You know, Ro, when I was getting ready for this interview, I actually read your first spotlight from the *Denver Post* all the way back in September."

"Wow." I manage a laugh. I can't even remember what it felt like to be myself back then. So much has changed that when I picture that girl in her fringed leather jacket, speaking from a swanky couch in the XLR8 office, she feels like a stranger. "I'm flattered."

"Oh, it was a great piece," Hoda says. "I mean, it's incredibly impressive—everything you'd already achieved then, and everything you've achieved since. To build something as impactful as MASH at such a young age." Her eyebrows rise like an exclamation point.

I don't know if I'm being paranoid or if she's picking her words carefully, but I notice the neutral way she says it all: what I've achieved, the impact I've made. None of it negative or positive, just stated as fact.

"I guess I'm just so curious," Hoda says, and I brace myself. "Everyone's talking about you as this oracle, seeing the future." Our eyes meet. "How does it feel to play god, Ro?"

There's a sudden, immovable silence—so heavy I'm scared, for a minute, that I won't be able to speak through it. Tears prick my eyes. The stage lights are hot, and I can feel the blood roaring in my ears. I told myself I wouldn't, but I look at Miller anyway: next to me on the couch, his shoulders squared off, his jaw set. When our eyes meet he doesn't blink, just nods at me. Serious and sure.

"I never wanted to play god," I hear myself say. "I never meant for any of this to happen. I was just trying to graduate high school."

Hoda blinks, surprised. "What do you mean, you never meant for this to happen? That you didn't expect MASH to take off the way that it has?"

"I mean, yeah, that." I draw a steadying breath. "MASH started as my senior project. Now it has this whole life without me, with people I've never even met. It's just this algorithm I wrote, but it's touching people's lives. Their real lives."

"Yes," Hoda says, clearly trying to keep up. I feel guilty for leading this conversation where she wasn't expecting it to go, for making yet another person uncomfortable. "Yes, MASH's promise is to"—she lifts the notes in her hand, reads right from them—"'predict the future and take the guesswork out of modern life.'" She glances up at me, then Miller. "I mean, that's no small task. But this app really is changing lives. Let's take a look."

Hoda turns toward the screen, and I clench my hands into fists. *This is it.* As the video starts to play, I realize with simultaneous relief and terror that Felix didn't let us down, that it's not XLR8's heartwarming testimonial video filling the screen. It's Maren's footage—right here on live television. The tape starts with Owen, his back to the camera, piano music filling the air.

"It makes me want to give up," the voice-over begins. He sounds young and afraid. "I've been playing forever. I mean, really forever—but if there's no future in it, what's the point?"

I glance at Hoda, but if she's confused, she doesn't let on. Miller reaches his hand out for mine, and I grab on for dear life. My heart's pounding so hard I feel like it's shaking my body, like I'm rocking forward and back on the couch with every single beat.

The video's already on Leila when I finally glance over my shoulder at the stage entrance. Jazz is there, whispering angrily at Felix, her arms waving around. But he's got her by the wrist, holding her back. I can't make out what they're saying—just the sharp shake of his head, one word on his lips. *No.*

And then, behind them, just rounding the corner: Evelyn and my mother. I whip around in my seat, and the video is still wrapping up—Maren's carefully chosen outro music—but I start talking because I know I don't have much time.

"Hoda, this is never what I intended." She turns to me, her mouth just parted. I point to the screen. "These people, this is just scratching the surface. Ever since the *New York Times* broke that story, Miller and I have been following this discussion all across the internet." I swallow, trying to keep myself calm. Miller's hand is still clenched in mine. "What we found is too big to ignore. MASH is hurting people. It's taking away their hope, and their joy, and it's making them stop believing in the things about themselves that they've always believed. Nothing is worth that."

Hoda's mouth closes, then opens again. "Are you—"

Behind me, I hear a commotion of voices. When I glance over my shoulder, Felix is trying to keep Evelyn from storming onto the stage.

"XLR8 wants me to tell you that this app predicts the future," I say, as quickly and clearly as I can. "And I'm here to tell you that it does—but only one version of it."

"What does that mean?" Hoda asks, leaning closer. "That there are multiple versions of our futures?"

"Yes," I say, nodding furiously. I probably look like a bobble-head, but I don't have time to care. "The survey isn't foolproof, because human behavior isn't."

I break the cardinal rule of this whole game, turning directly to the camera guy and staring straight into his lens.

"I can't end MASH now," I say. "It's bigger than me. I'm barely in charge of half of it. But you can stop using it. You can use your voice to get it off the market. Delete it from your phone, right now. Please." I glance over my shoulder, and Felix's eyes find mine. He's got one hand on Evelyn's elbow, and her face is fiery red. I think of Vera, who knew the truth all along, who isn't here to see this burning down. I think of what she'd want me to say, and then I look back at the camera and I say it.

"I made MASH because I wanted my life to make sense. I wanted to map it out like a math problem, like something I could solve. I wanted to understand why my mom left, and if I'd make it where I wanted to go, and if—" I glance at Miller, and he squeezes my hand, hard. "If my mistakes were forgivable. I thought that if I could predict the future, life would feel less scary."

My throat goes tight, and I have to scrape out the words. "But it doesn't. I thought MASH would make all our lives easier by telling us what's coming next, but it only captures what could be coming from this *one* moment. And even in that moment, it's only ninety-three percent accurate. I know now that everything that matters—everything we feel and the chances we take and all our mistakes and successes—they're in the seven percent left over. We exist in that gray area." I draw a steadying breath. "Listen to me: The human brain isn't set. It's malleable. It changes as you grow. Your answers to the MASH questions will change, and so will your path. That's the whole, entire point of being alive."

"*CUT!*" Evelyn's voice comes shrieking from backstage, and the camera I've been staring into swivels down to the floor. There's a rush of commotion as Hoda looks to her producers for direction, as Evelyn breaks from Felix's grip, as Miller tugs me toward him on the couch and wraps his arm around me.

"You did it," he whispers, right into my ear. I hold on to that, the soft rush of his voice, as Evelyn grabs my elbow and pulls me away from him.

"What are you doing?" she demands, her fingertips digging into my arm so hard it hurts. Her eyes are wide and wild. "What have you done?"

"Let me go," I say, yanking out of her grip. When I stand, Miller comes with me. Evelyn's chest rises and falls dramatically; she's out of breath with her anger. She opens her mouth to speak but I don't wait for it—I just sidestep her and make for the edge of the stage.

It's clear no one knows quite what to do: Hoda is still talking to a producer, and the camera crew is huddled together on the other side of the room. Evelyn stays there, paralyzed, as we walk away. When we reach Felix his eyes are glassy with tears, and he just nods at us. Jazz won't look at me. My mother stands in the hallway, waiting for us with her arms crossed.

I don't want to talk to her, and I know I don't have to. I'm done here: I've said what I needed to, and I've done the best I can with the only piece of this that's mine to control.

"Rose," she says, so long after we pass her that I don't think she's going to say anything at all. We're almost at the end of the hall when I turn back to her.

She's not smiling, but she doesn't look angry, either. More than anything, she looks like I've surprised her. And I recognize something else in her: that same resolve I felt after reading the *New*

York Times piece, when I knew what it was that I needed to do. When it's all crashed down, and there's no choice left to make but the hard one.

"You asked me, that first day, if I'd care about you without MASH." She hesitates, and Miller brushes his thumb over the inside of my wrist. "I've never known how best to connect to you, and MASH made it easy. It gave us common ground."

And now it's gone, I think. But then she says, "I hope you know you have my admiration and support no matter what you choose to do next."

Silence falls between us, blanketing the hallway. My mother sniffs a little, and for the first time, she looks nervous. "I don't think I did the best by you. But I do think it's what I was capable of then."

I nod slowly. Because maybe she's right—maybe she was meant to have one daughter, and it was meant to go like this. Maybe the space between what she could give me and what I wanted from her made room for my dad, and for Vera, and for Willow and Miller and even for me. I don't know who I'd be if she'd stuck around. But what I have is who I am now. Who I became, in spite of her: this person standing backstage with Miller, knowing I've done all I can.

"You two go," she says, finally. She straightens her watch, looks from me to Miller and back again. "I'll clean this up."

"Okay," I say, and it is. "Thank you."

My mother nods at me, holds my eyes over the empty length of the hallway. "Maybe I'll see you in California someday."

FOUR MONTHS
LATER

"It's funny," Maren says. She's smiling, all alone on the auditorium stage. "I thought I'd get all these serious photos of people with their secret, pensive thoughts. Some deep look at how we absorb into our own minds and retreat from the world in our private moments. But that's not what happened."

She hits a button and the slideshow starts: her beautiful, film-grain photographs, huge on the auditorium wall. The first picture is of her brothers, sitting at the kitchen table doing homework. One of them's chewing his pencil eraser, his chin tilted to peer at the other, whose head is bent over a textbook.

The next photo is of Felix, standing in a cardigan at the back of the XLR8 kitchen. He's swirling a spoon in a cup of coffee and half smiling at something out of frame. In the corner of the shot you can just see Jazz's elbow, a peek of her blazer as she leaves the room.

And then, the last one: that picture of Miller and me in the snow at winter formal, his eyes focused on my face in the falling dark. Now, sitting next to me in the last row of the auditorium, he squeezes my hand.

"Usually, when we think no one sees us, we're still looking at each other," Maren says. She clicks to the next slide, a full grid of photographs. I catch Autumn, and Maren's parents, and even my dad behind the espresso machine at Beans. Right in the middle there's a shot of Owen at the piano, his little sisters grinning at each other in the doorframe. "We're so connected, all the time. That's my big takeaway, I guess. Back in the fall, I titled this project *When They're Looking the Other Way.*"

Across the span of auditorium seats, Maren finds my eyes. I smile at her.

"But really," she says, "we're always just looking for each other."

When the panel of teachers starts their Q&A, I lower into my seat and lean my head against Miller's shoulder. His cast came off in March, and he's been in physical therapy to get his full range of motion back. When I hug him now, he wraps both arms around me.

He didn't get into Brown, which—all-in—has been the most incomprehensible thing to happen this year. Any school, any-where, would be luckier than hell to have Miller. But he won't have to pick just any school: Stanford wants him bad, and offered him a merit scholarship to come out to California.

It isn't XLR8's full ride, but he already has a four-year plan for getting an on-campus job, working over the summers, applying for grants. I mean, of course he does—this is Miller we're talking about.

It didn't even occur to me to want this, he told me when it happened. We were in his car, parked at the end of my driveway with the email open on his phone. *How is it possible that this feels better than what I've been dreaming of all along?*

Just life having its way, I guess. A little closer to San Jose, too—which I knew we were both thinking, but neither of us said out loud. *And you'll get to play gods forever*, I told him. We'd already scrolled through the Classics department's entire course catalog, our heads leaned close together over the center console. *Just like when we were kids.*

He'd grinned, a real one, just for me. No more Hidden Miller.

Sometimes I find myself missing him even though he's not gone yet, the backward echo of a future hurt. Like he said that night in New York, we don't know what the next year will look like, or any of the years after that. But Miller and I found our way back to each other once—we'll do it again, if we have to.

I'm trying, these days, to take it all as it comes. After MASH shut down, that felt like the only option: one second at a time. Turns out you can make it like that the whole way.

XLR8 shuttered their Denver office in February, moved everybody that wanted to come all the way out to Mountain View. Felix and Jazz didn't go—they're still here, and even come up to Switchback Ridge every now and then to meet us for coffee. Jazz took a while to come around. *She just feels guilty*, Felix told us, the first time we saw him without her. *She just really wanted to keep that job. And she knows she was wrong.*

I wanted to keep it, too, I told him. Still, all these months later, sometimes it punches the air straight out of me—how much I wish things were different. How close I came to everything I wanted, and how much it hurts, still, to have gotten it wrong.

Dad doesn't tolerate that kind of talk in the house; any time I start lamenting my losses, he reminds me of what I got from MASH instead. The knowledge that I'm capable of something so huge. The acceptances from colleges all over the country, curious to see what I'll do next from the home base of their campuses. I have a couple more weeks to choose where I'll go.

There's also the hesitant, sporadic line of communication with my mother, who's holding a job for me whenever I want it. It's nice to know the option's there, but I'm pretty sure I won't take her up on it. She told me I was just like her, back in that boardroom when it all came crashing down. But even if that's ninety-three percent true, I keep finding more and more of myself in the seven percent: with my dad, with Miller, with all my mistakes.

So much of what I loved about MASH was the part I created with Vera—not the code, but the questions. The survey we built to drill down on what people love, and what that means about them, and how it shapes the trajectory of their lives. My mother made me the kind of person who can write an algorithm, but Vera taught me life doesn't follow a formula. And that its unpredictability—all its surprises and its sorrows—are what make it worth living at all.

So I am like my mother, in a way. But I know now that there are lots of ways inside me. Maybe I'll pursue tech, just like she planned. But maybe I'll study behavioral science—that murky, mysterious world Vera opened up for me, the opposite of the order I found from writing code. It's like Maren said back in December: I get to decide, in the end.

311

Dad sold Vera's house in late winter, to a family with little kids who sled down our street when it snows. He used the money to finally, finally transform Beans on the Lake into the restaurant it was meant to be all along. *Mo's*, he named it, *because you two did something brave and impossible—which is what opening a restaurant's always felt like to me.*

I don't feel brave, not always. Sometimes I'm so scared it's paralyzing, like bare skin on black ice. I've spent the last few months acclimating to uncertainty—for a while there, I was so sure my future was all planned out. That I'd graduate, and work for XLR8, and stay in Denver close to Dad. It looked linear, like dots connecting on the map of my life.

Now, who knows. And we aren't supposed to know—I get that. The not knowing is the pain and the joy and the whole damn thing of it. We were never, ever supposed to know.

Vera said there will be different versions of me, stretching out across the years of my life. I imagine all those Ros like relay-race runners, passing on the baton of myself to the next version, and the next.

She said I'll become someone I can't even fathom yet. It's scary, to think about that. It's exciting, too.

Whoever she is, I can't wait to meet her.

ACKNOWLEDGMENTS

This book wouldn't exist without a huge cast of smart, talented people. I get to put my name on it, but they deserve all these thank-yous and so many more:

To my agent, Katie Shea Boutillier, who believed not only in Ro's story but in the stories that came before hers—thank you for being an unfailing advocate and for working so hard to make my dreams come true.

I've spent essentially my entire life dreaming of "having an editor" one day, and still I didn't think up someone even half as wonderful as my editor, Tara Weikum. When we met, I felt like a newborn baby deer in publishing—all nervous energy and trembling legs—and you've welcomed me into this business with incredible generosity and so much calm, kind guidance. I feel lucky every day to work with you. This book is so much better for your wise, thoughtful edits. Thank you for loving Ro and for taking a chance on me; words don't do justice to how much it means.

I'm grateful to the entire team at HarperCollins who brought *Seven Percent of Ro Devereux* into the world: Sarah Homer, for her spot-on notes and ongoing support; Chris Kwon, for this book's beautiful design; Caitlin Lonning, Alexandra Rakaczki, and Brenna Franzitta, for the brilliant, careful copyedits and the early enthusiasm; Lisa Calcasola and Katie Boni in marketing and publicity. Finally, of course, thank you to the talented Andrea De Santis for this book's showstopping cover.

I was lucky to have a deep bench of early readers for *Seven Percent of Ro Devereux*, who did me the enormous kindness of reading it like it was a real book before any of them knew it actually would be. Julia DeVillers, Kelly Duran, Emily Glickman, Andrea Massaro, Elyse Pomerantz, Laura Roettiger, Jamie Wiebe—thank you. For a book that's allegedly "mine," you sure helped me figure out what this story was supposed to say.

Thank you to Andrea Massaro, who sat next to me in Introduction to Fiction and Poetry when we were eighteen and has continued to sit with me and my writing all the years since. Andrea, you *get* every story I try to tell so eerily well that sometimes I worry you live inside my brain. You've done more for me and my work than I can ever truly articulate, so I'll just say: I'm so very grateful.

Thank you to Elyse Pomerantz, who read not only an early draft of this book, but drafts of nearly everything I wrote when we were kids. Your enthusiasm gave me hope and joy and gasoline then, as it does now. I'm so lucky to have you.

Thank you to the incomparable women in my critique

group—Crystal J. Bell, Maggie Boehme, Taylor Roberts—who make writing feel like a home that I don't live in alone. I'm so grateful for your insightful critiques, and even more grateful for your friendship.

Thank you to my agent siblings, Kelly Duran and Matthew Hubbard, for making me laugh and cry and for virtually holding my hand as we ride this roller coaster together. Thank you also to Harper Glenn, for your support and advice (and humor!) as I first figured out how to navigate this business.

Thank you to Kaitlyn Topolewski, who's helped me learn all the best things I know about myself and existing in the world. I don't know how I would have reached this finish line without you. I'm so, so grateful.

Thank you to my parents, who saw my love of writing and gave me everything I needed to help it grow. Thank you for driving me to every known writing camp in central Ohio, for buying me books that still live, beloved, on my shelves, and for not batting an eye when I chose to major in creative writing. Thank you for always trusting me to find my own way.

And thank you to Tucker, who told me years ago—when I had no agent and no book deal—that he wouldn't change a thing about me. Thank you for believing, even and especially when I didn't. Being a partner to someone chasing a creative career is no small task, and you do it all with incredible grace. I love you one hundred percent.